Kingdom of the Sun

stories

JAMES TERRY

D1316398

University of New Mexico Press • Albuquerque

© 2016 by James Terry
All rights reserved. Published 2016
Printed in the United States of America
21 20 19 18 17 16   1 2 3 4 5 6

Library of Congress Cataloging-in-Publication Data
Terry, James, 1970–
  [Short stories. Selections]
  Kingdom of the sun : stories / James Terry.
      pages cm
  ISBN 978-0-8263-5640-6 (pbk. : alk. paper) —
ISBN 978-0-8263-5641-3 (electronic)
  I. Title.
  PS3620.E7687A6 2016
  813'.6—dc23
                            2015018220

Cover photograph: *Roadwork*, 2009, courtesy of Robert Reck
Designed by Catherine Leonardo
Composed in Melior LT Std
Display type is Univers LT Std

For Patronilla, Irving, Josie, and Gene

Contents

IT WAS MY LAST SUMMER in Deming and I was feeling low. All I wanted was to get the hell out. But I had to work and save some money. In August I'd be in LA.

I was the grounds keeper at the municipal pool. I picked up the candy wrappers the kids chucked to the ground as they waited to get in. Sometimes there was a broken bottle, some cigarette butts, other stuff. I had to chop weeds too. When I ran out of easy stuff I worked on the shrub. It was old and dead. The City wanted it out of there. They said it was an eyesore. Sherry, my boss, didn't really give a shit. She told me to take my time. It wasn't any rush. She didn't want me having a heat-stroke. So I'd go out and hack at it every couple days with the pickaxe.

One day around lunch El pulled into the parking lot. I was in the pump room painting a sign. I watched her through the little window. She just sat there in her car. I wasn't sure what she was doing there. We weren't going out anymore. Then I saw Pete Measday walk over to her car. He was one of the life-guards. He was back from college. He stood there at her window talking for a while. Then he got in her car and they drove off. That fucked me up.

I found Eddie that night hanging out in his car in the parking lot of Napa Auto. We got his uncle to get us a six-pack of Mickey's and we went out and tried to run down some jackrabbits on the runways at the old airport. Eddie was still a junior and worshiped me. We usually did stupid shit together. Once we put a piece of raw liver on the steps of the First Baptist Church. Another time we cracked eggs into the golf-ball washers at the country club. Stuff like that.

Around midnight we snuck into the pool at the Mirador Motel. It was one of those nights when it feels hotter than the day. The pool was across the parking lot from the rooms, out of sight from the office. A low wall surrounded it, with some junipers at one end. A sign on the wall said no one was allowed in the pool after ten. There was a light switch that turned on the floodlight and the pool light. I unscrewed the bulb of the floodlight. Then there was only the eerie blue-green light of the pool.

I told Eddie too much. He's not the kind of guy you bare your soul to.

"There's more than one fish in the sea," Eddie said.

"Fuck you," I said.

He took it as a joke. I meant it.

After that I started going to the pool at the Mirador by myself. It wasn't every night. I only went when I felt a funk coming on. A couple times a week maybe. I'd sneak out of the house at midnight and get on my bike and ride all the way across town to the motel, right past the sheriff's station. They couldn't bust me for curfew anymore.

I don't know why I kept going there alone. It wasn't normal. I'd stay there for about an hour, floating on my back, looking up at the stars, or just treading water in the middle until my legs were on fire. One little thing I did was try to count the stars that I could see without moving my eyes or head. My record was three hundred. Every once in a while when my ears were above water I'd hear a truck passing on the interstate. Other than that the only sound was me breathing. The next day at work I'd barely be able to keep my eyes open. I'd cross the street to the park and take a nap on one of the concrete picnic benches in the shade until the ants woke me up.

One night I looked up from the water and El was there. She

was standing at the wall. At first I thought it was someone else. She'd cut most of her hair off and dyed it black. She was in her black one-piece with a yellow towel draped over her shoulders. She looked like a ghost in that blue-green light, appearing out of nowhere like that.

"Fancy meeting you here," she said.

It about broke my heart. We sometimes talked like that. She was into boring old books. I think she kind of pictured herself as one of those old-time heroines.

"Fancy that," I said.

She stepped over the wall. Her legs were a couple miles long and white as milk. They looked even longer with her hair so short. She tossed her towel onto a chair and got in one step at a time. I watched her. She dunked her head and smoothed her hair back over her skull and smiled at me. She had the best smile in the world.

We didn't say too much. There wasn't a lot to say. She asked about my job. I told her about all the weeds I was killing. She wasn't doing much herself, just hanging out with her mom and her sister and stuff. Her and Pete Measday were in the back of my mind but I didn't mention it. I think she was just checking up on me. Eddie must've told her.

Our fingertips were all wrinkled by the time we got out. I walked her to her car. You could feel the heat wafting up from the asphalt. It felt good. All the windows in the rooms were dark except one on the second floor. Gnats and moths were bouncing off the lights over the doors. The ice machine was humming under the stairs.

I put my hand on her cheek. The whites of her eyes were pink from the chlorine. I rubbed her cheekbone with my thumb.

"See you around?" I said.

She smiled a little and put her hand on mine.

We hugged for a while. All I wanted was to open up my heart and spill it out to her. Tell her how much I missed her. That I hated whatever she was doing with Pete Measday. That sometimes I thought of just saying fuck it and asking her to marry

3

me and staying in Deming for the rest of my life. But I couldn't say any of it.

I watched her drive off. My trunks were already bone dry.

———

We never called each other to set it up. Sometimes she'd show up, sometimes she wouldn't. Sometimes she'd already be there when I got there. That's what made it kind of magical. I never knew if she'd come or not.

We didn't talk about the past or the future. When we did talk it was small stuff, things our friends were doing, good new songs, stuff like that. We never tried to touch each other. Mostly we just floated around, thinking our own thoughts. It was strange and beautiful being with her in that blue-green light, the whole universe above us, the midnight air so hot. It seemed like we were all alone at the end of the world.

One night the manager caught us. He was nice about it. He told us we couldn't be in the pool at that time of night. He must've known we didn't have a room, but he didn't say anything. If he hadn't been so nice I would've kept going just to piss him off.

I tried the Bel Shore Inn next. That wasn't any good. The pool was right next to the road. I tried the Ramada Inn too. That was no good either. There wasn't any light in the pool. None of the other motels in town had pools. There was the Holiday Inn, but that wasn't even in town. I wasn't sure what to do.

It was July. I was starting to get nervous. I didn't know why I'd picked California anymore. Why that college in that place where Charles Manson killed all those people. Every day when the sun went down I'd feel this darkness seeping into me. I'd feel the need for a midnight pool.

Donna O'Neil was flirting with me. She was one of the lifeguards. She had a weird shape. She had these fat thighs but the rest of her was skinny. She had a good tan though. When she switched suits she had a bright white stripe around her crotch.

4

She was always reading one of those fat Danielle Steel paperbacks. She was pretty dorky. I asked her out one night. I borrowed my mom's car. We went to Sonic and took a few cruises. I gave her a blue-light special in the Kmart parking lot. It was awful. She pretended like it was great. It only made me feel like shit.

I hooked up with Eddie again. We split a bottle of peach Schnapps and dumped some leftover tuna casserole from his dad's house into the out-of-town mailbox at the post office. He told me he'd seen El with some dude at Video World. I acted like I didn't care. After we split I rode out to the desert behind the truck stop and yelled my head off and kicked some rusty beer cans. I yelled some more. When I stopped yelling all I could hear were the engines of the big trucks idling.

The next day I did some serious hacking on the shrub. It was at the corner on the Spruce Street side. The roots were hard as rock and all grown in under the wall so you couldn't get a good angle on it. I was working on it when El drove up. My shirt was off and I was drenched in sweat. I tried to ignore her but I couldn't. I dropped the pickaxe and walked up to her window and said, "He's not off yet."

It came out kind of mean.

She smiled a little. She didn't look happy. Her face and neck were sunburned. A big tight knot came into my throat.

"I know a good pool," she said. She said did I know where Barbara Robinette lived.

That threw me off. I barely even knew Barbara Robinette. I'd had her in freshman geometry but that was about it. She'd played the glockenspiel in band. A goody-goody. She meant nothing to me. I'd never seen El hanging out with her either.

It was hot standing there with the sun in my face. El's sunburned skin made it seem hotter. She put her hand on the steering wheel and stared off at the wall of the pool. I looked over there. I could see frickin' Pete Measday's head above the wall.

"I got work to do," I said.

I went and grabbed my pickaxe. It was rude. It felt good until she drove off.

Barbara Robinette's house was on Shelly Drive, over in the rich area between Florida and Walnut on the east side of town. It only took about ten minutes to ride out there, but it seemed a lot longer. It was another scorching night. I took Poplar all the way down. There were good long stretches of darkness on Poplar. They'd paved it a few years back and it was still nice and smooth. Passing this one streetlight I remembered me and Kyle and Tom sneaking out one night with our automatic BB pistols and all three of us unloading into it. The damn thing wouldn't break.

All the houses on Shelly Drive were pretty new. Brown brick. Two-car garages. Instead of a curb the sidewalks sloped down to the street like ramps. I used to ride my Huffy over there when I was small just for the cool curbs.

I didn't see El's car anywhere around. I turned into the alley behind the houses. About halfway down I got off my bike and leaned it against the wall and waited. It was quiet as hell. All you could hear were the air conditioners. After a while this black cat came over for a visit. I squatted down and petted it. It curled around my legs and arched its back. Its name tag said: "Chauncy, 1318 S. Saddler Street." I rubbed his neck until he purred.

Chauncy's ears perked up when El came walking down the alley. At first all I saw were her legs. Two white stalks out for a midnight stroll. Then the rest of her appeared.

"I didn't think you were coming," she said.

"I wasn't."

We petted the cat together.

It took us a minute or two to figure out which back wall was Barbara Robinette's. They all pretty much looked the same. El had to go back around and count the houses from the front.

"This is it," she said at a beige stucco wall to our right.

A little flutter went through my stomach. I could hear the quiet whine of a water faucet on the other side. Part of me was hoping she'd change her mind. She took her towel from her shoulders and flung it to the top of the wall.

6

"Help me up," she said.

She stepped into my hands and caught hold of the top of the wall. Her bare legs looked lovely against the rough texture of the stucco. I wanted to push my face into them. She pulled herself up, swung her legs over, then lowered herself down the other side. I heard her thump down. Her towel disappeared. I waited a second, listening for trouble, then I jumped up and pulled myself to the top of the wall and crouched there, catlike, checking out the house and the pool.

The pool was pitch black and perfectly still. It looked like a slab of cold, black marble. You could see the stars in it. It was long and rounded at the ends. The pavement around it was pretty wide and there were some white metal chairs and a round table on it. The back of the house had a big sliding glass door off to the left with a curtain drawn partly across it. There was a small window and two bigger ones to the right of it. The sprinkler was over in a patch of grass. It was one of those arching ones that kids like to run under.

I jumped down and looked at El. The wall was blocking the streetlight from the alley. The moon wasn't out either, so at first I wasn't sure what I was seeing. I stared hard. It was her nipples. And a darker patch farther down. My heart made a huge thump. Like a chunk of concrete dropped in the dirt. Then it sped away and there was a nervous tingle in all my joints. I stared at her. I'd never seen her whole body naked before, like that, from a distance. I'd seen her tits plenty, and a bit of bush, but never all of it at once. I stared at her like a blinded jackrabbit.

She didn't even look at me. She walked over to the shallow end and started inching her way in. The stars on the surface rippled, then vanished. I looked toward the house. A little green "12:00" was flashing somewhere in the darkness behind the sliding glass door. Some large flip-flops were sitting on the floor inside the door. I glanced over at the other windows. One of them was open a few inches. My skin went all goose-bumpy.

I slowly took off my shirt and shoes and padded over to the

edge of the pool. El's head was gliding across the water. I was just about to step in when she turned and looked at me. It was a challenge. I could tell, even in the dark. I took off my trunks as if I hadn't given it a second thought and slipped into the pool from the side, clutching the edge to keep from making any noise.

It was weird as hell being naked like that in Barbara Robinette's swimming pool. It wasn't normal. All I could think about was El's naked body. I knew better than to think it was for me. It was typical El. Some weird thing would come into her head and she'd do it, just like that, without a second thought. One night when we were still going out she'd decided she needed to spend the night in a hotel down in Palomas. White girl alone in a Mexican hotel. I didn't know anything about it. No one did. She was grounded for a month. She didn't care. She didn't even lie to her dad about it.

We kept to ourselves for a while then ended up down at the shallow end, squatting there with our backs against the wall, a couple feet apart. Our heads were the only thing above water. Pretty soon the water stopped moving. The stars came back. It was hard to feel the difference between the air and the water.

"Why Barbara Robinette?" I whispered. A cricket was chirping somewhere in the yard. That helped a little.

She thought about it a second.

"We were best friends in third grade."

That didn't make much sense, but I didn't ask more. We were too close to the windows.

"Do you want to smoke a joint?" I said after a while.

It was in the pocket of my trunks. I'd got it from Rudy Rivera, the funny little guy I'd worked with at the road department last summer. He was a stoner. Me and him would lounge in the big corrugated aluminum drainage tubes out in the lot, smoking his crap weed from his little pipe made of bolts. I had run into him the other day in his maroon Lincoln out by Dairy Queen and he'd given me the joint for old times' sake.

She turned to face me. Her eyes looked big and black. Suddenly that old feeling of love and hope was there again. We both must've felt it. We started kissing. It was heaven. It had been so long since I'd felt her. I came around in front of her. We went at it for a long time, pressed together in the water. I'd never felt anything like it. It was pure hell.

I reached down between her legs. She spun away from me and launched herself underwater out into the pool. There was a little splash. My heart was chugging. I looked up at the house. I kept looking. The windows stayed dark.

Then I went after her. It was pitch black underwater. I kicked off hard from the wall and glided out into the darkness with my hands stretched out in front of me, hoping to catch an ankle. There was a chill in the places where our skin had been touching.

I came up for air out in the middle and looked around. A few seconds later her head came up like the back of a turtle down at the deep end. I breaststroked toward her. She turned around and flashed me a smile. Just as I was reaching out she went down and launched off again.

That annoyed me. She'd always had a little cruel streak in her. One time in the early days she stopped in the middle of making out and said she had to tell me something. I didn't like the sound in her voice. She'd been quiet all night. We were in her mom's van in the desert behind the truck stop. I'd just taken off her bra. She turned down the radio and looked me in the eyes and told me she was pregnant. It was like someone jabbing a huge needle into me and sucking all my blood out. I sat there staring at this billboard for Bowlin's Teepee lit up by the interstate about a mile away.

"Aren't you happy?" she said.

I was dead. My life was over. I told her we had to think this through. She said she'd already thought it through and she was going to have it. With or without me.

"Are you insane?" I said.

She went quiet then started crying.

"I thought you loved me," she said.

"I do."

"Then how could you think of killing our child?"

9

I should've known at that point that it was a lie. But I was dead. I couldn't even think. I stared at the billboard and said good-bye to my life. Then after about ten minutes of unbearable silence she told me she was only joking. Ha ha. That's El Brdecko. Great-great-granddaughter of C. W. Brdecko, "the hanging judge."

I didn't go after her. I didn't feel like playing the game. A wave of sleepiness had suddenly come over me. I swam back down to the shallow end and ignored her and went to the steps and got out. I put my trunks on without drying off, afraid she'd catch a glimpse of my shriveled-up nub. After I'd dried off I went over and squatted down beside her head.

"You coming?"

She shook her head. She was in one of her moods, I could tell. There was no point trying to work it out when all we could do was whisper like snakes. I didn't want to leave her there alone.

"Come on, El. Let's go."

I squatted there, waiting for her to say something.

"I want to be alone," she said.

I felt bad. I should've played her game. I reached out and touched her wet hair. I was aware of myself doing it.

Then I put my shoes and shirt on and climbed over the wall.

I woke up at three in the morning with the sudden realization that she couldn't climb the wall without my help. I lay there wide awake, seeing her trapped in Barbara Robinette's back yard. I saw her dad driving the streets looking for her in a rage. My last thought before drifting back to sleep was that I had to go back and make sure she wasn't still there.

———

It was a week before I saw her again. In the afternoon when I was done with the weeds I'd stand out on the Spruce side of the pool, staring in the direction of her house. It made me all melancholy thinking of the sweet times we'd spent out on her front wall under the trees. She lived right across the street from the hospital. Sometimes we'd go over to the baby ward and check out the newborns through the glass. It was on her front wall that she told me it was over. The day after my birthday. We were sitting there holding hands. Out of the blue she says she can't go on. She says we're all used up. I didn't know what she was talking about. I kept waiting for her to say she was only joking. She wasn't. I knew because it felt like she'd just ripped my heart out and chucked it to the ground and poured some lighter fluid on it and set it on fire and stomped on it a few times before kicking it out into the street to be run over by a car. That was back in April.

Even with the sun in my face all I could think about was the darkness and the feeling of her naked skin against me. Every day it was like this. I couldn't shake the hunger for the midnight pools. The little girls helped a little. I'd go in and horse around with them before closing. They were about as big as my leg. They'd make themselves into a train. I'd be the engine. We'd do loops around the shallow end. Everything seemed all right when I was around them.

One day after work I saw Barbara Robinette at Farmer's. That was weird as hell. I went up and had a little chat with her but all I could think about was being naked in her pool at midnight with El. All these crazy emotions came over me, right there in the supermarket. I felt like hugging Barbara Robinette and telling her everything. It gave me an erection. I stood there staring into her eyes, saying "I love you" over and over in my mind. I didn't even know her. Finally I told her I had to bolt. I went and stood in the cereal aisle until I calmed down.

I knew I could never go back to Barbara Robinette's pool. It had to be someone else's. I kept thinking about what El had said when I asked her why Barbara Robinette. It was starting to make some kind of sense.

I knew some apartment pools. The Deluxe Apartments over on Orange, and these other ones on Florida that some friend of my grandma's had built in the '60s. I'd spent a lot of time in both of them. My best friend in fifth grade had lived at the Deluxe Apartments with his mom. Mario was a KISS freak. His room faced the courtyard where the pool was. He'd open his window and plant a speaker in it and blast KISS while we swam. He moved to El Paso in sixth grade. We wrote each other a couple times then lost touch.

The other apartments were an older memory. Me and my brother used to swim there. That friend of my grandma's, Ray Byrd, a weird, quiet guy with red hair, would sit there in a deck chair, skinny as a flattened cat, smoking and reading some library book. Every now and then he'd look up and mumble something to us about splashing and screaming. We just ignored him.

Neither of those pools grabbed me.

Then one day Kurt Brubek showed up at the pool and started showing off with all these fancy dives. I guess he'd been practicing at home. I stood there in the parking lot, leaning on the rake, watching him over the wall. This weird dark tingling feeling coming over me.

Brubek lived in a *Better Homes and Gardens* house on Tin Street, just down from the library. The alley was paved and the garbage cans didn't stink. I sat there on my bike, leaning against the wall. I watched the june bugs spinning around the streetlight. They made a quiet buzz. One of them landed on my shirt. Its legs kept snagging when it tried to walk. I cupped it in my hand. It made that funny little wheezing noise that june bugs do. I opened my hand and chucked it into the air.

Brubek had always been popular, even in grade school. He was our quarterback. Last season he'd led the Wildcats to their first victory over Silver City in thirty-two years. He was prom king. He was going to West Point. For a while in sixth grade I'd tried to be his best friend. I succeeded for a month or two, then I got bored with him. My knowledge of the Brubek home came from that period. His mother appreciated good manners in young men. I didn't have any. She was one of those moms that cleans your room every day.

I waited there for ages. El didn't show up. That hurt. I figured she was sore I'd left her at Barbara Robinette's. She hadn't sounded too happy on the phone. I walked up and down the alley for a while, then I said fuck it and went up the wall.

The moon was bright. The first thing I noticed was the blue plastic cover across the pool. The diving board sticking out over it looked like it was glowing. The house was one of those modern adobes. A sign on the back wall said: "OUR OOL HAS NO P IN IT: KEEP IT THAT WAY." Dark-brown wooden shutters framed all the windows. The swamp cooler was droning on the roof. There was some kind of cupid fountain thing in one part of the yard.

I jumped down.

It was a pain in the ass peeling back the cover. It was all stiff and kept crackling. Luckily none of the windows were open. I left it in a heap at the shallow end.

I went to the edge and stepped in. It was freezing! I was in a bad mood now. I just wanted to be done with it and get the hell out of there. I treaded water out in the middle, trying to warm up. Once I'd warmed up a little I began to relax. I took a nice long piss. It felt hot rising up my sides.

Then I heard a "psst" over at the wall. I looked up. Her head was poking over the edge. She must've been standing on my bike. All my annoyance vanished and I felt the magic of the midnight pools come over me again. I raised my arm and waved.

She came over the wall and took her shirt off and slipped out of her shorts. The sight of her naked body in that bright-blue moonlight killed me. I'd thought I was ready for it this time.

She waded in.

I took my suit off and wadded it up on the ledge.

"What kept you?" I whispered when she was close enough to hear.

"I was having a good dream," she said.

Then the weirdness of the whole thing set in again. Kurt Brubek was asleep in his bed on the other side of those walls. I pictured him in the room I'd seen in sixth grade. All those posters of cute dogs. I smiled to think that he'd be sleeping in a barracks pretty soon.

After a while we met out in the middle. We were standing with just our heads above the water.

"You look like Liza Minelli in this moonlight," I whispered.

She gave me a long look.

"You look like Winston Churchill," she said. I didn't believe her.

We stared into each other's eyes.

"I miss the hell out of you," I said.

She didn't say anything. She didn't have to. We went at each other like starving animals. There was something wild in her eyes tonight. She bit my shoulder. I had my finger right up in her. Then all of a sudden the sliding glass door filled with light.

We froze. Someone was in the kitchen. We bolted to the side of the pool closest to the house and pressed ourselves up against it. I tried to hold my breath but my heart was doing dropkicks against my lungs. The light was spilling all over the yard, lighting up the fountain and the back wall. I couldn't see them from that angle but I knew our clothes and towels were somewhere in the light. A big patch of the lumped-over pool cover was lit up too.

Then a shadow moved across the grass.

"We're fucked," I said.

We waited. Nothing happened. We waited some more.

After a while I turned around and grabbed the edge with the tips of my fingers and slowly raised my head up.

I could see part of the kitchen through the door. Some dark wood cabinets. One of those hanging wire mesh basket things with fruit and onions and stuff in it. The top part of a blender and some glass jars on the counter. Then Brubek came into view. He was wearing his navy-blue football shorts. His back was to me. I could see every mole on it. He was holding a bread bag in his right hand. He put it on the counter and took some bread out of it. He opened a drawer and took out a butter knife. When he moved a little to the side I saw a jar of peanut butter on the counter.

I dropped back down and looked at El.

"He's making a peanut butter sandwich," I said.

"Who is?"

"Kurt."

For some reason this seemed to relieve the tension. Not only that it was Kurt, but that he was making a peanut butter sandwich.

We waited. I'd never realized how long it takes to eat a peanut butter sandwich. The pool was starting to settle down from our panic. The water was feeling cold again. I looked over the edge again. He wasn't there.

We waited.

"I'm getting cold," El said.

I nodded.

"Maybe we should make a run for it," I said.

She turned around and looked over the edge herself. Her tits looked beautiful pressed up against the tiles. She came back down.

"What if he just forgot to turn off the light?" she said.

Our teeth were starting to chatter. We had to do something. We couldn't just stay there all night.

"I'm getting out," she said after another few minutes.

"Wait," I said.

She looked at me. I couldn't think of anything to say.

"You're shaking," she said. There was a lovely look of concern in her eyes.

That's when I spilled my guts. I told her that I didn't think I could go on without her. I said the craziest shit. I asked her to come to LA with me. We'd get a bungalow on the beach. We'd get married and have a kid. We'd grow old together. I told her she was the love of my life and that there'd never be another. All in this painful whisper.

She took my face in her hands and kissed both of my eyes.

"Come on," she said. "Let's go."

She turned around and pulled herself up as quietly as she could. I stayed there pressed tight against the side. Cold drops hit my head as she went around behind me. I turned. I wanted to see her.

Right then everything went black. I couldn't see a thing. It was like even the moon had vanished. I couldn't see El. I couldn't see the pool. I couldn't see my own hand in front of my face.

"El?" I whispered.

She didn't answer.

Gradually the shapes in the yard started coming back. The fountain. The walls. The hedge. I didn't see her at first because she wasn't where she should've been. She was standing on the diving board. Her arms were straight down at her sides. Her feet were together. She was looking straight ahead. She looked like a statue. It was the spookiest thing I ever saw.

Then she walked to the end of the board and did a little hop.

You know when you're in the kitchen and you turn to do something and you knock a glass over the counter? You see it falling and you hear it shatter long before it reaches the ground. But it just keeps falling. All you can do is stand there and watch it fall. That's how it felt watching El spring out over the pool.

She pulled her knees up into her body and wrapped her arms around her shins and floated there against the stars like that fetus in *2001*. I sucked in a lungful of air. My hands flew up as if to beg her to go back, go back. Maybe I thought I could even catch her.

Then she dropped.

———

It was a relief to be back around normal people. Lifeguards and kids and moody mothers. By ten o'clock it was a hundred degrees out. I got the pickaxe from the pump room and went out to the shrub. I hacked and hacked with the pointy end of the pickaxe and fired the blade of the shovel in under the roots and torqued the handle with all my weight.

I kept hearing that horrible smack in my mind. That deep *k-thunk*. That sound like falling rain. I kept feeling that sheet of water falling over me, kept seeing myself trying to run but the water not letting me. Plowing with my arms and legs against the water but not moving at all. The shock wave shoving me forward and sucking me back. Then somehow getting out, running crazy, firing my legs into my trunks, grabbing my shirt and towel, trying to get my wet feet into my shoes. She was still underwater. The pool was heaving and slopping all over the place. I was hopping back and forth at the edge of the pool, waiting for her crazy ass to come up. I had her clothes and her towel in my hands. Then the light flicked on in one of the windows. The curtain drew back. It was the dad. Larry Brubek. President of Home Federal. I was looking right at him. That's when I panicked. I threw her stuff to the ground and ran. I jumped to the top of the wall in one freakish leap and went over.

I'll never forget the sound of his voice.

"Get the hell off my property!"

It sounded like it was right in my ear. I jumped on my bike and flew the hell out of there.

I'd only gone about two blocks before I started laughing. I kept picturing El stepping naked out of Kurt Brubek's pool. I was laughing so hard I couldn't even ride. I eventually had to stop at the vacant lot by the junior high that I used to walk to school through every day. I went down in the dirt and stared up at the moon and laughed so hard I thought it was going to kill me.

The whole tangled mess of roots finally came out around four o'clock, leaving a big gaping hole in the dirt. I was ready to collapse. I was caked with sweat and dirt. My shoulders and lower back were on fire. I left my tools there and went in and jumped into the pool.

I stayed down there as long as I could with all those quiet little legs, wishing I could just stretch out on the bottom of the pool and stare straight up at that sheet of liquid mercury rippling above me forever.

IT BEGAN THAT EVENING IN early June when just east of Deming he noticed a movie playing at the drive-in on the outskirts of town. The towns along the interstate were littered with old drive-in theaters, more often than not a few tattered scraps of screen clinging to a wreck of gray boards, their lots overrun with weeds and garbage and broken-down cars, but he couldn't remember the last time he'd seen one up and running. As he watched that luminous rectangle softly flickering in the distance, he felt again the innocent wonder of his boyhood years, the contentment of those old family outings, the joys and trepidations of exploring the bodies of girls for the first time, all those old drive-in memories balled up in a warm little knot behind his heart, and he wished there was something he could do with this feeling, for he was a practical man and liked there to be uses for things. He watched until all that remained of that window onto a bygone world was a thin shaft of light, then darkness. But the feelings it awoke stayed with him long into the night.

Two days later, eastbound from Phoenix in the glaring dullness of late afternoon, Riggs found himself exiting the interstate at Motel Drive and pulling into the big lot of the Deming Truck Terminal on the west side of town. He'd stopped there once or twice before and seemed to remember they served a decent cup of coffee. He eased the rig in line with the others and climbed down from the cab, stretched his aching back, and made his way with a slight limp across the scorching lot.

There weren't but a few other truckers at the tables and booths in the restaurant, each sitting alone. They glanced up as he entered, but he didn't know them. He sank into one of the booths along the big tinted windows facing the interstate, the road still flowing through him, through his boots and through his bones. It was nice and cool in there and smelled of steaks and fries. Waiting for the waitress to come around he flipped through the songs in the miniature jukebox on his table, turning the pages with the little chrome lever. Good old songs, nothing later than the '70s. He fished around in his front pocket for some loose change and dropped a few quarters into the slot and chose a couple of Conway Twitty standards.

"What can I get ya?" the waitress said.

She looked about eighteen and was boredly pulverizing a piece of gum. Her name was Becky. Her plastic name badge said as much. Skinny girl. Blonde hair. Sort of pretty in a run-of-the-mill way. She didn't seem right for the place. In his experience it was the mean old bats who ended up at the truck stops, women who looked like they'd sooner stick a fork in your eye than replace the one on the floor.

He ordered a cup of coffee and a piece of apple pie. It wasn't too often that he had a piece of pie but the notion just popped into his head and he saw no reason not to. He'd made good time across Arizona and would easily reach Van Horn in time for a late dinner at Love's.

Becky walked off with his order, in no particular hurry herself. Riggs watched her hips sally as she went, as was his habit and his privilege. Conway Twitty crooned manfully through the dull afternoon.

"I saw you here before," she said, coming back around to pour his coffee.

He doubted that. He hadn't been in that restaurant for a good six months at least. It was an odd thing to say anyway, even if she had seen him. But it wasn't worth arguing about.

"Yeah, it's a good little town," he said.

"Is it?"

She didn't even smile.

"Good as the next one, I expect," he said.

She made a face, unconvinced. She was a sullen little thing.

"Say," he said as she was walking away. "What's the story with that drive-in out there?"

She didn't know what he was talking about.

"Yeah, I saw it the other night as I was passing through," he said, aware now how this little enthusiasm for something local would grate on her. "I ain't seen one of them up and running since long before you were born."

She shrugged. "Beats me."

She went off and came back with his piece of pie and stood there beside the table.

"Where you headed?" she said.

"Back to Waco, Texas. Just come from Los Angeles."

All of a sudden she was transformed. She set the coffeepot on the table and beamed at him with a mouth and eyes that did something unexpected to his insides.

"What's it like in Los Angeles?" she gushed. "It must be so amazing."

He took a swig of coffee and scalded his tongue.

"They can have that place far as I'm concerned." He winced.

But she wanted more. Had he ever seen a movie star? What was it like on the beach? Was it always warm and sunny there, even in the winter? He supplied her with a few stark images of the trucking yards of Long Beach, but this did little to temper her enthusiasm for that city he loathed.

At last she was called away to another table. He sat there in a daze, his heart softly thudding.

———

With a name like Riggs it would seem he'd been destined from birth to drive eighteen-wheelers, but in his youth he'd dreamed of being a country singer. He'd given it his best shot, singing for a year in the bars around Wichita Falls, but he'd never managed to overcome his stage fright. The road he'd taken from artist to trucker was strewn with jobs that in retrospect revealed a steadily decreasing tolerance for bosses and coworkers, a journey that ended in his late twenties in the solitary confinement of a rebuilt '64 Peterbilt. Since then he hadn't slept in his own bed for more than a week at a stretch. It had been a good long run, best job in the world as far as he was concerned, but he knew his days were numbered. His sciatica and bum right heel could attest to that. Over the years he'd seen all there was to see on the great American highway, things he'd never forget as long as he lived: a pear-shaped moon the color of dried blood oozing out of the predawn sky above the Mojave; a polar bear in a farmer's field outside Oroville, Washington; an orgy in the back of a hippy van crossing the Memphis Bridge; UFOs; dogs at the wheel; bicyclists in blizzards—he'd seen it all and more. He'd driven through every kind of weather imaginable, rode out tornadoes and hurricanes and earthquakes and forest fires, listened to the strange life stories of a thousand and one hitchhikers, came to revere men whose real names he'd never know, men like "Sasquatch" and "Tarbelly Ace" and "The Gringo Kid" and that golden-throated Zen Buddhist ex-con "Moondog Jones," who plunged to his death in the Rio Grande Gorge. In this way the days and nights of thirty years had passed into the slow backward flow of time, never to return.

That summer he was making the California run every other week or so, hauling reefers of frozen chicken from Waco to Los Angeles and coming back with whatever he could get a hold of, and it so happened that the sun would just be starting to set around the time he crossed the state line westbound into New Mexico. It was another hour and a quarter before he reached Deming, by which time only a faint band of blue would still be left in the western sky and the movie at the drive-in would already be underway. Something about the Deming drive-in, maybe the rosy quality of the light, too far away for him to make out the actors' faces, had taken hold of him and wouldn't let go. It was the same every time he passed it, a deep ache right behind his heart. As if that rectangle of softly flickering light in the distance were a window onto his own past, and if only he were close enough he would see that it wasn't a movie at all but his very own memories being projected on to the screen. Memories of his mother and father, of his brother and sister. Out there in the desert night, just beyond his reach.

He'd pull into Deming around four in the afternoon on his way back through, six hundred miles flat out across the blast furnace of the Sonora, and at that moment there was nothing better in the world than stepping into that restaurant and settling into his booth beside the window with his cup of coffee and his piece of apple pie. She called him Duke—"So what's your handle?" she'd asked him the second time—and from her he didn't mind it. The conversation was always the same. She: "Hey, Duke. How's the weather in LA?" He: "Warm and smoggy." She: "See any movie stars?" He: "No, but I did see a red Ferrari." Or a man with a purple mohawk, or the sunlight dancing on the water. Beaches. Flashy cars. Movie stars. She yearned for the clichés. He knew her smile had a certain price, proof that the fabled city of angels really existed, and he was happy to pay.

Soon enough he found himself seeing things through her eyes when he was in LA, imagining her there in the truck with him, gushing and gasping. And sometimes he had to admit that indeed there was something exhilarating in the air when you were in sight of the ocean. The hazy blue. The glittering sunlight. It did give you a sense of possibility. Each time he saw her he tried to give her a new image, something she could savor during her long, dull hours at the Deming truck stop. The mere mention of palm trees was enough to make her smile, and that was enough for him. If he happened to learn that she had a brother and a sister, that she'd been terrible at algebra but excelled in drama, that the Deming Wildcats were a sucky team, that her former friend Barbara was a bitch, that truckers on the whole weren't very good tippers, and a dozen other pieces of local trivia, it wasn't through any effort of his own but because like nearly every woman he'd ever met, Becky had a compulsion to say every damn thing that came into her head. He would've preferred she said nothing at all. Just smiled.

———

"Well, that's a mighty shame," he said. "You ain't lived till you been to a drive-in movie."

It was late July, searing hot, the summer's first thunderheads drifting up from the south.

"Why don't you take me then?" she said and went on smacking her gum like a sassy little calf chewing her cud.

Riggs grinned sardonically, but from that moment on there was no getting the idea out of his head. She'd said it as a joke, he was certain of that. Only moments before, she'd blushed after an unthinking comment about old people, which made it pretty clear how she classified him. She also knew he was married—he'd mentioned his wife more than once—and it was better that way, for he didn't want her getting the wrong idea about his friendliness. When, on his next trip through, Becky made no mention of the drive-in or her proposition, it confirmed his suspicion that it had only been a joke, that she wasn't the least bit attracted to him—it was Los Angeles she was crazy about, not him—and he was relieved to be rid of the thought. He was a fool to have considered it at all.

It was easy to reach this conclusion in the glaring sunlight of late afternoon when all he could see as he was leaving town was the dull gray beams of the back of the screen, dwarfed by the ridges of the Florida mountains off to the south, but then, a week later, just after sunset, the sky finally getting easy on his road-weary eyes, he'd find himself once more on the outskirts of that dull little town that had so bewitched him, the movie playing softly in the distance, and the urge to be there at the drive-in would be overwhelming.

Such was the case one balmy evening in early August. He'd been battling thunderstorms clear across West Texas, and it was a relief to finally see the fading pink in the clouds beyond Deming. He rolled down his window and turned off the air conditioner. The hot, humid wind blew across the side of his face. Once more he turned his eyes to the drive-in theater, and his yearning to be there watching it was almost unbearable. A big hot stone right in the middle of his chest. It seemed to him that everything—him and the truck and the eight tons of frozen chicken and the whole world around him—was being sucked into that pale flickering light in the distance.

A long, shrill honk pierced his daze and he looked to the road to see that he was halfway in the other lane. He yanked the wheel hard right. The little red car in the mirror fishtailed, braking and squealing. The trailer listed ominously left and seemed to hang there tilting between the sky and the road for a good three seconds before at last it fell back and the whole cab bounced and shuttered. He clenched the wheel and straightened her out and only started to breathe again when the broken white lines were flowing once again straight and true down the left side of the truck.

"Sweet Jesus."

A quick glance in the far mirror confirmed his clearance. He flicked on the turn signal and the hazards and downshifted slowly, bringing the rig to a smooth stop on the shoulder. He sat there for a while, his insides all feathery.

The man in the red car flipped him off as he passed.

The CB squelched.

"Any trouble, Chicken Little?"

He turned down the stereo and picked up the handset.

"Naw. Just takin' care of a little business."

———

She said yes.

"Becky," he said with a little quiver in his voice. "I've got to have some work done on my truck, and I'm in town overnight. I was thinking about going to that drive-in later on and I was wondering if you'd like to come along . . ." and without giving her a chance to say yes or no he set about explaining in a not very convincing manner that he didn't want her to think he was asking her on a date or anything, but rather that over those past few months he'd come to think of her as a friend, and he didn't really know anyone else in town, and he couldn't exactly drive an eighteen-wheeler into a drive-in theater, and because he knew how much she loved movies and all . . .

"I've got a car," she said.

"Well, I'd hate to trouble you."

She only smiled.

When he'd finished his jittery coffee they stepped out into the parking lot and he pointed out his truck.

"Just knock on the door around sunset."

He spent the remainder of the afternoon watching stock car races on the big-screen TV in the lounge, wondering during the commercials what in the hell had gotten into him. And what her own thoughts on the matter were. Around seven o'clock he went out to the rig and took his boots off and had a little nap. He awoke with the sun in his face, and it occurred to him that she wasn't going to come, and that it was probably for the best.

But she came. Three little taps on the driver's door.

"Wake up, Duke."

"I'm up, I'm up," he said and opened the door and climbed stiffly down.

Out of her uniform she looked ridiculously young. She was wearing tight, faded jeans with premade holes in the knees and a frilly white T-shirt with some kind of gibberish emblazoned across it, and her lips were shiny with lip gloss. He'd known it was going to be awkward as hell, but nothing could have prepared him for the way he felt when he sat back in the passenger's seat of her little white Mazda hatchback with maroon upholstery, so low to the ground that he might as well have been in a go-kart.

A bombardment of screeching noise masquerading as music erupted as she started the car. She turned it down—not nearly enough—and backed out, and they were on their way.

"I hate this car," she yelled above the music. "It's a piece of shit."

Riggs made no comment. A pine-scented air freshener in the

shape of a Christmas tree dangled from the rearview mirror. The ashtray was pulled out and there was loose change in it and red-and-white peppermints. Part of the button of the glove box was broken and the faded plastic of the dash was all cracked from the sun. None of these things in and of themselves were of any significance to him, but taken as a whole they had the effect of plunging Riggs into Becky's private universe, which only exacerbated his unease.

"Looks like we might get a little rain," he hollered with forced casualness.

The front was closing in from the southeast, an armada of great blue-black thunderheads shaped like anvils.

She nodded and smacked and swung her head with the music.

The drive across town took forever. She drove down tree-lined Pine Street, past the Sonic and the sky-blue water tower and the municipal swimming pool. Motels and fast-food restaurants and filling stations on the north side of the street, old houses with big porches and shade trees on the south. Two lanes in both directions, a divider up the middle, only a handful of cars on the road. And yet it took forever. They sat for years at the intersection of Pine and Gold, waiting for the light to turn green. Three cars and two pickups idling in the torrid heat. Not a soul on the sidewalks. The tape softly hissing in the emptiness between songs.

"Your wife must get pretty lonesome with you gone so much."

Riggs smiled. More a wince than a smile.

"Well," he said, and let it stand at that.

The light turned green. The next song exploded. The journey resumed.

They crossed a railroad track near the country club, a lone golfer out there in the yellow-green fairway. She picked up speed. In time the back of the screen came into view, and a few minutes later she was pulling up behind a row of half a dozen cars and trucks lined up outside the blue-green sheet-metal fence. *Last Train to Yucca Bluff* and *The Moonbeamers,* announced the sign rising above the fence, neither of which Riggs had ever heard of.

Glancing out his window he noticed a cemetery on the other side of the road. Big old thing, enclosed by a low stone wall and full of enormous trees, giving it the quality of a wooded park or the grounds of an estate. The golden light of the setting sun was blazing against the leaves and trunks, making the deep-green shade it cast seem all the cooler. Riggs stared into the shadows, seized by a feeling that he'd been there before. His eyes lingered for a long time in the soothing green darkness deep within.

Becky pulled forward. It was their turn to pay. An old goat in a red ball cap and suspenders stooped down to count their heads and declared the damage to be five smackeroos.

"I'm getting this," Riggs said and reached for his wallet, grateful at last for an opportunity to assert himself.

Becky paid the man and handed Riggs the coupon for a 10 percent discount on any haircut at Fermina's Coiffures, and she drove in.

His first glimpse of the enormous screen towering above the wide dirt lot made Riggs smile. He'd nearly forgotten the reason he'd come there. He reached over and turned down the stereo so he could hear the sound of the tires in the dirt, that wonderful quiet sound of arrival at the drive-in. He let his arm hang down outside the window, and the heat rising from the dirt kissed his fingertips.

She coasted down the dusty path along the back fence.

"Where should I park?"

There weren't more than a dozen vehicles there yet, each parked at the greatest possible distance from the other. That they were all current or recent models seemed strange to Riggs, so vivid were the fins and chrome bumpers of his memory. He pointed out a spot off to the right. Becky pulled up to a pole and cut the engine.

"Well, here we are," she said.

She reached for a peppermint and unwrapped it and popped it into her mouth and dropped the little wrapper out the window. She offered him one and he took it and fiddled with the wrapper but didn't open it.

The sun was down now but it would be a while yet before it was dark enough to start the movie. A low rumble rolled across the sky and touched down gently far away. The first hint of coolness slipped into the balmy evening air.

"My turn to wait on you," he said and asked her what she wanted.

Making his way across the lot over to the little white concessions building, he felt as if he were hovering above the ground. A pimply kid with glasses and a paper hat was standing behind the stainless steel chutes lined with hamburgers and hot dogs and boxes of fried chicken. Plastic bottles of ketchup and mustard and mayonnaise lined the counter. A big jar of fat green gherkins. A bowl of sauerkraut. Nachos. The popcorn machine churning oily yellow popcorn. Riggs glanced up at the red-lettered menu.

"Last time I was at a drive-in the burgers were a quarter," he said with hometown conviviality to the man and woman ahead of him at the counter, an old married couple by the looks of it. The man had a goiter the size of a ping-pong ball, and his pants were too short, revealing the threadbare ankles of his pale-yellow socks.

"And girls were ladies and boys were gentlemen," said the woman, whose big white poker-chip earrings wobbled with every turn of her head. A monogrammed leather purse hung loosely from her finely wrinkled forearm.

"We've been out here nearly every night since he opened it," she said. "It's such a great idea, don't you think?"

"Yes I do, ma'am. Yes I do."

"It's funny how things work out. He thought he was doing it for the youngsters, and it turns out it's all us old-timers trying to relive our youth!" She laughed.

"No danger of that," the man grumbled with good-natured irascibility.

"We bring the grandkids out and let 'em run wild. It's so nice to be out under the stars of a summer night."

Riggs nodded. A feeling of great peace rich in the moral certainties of yesteryear was washing over him. He wished his wife were there with him.

Another old couple came in. Hispanic. Riggs glanced out the window. The woman was right. He didn't see a single young person anywhere on the lot.

A few minutes later he emerged from the building holding a cardboard tray with two drinks, two cheeseburgers wrapped in foil, and a big tub of popcorn in it. In the interim the sky had grown dimmer, the night's first stars sneaking through, and now the cars were flowing in, filling up the empty spaces, churning up the dust. Off to the south the sky was scribbling silent blue lightning beneath the leaden thunderheads. When he saw the children in the playground up near the screen he had to stop and revel in a warm gush of memory. He and his brother and sister leaping out of that old Chrysler, leaving their mother in brief, blessed peace, running up between the parked cars to the swing set and merry-go-round at the base of the enormous screen. You had to be careful when you ran between the cars not to lynch yourself on the speaker cables stretched between the pole and the window of the car, not so much out of fear of injury as fear of the consequences if you broke off someone's window. After a while their mother would stalk up, irate that they hadn't come back for their supper like she'd told them to, and they would all file back together. It was strange and exciting walking in between all those other people's cars, seeing other families inside, everyone eating and drinking just as if they were at their own dinner table. Other mothers and fathers, other kids, all side by side in their different cars, facing the screen, eating. Back in the car, he'd gobble down his hamburger, then rush back out to the playground, and he wouldn't even realize it had gone dark until the first strains of music began to echo out of the speakers.

Riggs stood there for a while, eyes glazed over, then he carried on back to the little white car.

"Got us some popcorn," he said, handing the drinks to Becky through her window.

She looked bored.

He got back in and set the tub between them.

"I hope you don't mind," she said as she pulled a half-pint bottle of Wild Turkey from her purse.

This took Riggs by surprise. He wasn't sure why.

"Why should I mind?"

She poured half an inch of the whiskey into her Coke and put the lid back on and swirled it around a little and took a sip through the straw, then handed Riggs the bottle.

"I'd considered it myself," he lied, pouring some into his drink.

The warmth spread leisurely down into his stomach and out to his hands and feet. A humid breeze made off with the dust from the arriving cars. A honk lingered in the air.

"So, Becky," he said, "what do you aim to do once you get to Hollywood?"

She gave him a little look barbed with sarcasm.

"Be a movie star, what else?"

He nodded.

They sat there in the quiet. He told her about the time he'd nearly sandwiched two kids on a motorbike on the Santa Monica freeway, and that was enough to put a twinkle in her eye and a smile on her lips.

She must have seen the look in his eyes, for she quickly looked away, and it was awkward and quiet again. They sat there eating their burgers, sipping their drinks, waiting for darkness to fall.

At long last the screen blazed alive with the mayhem of a coming attraction. A great, tinny mishmash of violins and voices swept across the lot, echoing wildly, and a hundred arms reached out in unison for the speakers.

"I love those old things," Riggs said as Becky hooked the big hunk of gray metal, like something salvaged from a U-boat, on to her window and turned up the volume, bringing the drive-in squarely into the car. Off to the south the lightning was flashing brighter, and now he could smell the rain.

The preview they were watching, if the fashions and the

cars and the faded pinkish quality of the film itself were any indication, must have been at least fifty years old.

"Where in hell'd he get hold of that?" Riggs said.

"Is that a real movie?"

The preview finished and another one equally old came up.

"You ever heard of *Last Train to Yucca Bluff*?" Riggs asked her.

She hadn't. Nor *The Moonbeamers*.

"Oh God," Becky said when the movie finally started. "I hate black-and-white movies."

Opening credits. A lone rider traversing a vast desert plain. Soaring orchestration. "Lorna Jones . . . Douglas Franklin . . . in a Harold Wertzmeyer Production . . ."

"Hell, if I knew it was nothing but old movies," Riggs said.

"Barf," she said.

"No wonder there aren't any kids out here."

It was only for her sake that he felt bad. He wasn't averse to watching an old Western himself. He kind of liked the idea.

They sipped their drinks and took turns reaching into the tub of oily popcorn between them and pretended to be getting sucked into the scratchy old C-grade Western.

About ten minutes into the movie, which featured a gang of scowling Mexicans—played by painted whites—terrorizing an isolated ranch family, and which Riggs had convinced himself wasn't half-bad after all, Becky reached over and set her hand in his crotch, as casually as if she'd misjudged a reach for the popcorn, and there she left it.

Neither of them said anything. He took another swig of his drink and kept his eyes on the movie, which all of a sudden changed into something altogether different, the soundtrack and the action on the screen suddenly taking on a strange, unreal quality, somehow of a piece with the warmth flowing from Becky's hand, and an image flashed through Riggs's mind of being in the truck at that very moment, just outside of Deming, watching the movie as he drove along, aware that he was actually there, on the road, and also there, with an eighteen-year-old girl presently unzipping his fly and inserting her chilled hand into his underwear and taking a firm hold of his tool and pulling it out into the warm, humid air, certainly not the first time she'd performed this operation, a thought that filled him with strange jealousy.

Then it began to rain. At first slow fat drops that smacked the windshield like splattered bugs. Then a real downpour. A real summer thunderstorm. Lightning flashing and forking a million times brighter than the screen. Thunder cracking and battering the earth.

"Shit! I'm getting all wet," Becky said.

She put the speaker back on the pole and rolled up her window. Now the rain pummeling the little car all but blotted out the soundtrack. The runny gray blob of a movie dripped down onto the hood and spilled across it.

Riggs told himself he'd better just zip himself up and say in a firm tone that while he thought she was a good-looking gal and all, she was mistaken if she thought he'd asked her out there to take advantage of her. But he said nothing. Moving the popcorn out of the way, Becky scooted over onto his seat. Riggs took a firm hold of her and closed his eyes. He rubbed his hands up and down her impossibly smooth young arms. His fingers slipped up into her sleeves and around her shoulders. She pulled up her shirt. Her nipples felt hard and soft and tiny against the meat of his rough palms.

"Do me, Duke," she quivered, and somehow that cheesy Hollywood line sounded just right in Riggs's ears.

But the moment he felt himself inside her he was overcome by disgust. With her, with himself, with being there at that drive-in when he should have been on his way back home to his wife, with the thrumming of the rain on that pathetic little car, with the sound of her sincere little whimpers, but most of all with the fact that this very disgust was part of the cheap thrill of it all. To make matters worse the alcohol had been stronger than he'd realized and he found himself giving everything he had in an effort to be done with it, only to find that he was making no progress at all, and it seemed to him, not without an odd twinge of pride, that at this rate he would outlast the movie. Her whimpers were driving him nuts, so certain were they of their intended effect. She sounded like some over-blown porno, less so the sound of her voice than the implication in it that behind his exertions was a desperate desire to please her when in truth he simply wanted to get it over with. But even that simple dignity seemed beyond his reach.

He battled on for a few more minutes, her fake orgasms growing ever raspier, and then he felt himself begin to deflate. Finally, cashing in the remainder of his pride, he faked a spasm himself and collapsed back in the seat.

They lay like that for some time, her heartbeat tapping lightly out of sync with his own, the rain still pounding the little car, and through it all the faint squeal of violins.

Half an hour later the storm had blown over and they were back in their own seats, watching the movie just like all the other old couples in the cars around them. Eating popcorn and watching the movie, as if nothing at all had happened. It was the longest movie Riggs had ever seen.

When it was finally over and people started heading back to the concessions building to get more food, Riggs asked Becky if she had her heart set on staying for the second feature.

She seemed to give it some thought, then said, "Whatever you want."

She drove him back to the truck stop through the dark wet streets. The town was completely dead. She pulled up beside his truck, like a boy delivering his girl to her front door.

Riggs thought he should say something but he didn't know what. The restaurant looked inviting through the windows. A man in a booth raised a white cup to his lips and took a sip. A waitress came over and the man smiled at her and she smiled back at him.

"Penny for your thoughts," Becky said.

Riggs looked at her. In the darkness her eyes looked too big for her face. He went on looking at her.

"They ain't worth that much," he said.

She leaned over and kissed him on the cheek. A preposterous little peck that seemed to say it all.

Darling Courts

FREDDIE YORK WASN'T MUCH TO look at. He had bad teeth, his eyes bulged, and his Adam's apple jerked up and down like something trying to claw its way out of him. His hands were always filthy and his hair was as greasy as a restaurant mop. Ed never would've hired him in a million years. Riffraff, he would've called him. I wasn't too sure about him myself that day he came for the job. When I asked him what kind of experience he had, he closed his eyes and pursed his lips and began stroking his chin like I'd asked him what the meaning of life was. Eventually he opened his eyes and said: "I'm good at building stuff."

He claimed he'd built a washing machine once out of old car parts. Apparently it hadn't worked, I felt like saying, but I held my tongue. "I like working with my hands," he said. He spoke in a slow, monotonous baritone that rattled your backbone.

I asked him if he had any references. He thought about it.

"None as such, Ms. Basch."

I waited for something more. He went on looking at me. He didn't blink nearly enough.

"Are you working now?"

"I'm digging graves out at the pet cemetery."

It was the first I'd heard of a pet cemetery in Deming and I'd been here forty years.

"Who runs it?"

"Shrimpy Hendrix. You could call him but there's no phone out there."

We stared at each other.

"Well, is there anyone I can call for a reference?"

He closed his eyes and pursed his lips.

"Shrimpy Hendrix," he said.

I smiled cordially. I went ahead and told him what I was looking for—he nodded with conviction at every point—but I'd already made up my mind I didn't want anything to do with him.

Just to be civil I asked him how he could be reached.

"I could stop back by," he said.

"Well . . ."

"How about Wednesday?" he said with such hope in his voice that I couldn't say no. He put out his filthy hand and I went ahead and shook it.

It was Mary Jo Nicklas who'd told me I ought to take in a handyman, let him live in one of the units in lieu of pay. I wasn't too keen on the idea at first. Sooner or later he'd want the money. Or else he'd have to take on other work. Then he wouldn't be around when I needed him. But it's hard to get someone over for these piddly little jobs like fixing a busted window crank. My husband used to do all the repairs himself, but he'd been dead ten years. Ed never would've hired Freddie York in a million years.

Ed and I had bought Darling Courts from Walter Measday when we moved out from Pottstown, Pennsylvania, in 1952. It was a motor court at the time, constructed from buildings brought from the Japanese internment camp outside Lordsburg. They hadn't changed much over the years. They were still white stucco with broad, rounded corners, like adobes. A shallow awning ran along above the doors, giving the three buildings a touch of modern style. The doors and window frames were aqua green. Every unit had its own squared-off juniper shrub and a bed of tulips. In the early days, when it was still a motor court, we had a big, heart-shaped neon sign in the courtyard to help attract the highway traffic. This was before the interstate was built and it was just the old two-lane highway going west to Lordsburg and east to Las Cruces. There'd also been a big red heart painted on the outside wall of the office, with "Best Assured at Darling Courts" painted inside it. I loved the heart theme. It wasn't just a gimmick. It really made people feel welcome. I always kept a batch of homemade cookies on a plate at the check-in desk. Our girls were kids then. They helped people with their luggage and showed them to their rooms. We got travelers from all over. I loved hearing about where they'd been and where they were headed to. It was different back then. People on the whole were more decent.

We kept the motel going for nearly twenty years. Ed was still working full time at Paul Revere in those days, so I pretty much ran it myself, with the help of the girls. But by the end of the sixties I'd had enough. All we ever got anymore were the hippies and weirdos. All the normal people were staying at the new Holiday Inn and the Motel 6 on the other side of town. The hearts didn't mean what they used to. People thought it was a love motel. It wasn't a good environment for the girls. When I discovered the kind of stuff they were finding in the rooms I took them off the job and hired a Mexican lady to do the cleaning.

In 1971 we converted the twelve rooms to eight apartments. It never was the sort of place to attract families. The units were too small, all one-bedrooms with a small kitchen and living room, the kind of place for poor young couples, bachelors, and widows. As strange as some of the tenants were, it always felt like a little community at Darling Courts, and I was happy to be a part of it. On summer nights we'd have barbecues out in the courtyard, and everyone would sit around on lawn chairs long into the night, drinking beer and talking under the stars. We had people from all walks of life. Bud Lewis lived in number 4 for fifteen years. He sold orthopedic shoes. There were the Ruebush twins, Jean and Deloris, in number 2. They were nurses. They were a great help after my hysterectomy. There was Yolk and Lew See Lew in number 7. They had the China Garden. We had some weird ones too. Like the guy who ran the rock shop, Rex Koleer. He had us take the bed out because he preferred sleeping on the floor. And Ms. Carmack, the junior high band teacher. She got arrested for shoplifting. All those people were gone now, dead or moved on.

Now it was my turn. I was damn near eighty. I was tired of the hassles and the upkeep. I wanted to have a little money to leave my daughters when I croaked. They were all married, one of them on her second husband, and living in different states. They didn't want me coming to live with them. I didn't blame them. I'd done the same thing to my mother. Besides, they knew I'd never leave Deming.

I saw a few more people. One guy after looking around had the gall to tell me I'd be robbing anyone dumb enough to work for rent. In his next breath he told me he'd be happy to do "the whole job" for ten thousand dollars. I told him where he could stick his ten thousand dollars. Another man had three kids and was looking for a salary. Freddie hadn't mentioned money once.

He showed up around eleven on Wednesday wearing the same clothes he'd worn on Monday: green jeans and a red-and-white flannel long-sleeve shirt buttoned at the wrists. I watched him gangle across the courtyard to my door, wondering what the hell I was getting myself into.

"Here's the deal," I said, holding the screen open. "If I like your work we're in business. If not I'll pay you for your time but that's the end of it."

"Thank you, ma'am," he said.

I took him over to number 6. Ernie Hofackett had been in there for years. He'd recently remarried and moved in with the woman. There was a lot of work to be done. The walls needed cleaning and painting. You could see where Ernie used to sit and smoke his cigars. The linoleum was buckling in the kitchen. The closet door in the bedroom had come off its rails. I don't care to mention the state of the toilet.

I asked Freddie how long he thought it would take. He seemed confused. I think it hadn't dawned on him until then that he was the one who'd be doing the work. He took another look around.

"Oh, not too long," he said.

"Well, how long? A week, two weeks, what?"

"A week."

It took him two. I checked up on him now and then but mostly left him alone. If he couldn't do the work without me looking over his shoulder then I didn't want him. He didn't have all the stuff he needed, so I had him use my account at Foxworth-Galbraith. I called Kenny down there to let him know I had someone coming in. He called back after seeing Freddie, just to make sure.

Freddie drove an old green Datsun pickup with all kinds of crap in the back. Boards, rope, pipes, old shoes, dead cactuses, a lamp, mud-encrusted towels—you name it, it was back there. The front was full of crap too. He had a worn-out biography of Leonardo da Vinci on the dash. When he wasn't working for me he was usually working on that truck.

The tenants gave him strange looks whenever they crossed paths. They were a nosy lot. Most of them had been with me for years and felt they had a stake in everything that went on at Darling Courts. They were anxious about who'd be taking Ernie's place. I didn't mention who it might be. I still wasn't sure myself.

As it turned out, he did good work. It was the best the unit had looked in decades. Everything was brilliant white. He'd fixed everything. Every hinge, every knob, every socket. He'd even managed to salvage the toilet. All for less than a hundred dollars.

"You outdid yourself," I said, careful not to sound too pleased.

If he was proud, he didn't show it. He just scratched his neck and looked around like he'd never seen the place before. He was even filthier now, but I couldn't argue with the results. I told him it was his if he wanted it.

He put his hands in his pockets and nodded to himself.

———

He was odd. There's no denying that. The ladies steered well clear of him. Lucie Cobb was always going on about how much he stank. I honestly never noticed it, but I never did have a good sense of smell—it used to drive Ed crazy that I was always burning the toast. Bessie Puckett was just plain afraid of him. That deep, monotonous voice of his gave her the creeps. Ms. Craig couldn't stand him, but she was a bitter old bitch who couldn't stand anyone. The men didn't like him because he was slow and shifty. In the beginning they tried to get chummy with him. He'd be out pruning the hedges or raking the gravel and they'd step over to say hello and put their ten cents in like men always do, but he didn't have any use for them. He'd stop what he was doing and listen to them in that intense way he had, then he'd just nod and carry on with his work. Vern Mosier thought he was retarded. I didn't know what to say to that. Maybe he was a little slow, but I was the one who'd hired him, who'd given him Ernie's apartment. I wasn't about to start bad-mouthing him behind his back.

It wasn't that he did anything particularly strange. It was just his manner, that slow inward earnestness of his. It always seemed like he was straining to hear some argument going on deep inside himself. You'd be talking to him and you'd see he was more interested in whatever was going on inside his head than what you were saying. I usually had to repeat myself two or three times before what I was telling him began to sink in. Then it was like a revelation, and I could see the sense of purpose come into his eyes.

In the summer, when he was working on something outside, I'd make him take a break and come in for a drink. It was like pulling teeth that first time.

"Can I get you some ice water?" I asked him. He'd been out scraping the walls in preparation for painting. I was afraid he'd have a heatstroke and fall off the ladder and break his neck and sue me.

"No, ma'am."

"Just call me Bea, Freddie."

"It's not good manners."

"Good manners are for strangers. How about some iced tea?"

He thought about it.

"No thank you."

"You've got to drink something, Freddie. It's a hundred degrees out there. What do you like? I've got juice, pop, milk."

I could see that all he really wanted was to get back out to his work, to be alone, but his notion of good manners wouldn't allow it. He was stuck. He gave in to the cola, and I put some ice cubes in a glass.

"No ice, please," he said.

I looked at him.

"But it's not cold. You can't drink it warm."

"I don't mind."

"Suit yourself," I said and poured the warm cola into a glass and set it on the table in front of him.

He sat there with his hand around the glass, stiff as a mannequin. He had other peculiarities. Like always wearing heavy leather gardening gloves when he watered the shrubs and tulips. I hadn't noticed until Elmer Boehm pointed it out. I thought it was just because he was pruning and pulling weeds.

"He wasn't doing any pruning or weeding," Elmer said. "He put those gloves on just to water."

"Well, what's so strange about that? Maybe he just likes to wear gloves when he works."

"It's peculiar," Elmer said.

Elmer had no business talking about other people's peculiarities. He was a retired mailman who still walked his route every morning. He'd done it for twenty years before retiring and ten years after. "Seeing as they're still paying me," he'd say when anyone asked him why he did it, but he'd never finish his sentence, as if it was obvious that the only decent thing to do with a pension was to go on doing what you did to earn it.

Lucie was convinced that Freddie never bathed. She lived in number 7, directly to the right of him.

"I never hear the shower running over there."

"I'm sure he takes a bath or something," I said.

"I would've heard it. A bath runs louder than a shower. I hear LaVerne's all the time."

"Well, it's no concern of mine if he bathes or not. That's not what I hired him for."

Of course she was right. You could see it just looking at his hands. They were the color of a dirty street, with patches of pale skin showing through here and there. I hated to think about the state of the apartment after how nice and clean he'd gotten it, but I wasn't about to get rid of him just because he was dirty. He was saving me a lot of money.

I often found myself defending him, sometimes for things I didn't care for myself. Like how damn slow he worked. It took him three times as long as a normal person to finish anything, mostly because he spent half his time staring into space. It didn't matter as much when he was outside, but I had a hell of a time with the tenants when he was working in their apartments, especially the women.

"I don't want that man coming into my apartment again," Bessie came in whining one day, all in a fluster.

"What happened?"

"He stares at me."

Bessie was a faded glamour queen who'd been stared at her whole life and wouldn't have known what to do with herself if she wasn't. She still went around in miniskirts at sixty years old.

"He stares at everything," I said. "He stares at walls and rocks and dead spiders. The only way to keep him from staring at you is if you're not there."

So he could only go into Bessie's when she was out at the country club or Golden Gossip, which slowed things down even more.

All of them had some kind of problem with him. Herb Guzon, who was paid to stand around looking solemn during services at Garcia's Funeral Home, was convinced he was a psychopath. Vern and Lucie, who lived on either side of Freddie, were constantly reporting odd little noises coming from his apartment, clicks and hums and scrapings, which only confirmed their suspicions that he was building a bomb to kill us all. None of them could understand why I'd hired him, much less given him an apartment to live in. It was like I'd welcomed a wolf into the flock.

He was an affront to the senses, I'll grant them that, but I liked him all the more for it. I don't know why. I value cleanliness as much as the next person. He only had two pairs of pants that I ever saw, the green ones and the gray ones, and the more work he did for me the more indistinguishable they became. I found that oddly comforting. Sometimes I'd stand at the window watching him work. It was like watching some strange sea creature floating in an aquarium, he moved so slowly. I liked the way he stared at things too. It made you give a second look to things yourself. Maybe it came down to the fact that the longer he took to finish the work, the longer I could put off selling Darling Courts.

———

Once it got cold there wasn't much for him to do. Just little things like relighting the pilots, changing kitchen light bulbs, dealing with the odd broken curtain rod. I saved the big projects for the warmer months. Freddie didn't like being idle, which was partly why he took so long to finish anything. So when winter rolled around and he found himself with nothing to do, he took a job as a cook at the Ramada Inn. I couldn't believe any eating establishment would hire him, but apparently he'd been a cook at one time or another in nearly every restaurant in Deming. I found that out later from Dan Chadburn, who did the deliveries for the meat-packing company.

I was a fairly regular diner at the Ramada Inn buffet. Me and some of the ladies would go there occasionally after church. It gave me pause to think that Freddie was the one cooking our food. (I didn't mention it to the ladies. They would've stopped going if they knew.) Of course he'd had to clean himself up. Even Deming restaurants have hygiene laws. It was strange seeing him leaving for work in his clean white cook's uniform, his hair cut short, his mustache trimmed. Even the skin of his hands looked unnaturally bright. He didn't seem like the same person. It wasn't just the way he looked, though that was part of it. It was more that I just couldn't picture him as anything but my handyman. Even if there wasn't a thing for him to do, it seemed like he should've still been around, in case something did come up. He was living rent-free after all. That was just selfishness on my part. The man had a right to survive. The first time I ate at the Ramada Inn while he was the cook it took an hour for the roasted potatoes to reappear in the buffet. The ladies were fuming. I couldn't help laughing inside.

One Saturday afternoon in February an old friend of ours, Tom Cline, a CPA who lived in Las Cruces, stopped by to help me with my taxes. He'd lived in number 3 for a few years back in the late seventies.

"Isn't that Freddie York out there?" he said on his way in. It must've been one of Freddie's days off from the restaurant. I had him working on Herb's doorknob.

"You know Freddie?"

"Not really. I know his father. Does he work for you?"

"He's my handyman."

I made us some coffee and asked him what all he knew about Freddie.

"His father's Tad York, the cactus guy. His original name was Tadeusz Jankowski. He was from Poland. He spent three years in Gross-Rosen. He's still got the tattoo on his forearm. He emigrated in the early fifties with his wife. "

Tom watched Freddie through the window.

"His mother died of cancer sometime in the '80s. She never spoke much English. Her name was Sylvia. Painfully shy. An enigmatic creature, like Freddie."

I glanced out the window trying to picture Freddie in the bosom of this family Tom was describing.

"He had a falling out with his father some years back," Tom went on. "I don't know the details. He tried having Freddie work for him for a while, but Freddie either scared off the customers or just gave the cactuses away."

44

Tom wasn't looking well. I'd heard from a mutual friend that he was drinking a lot. His skin looked deathly pale in that winter afternoon light.

"The story that always stands out in my mind about Freddie," he said, "is that he was bitten by a dog when he was a kid and had to get rabies shots in his stomach. According to Tad he was never the same after that."

"How awful." A shiver ran through me as I pictured enormous needles puncturing little Freddie's stomach.

"You know he's afraid of water," Tom added.

"What?"

"Yes. He won't go near it. Won't even drink it," Tom said. "The hydrophobia never actually set in or he'd probably be dead. It's psychosomatic. Somewhere along the way he convinced himself he was afraid of water, and it's been with him ever since."

We both watched Freddie doing nothing for a while.

"So," Tom said, "how are the girls?"

———

Those sad little glimpses into Freddie's childhood deepened my protective urges toward him. What a terrible thing to be burdened with. Fear of water. In a desert. And here everyone was thinking he was just too lazy to bathe. I felt sorry for him. He didn't have any friends that I ever saw. The other tenants went out of their way to avoid him. His own father had disowned him. His mother was dead. He didn't have any brothers or sisters. I felt like I was about the only family he had, and that sure as hell wasn't worth much. What he needed was a little human kindness. He was like a dog that's been kicked so many times it's forgotten how to relax in human company. Knowing how much he liked candy bars—when he did take breaks it was to sit and eat some gloppy thing in the full glare of the sun—I baked a batch of chocolate chip cookies for him and took them over to his apartment in a big Tupperware tub. He tried his best to refuse them but I wouldn't have any of it. He thanked me begrudgingly and took the tub. He never mentioned whether or not he ate them, and I never got the tub back. I racked my brain trying to think what else nice I could do for him, but any sign of interest in him made him so uncomfortable. I certainly didn't want to mention that I knew about his phobia.

I knew from the gossip mill—Ms. Craig had "noticed" his trash in the dumpster—that all he ever ate for dinner were microwave TV dinners, so I decided to ask him if he'd care to come around some night for a proper meal. It was another three months before he accepted. By that time he'd been fired from the Ramada Inn and was back full time with me. He'd been with me for a year now, and the day was approaching when there'd be nothing left for him to do. I was already thinking up projects just to keep him busy.

I made my special meatloaf that night, the way Ed always loved it, with onions and peppers in it, and my secret ingredient, a few fresh mint leaves. I went out and bought a six-pack of Coors. (I'd seen some empty cans in the bed of his truck.) I felt like a real ass standing at the counter in Bob's Bottle Shop, especially when the man asked to see my ID.

It was a peculiar dinner. Freddie tucked his napkin into the collar of his shirt. What a sight! The odd elegance of that paper napkin against the smeared and speckled crud all over his flannel shirt. He chewed with his mouth open. Bits of food kept sticking to his mustache, which he'd wipe off with the back of his hand in the middle of chewing. He drank a few beers. It made him a little more talkative than usual. I had one myself. Somehow we got on the subject of the water tower.

"There's about a million gallons in there," he said with a glimmer of boozy awe in his eyes.

The water tower stood about half a mile to the north, over next to Sonic and the interstate. It was about the highest thing in town. You could see it from the courtyard. It was pale blue, with "DEMING" written on it in big black letters.

"I doubt it's a million," I said.

"It's a million," he insisted. "All that water's pumped up

from the Mimbres aquifer. There's not a running river within sixty miles. If that water tower wasn't there, all these faucets in town would be bone dry. Deming would dry up and blow away like a tumbleweed."

He grinned like a fool, as if the thought of Deming drying up and blowing away was one of his most cherished dreams. I indulged him. I was just happy he was talking. I don't think he'd said that many words the whole time I'd known him.

"The Mimbres runs after a good storm, don't forget that," I said, showing a little pride in our own sometimes river.

I brought out my butterscotch pudding for desert. He really liked that. He ate nearly half the bowl. I caught him out of the corner of my eye licking his bowl while I was in the kitchen.

I put on the radio and we went and sat in the living room. I had the front door open and you could hear the sparrows chirping away out there in the last of the light.

"Are you happy with our arrangement here, Freddie?" I asked him. The beer had made me a little forward as well.

He didn't seem to hear.

"I mean, it's not a burden, is it, financially? You do do an awful lot of work."

It was good seeing someone sitting in Ed's recliner for a change.

"I like the work," he said.

"But how do you get by?" I couldn't contain my curiosity any longer. It was guilt too.

"My father helps me," he said. Something came over his face as he said this. A flicker of something sharp as glass behind that blank, bug-eyed expression. Then it was gone and he was back to normal.

I shouldn't have asked.

"Well, I just want you to know I appreciate all the work you've done for me. I hope you're happy. If there's anything you ever need just let me know."

He nodded but he wasn't really listening. He was staring at my butterfly. It's one of those that's perched on a twig in a little glass dome. My youngest had got it for me on a field trip to

Washington, DC. I had an urge to give it to him, but it didn't seem right.

———

After that night something seemed to come over him. I didn't see him for a few days, though his truck stayed there in front of his apartment. Thinking he might be sick, I went over to see if he was okay. It took him a long time to answer, and when he did he wouldn't look me in the eye. He was supposed to be digging the hole for a little decorative pond and fountain I wanted to put in the courtyard, so I asked him how that was coming along. It was obvious it wasn't coming along at all, but I had to say something.

"Good," he said.

I couldn't help feeling that he was upset with me for something. I lingered there at his door for a few more awkward moments, then went back home.

He was nearly three weeks digging that hole. He'd do two or three shovelfuls, then go back into his apartment. His routine had always been to stop by every few mornings to see what I wanted done. That had stopped altogether. I couldn't help thinking that the look I'd seen when I'd asked about his finances had something to do with the change that had come over him. It sharpened my guilt over how much I'd taken advantage of him, which I'd been feeling more and more since Tom's visit.

One evening, about a month after our dinner, he knocked on my door. It was just past supper and I was watching an awful program on TV. I turned it off and went to the door.

"What can I do for you, Freddie?" I said cheerfully, as if to show him how easy I was with things.

He didn't say anything. We stood there facing each other across the screen. I asked him again what it was he needed, but he just went on looking at me. All of a sudden, as I was looking into his eyes, my knees went a little weak. I hadn't felt anything like it in a long long time. I looked away, pretending not to feel it.

Finally I said, "Well, I can't just stand here all night, Freddie." I started to close the door.

"Ms. Basch," he said and cleared his throat.

I opened the door again. This time when I looked at him all his filth and ugliness seemed to fall away, and standing before me was a lovely young man, too bashful to speak his heart. The sunset was pale orange and pink behind him. The air was nice and cool coming through the screen. It was such a lovely feeling. As I was standing there gawking at him like a lovestruck girl, an image came into my mind that set my spine tingling. He was naked in my bathtub and I was washing him, my hands running all over his body, seeking out every hidden pocket of dirt and freeing it from his skin. All his fears and anxieties were pouring out of him, and he was relaxing at last in the water, in my hands.

We stared at each other for a while, my heart knocking like I'd just climbed a flight of stairs, then he cleared his throat again and said, "I hate to bother you, Ms. Basch, but I was wondering if I could borrow ten dollars."

It took me a second to come back to reality. I smiled, if only to conceal my true feelings.

"Well, of course you can, Freddie." I went and got my purse and took a ten out of my billfold. The color was already draining from the sky by the time I returned to the door.

"Just keep it," I said, opening the screen and handing him the bill. I couldn't look him in the eye.

"No, ma'am," he said. "I'll pay you back."

"I don't want you to."

We went back and forth about it for so long that I finally got irate and said, "Keep the money, Freddie, for Christ's sake." He put the bill in his pocket and thanked me and left.

I stood for a long time at the kitchen sink, feeling like a fool. I decided then and there that after he finished the fountain I'd tell him I didn't have any more work for him, that our arrangement was over. He'd have to find somewhere else to live.

49

It never came to that. On the morning of June seventeenth, while I was in the shower, I heard an explosion. It was big. It jolted the window panes and shook the walls. I turned off the water and stood there in a fright. There was an eerie silence outside the window. Even the sparrows had stopped chirping.

I got out and dressed quickly and headed for the front door. The note was there just inside the sill. It was folded in a small square. All it said was: *Tell them it was me. Freddie.* Whatever blood was left in me sank straight down to the floor.

Everyone was standing out in the courtyard, facing north, the strangest expressions on their faces. I turned to look. First I saw the long smudge of black smoke way up high. Then I saw the tower. The metal of the bulb was peeled back like an orange rind, and there were streams of water pouring out of it, long continuous streams running all the way to the ground, glittering like liquid gold in the morning sun. It was the awfullest thing I ever saw.

We all just stood there with our jaws hanging open. I still hadn't connected what I was seeing with Freddie's note. It wasn't until someone said, "A water tower don't just blow up," that it hit me. I went back in and stood at the kitchen sink, my hands shaking. Then I called the sheriff.

He was there in about ten minutes, asking to see the note. We went over to Freddie's apartment together. I remember the looks of self-righteous vindication in the eyes of the tenants, seeing me and the sheriff going into Freddie's apartment like that.

It was cleaner than I thought it would be, just some candy bar wrappers on the coffee table and some grime around the light switches. The sheriff looked around the living room, then went into the bedroom. I was staring out the window, unable to take my eyes off the water tower. I hadn't felt anything like it since the morning I'd found Ed dead on the bathroom floor. You see it with your own eyes, but you just don't believe it.

"Ms. Basch, can you come here a minute?" the sheriff called from the bedroom.

There were a bunch of small cardboard boxes scattered all over the floor. He was holding a few, reading the labels.

"What is it?"

"Chemical suppliers," he said. "A whole mess of 'em, by the looks of it."

He asked me a few more questions, then said he had to get back to the tower. The whole town was on their way down there to see it.

"I'll have to keep this," he said about the note. That probably upset me more than anything. I knew he had no choice, but I couldn't help feeling that Freddie's note had been for me alone. He'd given it to me, not anyone else. The sheriff told me not to touch anything, not to go back in. He'd be back later to get a statement from me. Then he got back in his car and drove off, leaving me to deal with that look in the tenants' eyes.

"I don't know anything!" I snapped at them.

Then they all started going back into their apartments to call people and spread the news that Freddie York had blown up the water tower. I don't think it even crossed their minds that he might be dead. They wouldn't have cared anyway.

The water was back on by noon. All they did was divert it from the eastside tower. Deming didn't dry up and blow away.

———

I sold Darling Courts to Bill McKinley later that year and moved into the Kingdom of the Sun Retirement Center, right next door to Mary Jo Nicklas. My daughters come to visit once or twice a year. I'm happy enough, I suppose.

It seems to hit me most when I'm brushing my teeth before bed, with the faucet running. Sometimes it's sadness. Sometimes it's a feeling of betrayal. I stop brushing and I see Freddie standing there on top of the tower, holding my Tupperware tub, way up above everything. He's staring out across the desert. The sun is just coming up, striking the northern ridges of the Floridas. The sky is all around him, Deming sprawled out far below. Then he just turns the tub and pours all that pure sodium metal through the hole he made with that ten-dollar hacksaw. The worst thing is, I know I didn't even cross his mind.

Road to Nowhere

THE MARKERS RAN DUE EAST from an unused dirt road named Maverick straight toward the mountains, their fluorescent orange ribbons bright as poppies against the pale browns of the desert. It was mostly mesquite bushes and grama grass on this side, the occasional yucca and dried-up ocotillo. Clarence's new bulldozer plowed through it all like a hot spoon through margarine.

It had been nearly a year coming. First the County had cut his budget, leaving him barely enough money to maintain his existing equipment, let alone buy anything new. So he'd applied for a project completion grant from the State. The only problem was that there hadn't been any projects in need of completion. Clarence had remedied that by creating Enchanted View Road SE. He knew there to be a tract of county land seven miles southeast of town, out near the base of the Floridas, already platted for development. Sooner or later it would need an access road. He'd gotten the records from the county clerk, had his usual guy do the survey, drafted the bid himself—he requested $100,000 knowing he'd be lucky to get half that—and got his old high school drinking buddy Tom Reed, now the county commissioner, to backdate the proposal by a year. Next he'd phoned Ike Crawford, who, in his autumn years as state senator, was trying to seal his legacy as the champion of Luna County roads. Crawford said he'd see what he could do when the legislature reconvened in January. Road projects being low on the list of priorities for the State in a recession, he wasn't able to get a slot in the capital outlay calendar until late February. At the urging of a personal memo from the governor, who owed Crawford a favor for his help in the last election, the chair of the finance committee made sure that the merits of financing the completion of a rural road in one of the least populous counties in the state, a road that probably wouldn't have a tire anywhere near it for decades to come, were not seriously debated. In the end, "Enchanted View Road Completion" was apportioned $50,000. Clarence called in his order the very next day, only to be told that there was a backlog on the track loaders—"The Israeli army cleaned us out"—and he'd have to wait six to eight weeks. Four months later the bulldozer finally arrived.

Some people might have said that what he'd done was dishonest, but Clarence didn't see it that way. The department had needed a new bulldozer and he'd found a way to get it one. To his mind, taking advantage of the law was a whole lot different than breaking it. And to prove, if only to himself, that he had every intention of using the bulldozer to complete the road he'd invented, he chose the very next morning to take it out to the site and get started on it.

The mesquite roots were the only thing that gave him any resistance at all. Some of them were as long as thirty feet, snaking out stiff as dead tree branches just below the surface. He snagged the bushes in the teeth of the rippers and gunned it straight up, and the roots leapt through the dirt, thumping and snapping as he dragged them off to the side of the road path.

The sun beating down hard on him, baking his cracked knuckles a deep coppery brown, Clarence took a break just after noon. He lifted his hat and wiped his brow with his sleeve. As he was digging out the used-up dip from his right cheek to pinch a fresh one in, he noticed something in the distance, some little man-made structure. It was white, or close to it. He took off his sunglasses and squinted but still couldn't make it out clearly. Whatever it was it looked like it was right in the path of his road.

He cut the engine and got down and set out walking up the

gently sloping bajada, weaving around the bushes as he went. Up close Clarence wasn't as big as he looked from a distance. It was his belly that gave people the impression that he was a man of stature. The pride and confidence that ten years as head honcho of the Luna County Road Department had given him exaggerated his natural swagger, pulling his shoulders back, curving his arms parenthetically around him as they swung through their arcs, shifting the brunt of his weight to the back edge of his boot heels, all of which tended to push his belly out tight against the long-sleeve polyester business shirts he favored. It wasn't a beer gut, for when he did drink, which wasn't as often as he liked to let on with the men, he went in for the harder stuff. Nor was an unhealthy diet to blame. Barb made sure of that. She always trimmed the fat from their steaks, used low-fat margarine and two-percent milk. The fact of the matter was that, like Clarence himself, his belly wasn't actually as large as the impression it left in people's minds.

It turned out to be a small camping trailer, a sixteen- or eighteen-footer by the looks of it, white, the lower third of it banded aqua green. The door in the side appeared to be open, or missing altogether. As Clarence came nearer he observed that the hoist was resting on a stack of rocks and that the tires appeared to be inflated, indications that this wasn't just another old wreck that someone hadn't bothered to dispose of properly. Even so, he wasn't expecting it when someone stepped across the doorway.

Clarence stopped and stood there for a moment, eyes fixed on the camper. He turned his head and spat. He wasn't fond of coming across people out in the desert. Nine times out of ten there was a good reason they were out there instead of with the rest of civilization, namely that they weren't normal. They were outcasts—fugitives of the law, wetbacks, religious fruit-cakes, kooks of one stripe or another. The last thing he wanted was to spook some nut case with a gun.

He considered things for another moment or two, squinting against the sun, marveling how out of all the miles of open desert to choose from they had gone and parked the thing directly in his road path, then he carried on up the bajada, clearing his throat every now and then so as to make his presence known.

When he was an easy stone's throw from the camper, he stopped and hooked his thumbs over his front pockets and called out.

"Hey there."

A moment later a woman appeared in the doorway. The first thing Clarence noticed was her belly. By the looks of it she was a good six or seven months pregnant. She looked young but there was a hardness in her face, something gaunt and weary in the way she peered out at him, her black hair tied back tight against her skull. She was wearing a pale-yellow cotton print dress that went clear down to her ankles, like something worn a hundred years ago.

Clarence stared at her for a full five seconds, then he lifted his hat a little to show his cordiality and said, "Afternoon, ma'am."

"Howdie," she replied, staring back at him suspiciously.

"This your trailer?"

"Me and my husbunt," she said.

A bunch of plastic milk jugs and various other plastic containers full of water were lined up along the front of the camper. Off to one side sat some apple crates that appeared to be full of rocks.

"Name's Clarence Bowman. I'm with the road department."

"Howdie," she said again.

He waited a moment for her to say her name or anything at all to explain what she was doing out there in a camper in the middle of nowhere. She didn't.

"Is your husband around?" Clarence asked.

"He's out."

Clarence scuffed his boot around a little in the dirt.

"Well, we're fixin' to put a road through this way," he said, nodding toward the camper and beyond. "See them stakes over yonder?"

She squinted.

"What for?"

"Oh," Clarence grinned, as if letting her in on some private joke, "just plannin' ahead."

Her expression didn't change. Clarence turned his head to spit but caught himself in time.

"Mind if I have a look around?" he asked.

"Make yourself at home," she said.

He thanked her and walked around to the back of the camper. It had an Oklahoma license plate with an out-of-date registration sticker. Some blackened tin cans and half-melted plastic marked the spot where they had been burning their garbage. He spat there, then walked around to the hoist. The tire tracks led off to the north.

A few minutes later he came back around to the front. She was still in the doorway, leaning her right hip against the frame. He noticed now that she was barefoot. She raised her hand again and looked down at him. Clarence kept a respectful distance.

"Your husband workin' in town, is he?" he asked her.

"Nah, he's up there gettin' rocks," she said, referring with the back of her head to the mountains.

"Rocks?"

"He's a rock collector. We had us a place in Muskogee with a museum and all but it burnt down."

"Sorry to hear that."

She didn't look all that sorry herself.

"When ya'll startin' on that road?"

"I'm down there now doing some clearin'."

"You want us to move?"

"Well," he said, giving it a little thought, "it'll be a while yet before I'm up this far."

"We ain't supposed to be here much longer," she said.

Clarence nodded. He raised his hat.

"You have a good day now, ma'am," he said and turned to leave.

"I'll tell my husbunt you stopped by," the woman said.

Clarence turned back and winked, then carried on down the bajada.

———

"Modern-day Okies," Ruby cackled when Clarence told her about his encounter in the desert. He knew it would get a rise out of her. She was forever reading some trashy paperback novel about trashy people doing trashy things to each other. She was sixty-two years old and had spent thirty of them running the office at the road department, which mostly entailed filing papers and talking to her daughters long-distance on the County dime. On her desk sat an array of framed photographs of her grandchildren in their infancy, red-faced babies not long from the womb, their eyes and mouths and nostrils identically shaped little lozenges of perplexity. She had a big jowly face with a mass of bronze hair that she tinted herself every three months and sculpted every morning with a wire hairbrush and a fog of hairspray. She smoked two packs of menthol cigarettes a day and had a voice like a bullfrog.

The one thing Clarence could always count on from Ruby was her cynicism. It was perfectly in tune with his own. She expected only the worst of people and was seldom disappointed.

"The husband's some kind of rock hound," Clarence said.

"Rocks for brains sounds more like it."

Sometimes Clarence wished Barb could take a few lessons from old Ruby. When he told her over supper about the people in the camper she started right in with the pity.

"That's no place for a pregnant woman to be stuck all alone." She set her fork on her plate and looked at Clarence as if he had parked the woman there himself. "Out there without a car. That isn't right. She could fall down and hurt herself and there'd be no one there to help her. No phone, nothing."

"Well, I don't think they intend on startin' a family out there," Clarence said.

"What kind of a man goes and leaves a pregnant woman

alone all day in a camper in the middle of the desert at the height of summer without any electricity or running water?"

"Them old things run on propane," Clarence said, cutting into the foil of his baked potato. "Matt Hertz used to have one. Refrigerator and everything. They'll probably only be there a couple days anyhow. The husband's some kind of rock collector."

"I don't care if he's John D. Rockefeller. That's no way to treat a pregnant woman, Clarence."

Barb believed that the world was a good place and that people were good too, even when they did bad things. She had a knack for talking to complete strangers as if they had been next-door neighbors all their lives, and more often than not the stranger couldn't help but respond in kind. This frustrated Clarence to no end whenever they went to the mall in Las Cruces. Inevitably she would strike up a conversation with the cashier in Sears, or the people in line with them at the corn-dog place, or some old man resting beside her on the bench. It didn't matter what the subject was—the weather, the price of gas, her aching feet—she always got them talking. Sooner or later she would start talking about Clarence or their daughter, Shelly, or some other private matter that Clarence didn't feel was any stranger's business, and he would shift around and clear his throat in an attempt to remind her that they didn't know this guy from Adam. The worst was when she started rattling off the names of friends and other Deming people as if they were common knowledge to the whole of humanity. "How the hell is he supposed to know who Rhonda is?" Clarence would say irately once they were alone again. But these small frustrations aside, it was this trusting, generous, sometimes downright naive nature of Barb's that had captured Clarence's heart nearly twenty-five years ago and never let go.

"Did her ankles look swollen?"

"How should I know? I wasn't lookin' at her ankles."

"Well, was her face all puffy?"

"No, she looked half-starved if you ask me."

"Good Lord." She shook her head. "Doesn't that just make you sick?"

"Why should I give a damn if people want to live like gypsies? It's a free country."

Barb shook her head sadly and picked up her fork and stabbed her potato to let out some of the steam.

Clarence figured that was the end of it. He should have known better. The next morning as he was pulling out of the driveway, Barb scuttled out in her pink housecoat with a carton of Vivaway "Female Vitality" in her hand. Clarence stopped the truck and rolled down his window.

"Here," she said, "take this out to that woman."

"Oh, for Pete's sake."

"Just do it, Clarence. She needs it."

"I'm not out there makin' house calls."

"It won't kill you." She gave him her irritated, maternal glare. He sighed and grabbed the carton and put it on the seat. She stood in the driveway and watched him drive away.

The sight of the new bulldozer basking in the morning sunlight, yellow as the yolks of fresh duck eggs, filled Clarence's heart with gladness. The feeling stayed with him all morning as he worked clearing the brush. For Clarence there was no greater joy than starting a new road. There was something so promising about it. It was the work of civilization, of man taming unruly Mother Earth. What could be more important work than that? Whatever frustrations he may have had to suffer along the way, it was all worth it when he looked out and saw that nice straight stretch of fresh, clean dirt cutting across all that wild desert brush.

Shortly after noon he cut the engine and walked back to the truck to have his lunch. He sat in the hot silence of the cab, eating his turkey sandwich, a carton of Female Vitality resting beside him on the seat.

"Vivaway," it said in bold white letters across the blue-and-pink box; and beneath it, in smaller letters: "For a New Tomorrow."

Clarence picked up the carton.

"Female Vitality," he grumbled, shaking his head with sufferance. He turned the carton around and read: "Designed to support proper balance of the female reproductive and glandular systems." He read the ingredients, a long list of strange-sounding roots and herbs. He read everything else, the recommended intake, the claims and disclaimers, the company's mailing address, etc.

The desert heat wafted in through the open windows, stinging Clarence's cheeks. He sat for some time, staring at the mountains, trying to picture some guy out there looking for rocks, leaving his pregnant wife stranded in a sweltering trailer. Then, with an annoyed grunt, he grabbed the carton and set out up the road path.

He stopped about twenty feet short of the camper and loudly cleared his throat. The woman came to the door. She was in the same dress as yesterday.

"Afternoon, ma'am," Clarence said. "Sorry to bother you again. My wife asked me to give you this." He walked up to the door. The woman went to take a step down then yanked her bare foot back from the hot metal.

"Watch yourself there," Clarence handed the box up to her. She took it and looked it over curiously. Clarence's face was almost level with her belly, and he couldn't help but notice how her navel was poking out against the stretched fabric of her dress.

"It's supposed to be good for . . . well, uh, somethin' or other," he said with an embarrassed little smile.

She thanked him.

"I don't know if it works or not," he added. "I guess some people think it does or she wouldn't be sellin' so much of it. Our garage is full of the stuff."

"I'll give it a try," she said, slipping her feet into a pair of blue plastic flip-flops just inside the door.

Clarence stepped back and surveyed the desert.

"It's a hot one today, ain't it," he said.

She stepped down cautiously on to the metal step, then settled down in the doorway in a familiar way. He noticed now

61

that her eyes were an unusually light brown, almost the color of the desert sand, as if their natural color had been bleached out of them.

"I told Trevor you was puttin' a road through here," she said. "He got a kick out of that. Puttin' a road out here."

"You'd be surprised at some of the places we've put roads," Clarence said. "My crew's down near the border as we speak, workin' on a five-miler. That one's just about nowhere to nowhere too. You got a road department, you got to make roads. Sooner or later someone'll need them."

She looked at him and scratched her ankle. Clarence took note that they weren't at all swollen.

"Why ain't you with them?" she asked him.

"Huh? Oh. Well, I figured I'd give this new dozer a spin, have a look out this way," he said, glancing out at the desert.

She didn't say anything.

Clarence was just about to say he'd better be on his way when she asked him if he was thirsty. He gave it some thought.

"I can't say as I am at the moment."

"We got some cola. I'm gonna get me one. You want one?"

"Well," he said, stroking his mustache, "if you're going to the trouble."

"It ain't no trouble," she said and smiled. It was the first smile he'd seen on her, and it put him a little more at ease.

She stood up and went in. Clarence turned his head and spat and scuffed some dirt over the wetness. He stepped over to one of the apple crates and had a look at the rocks. There were a few rough geodes, but most of it looked worthless to him: shale and quartz and plain old chunks of granite. She came back to the doorway, handed him the can, and sat back down.

"Nice and cold," Clarence said, opening it and taking a sip. It was awful. The can said "Cola" on it. "Mighty nifty, these old campers, runnin' on propane."

She sipped her cola and looked at him.

"How long you been married?"

That took Clarence aback a little. He reached up and adjusted his hat.

"Oh, going on twenty-two years, I reckon."

"Shee, now that's a long time. We only been married a year," she said. "Seems like a lot longer," she added a moment later with a twitch of her lips. "Any kids?"

He told her about Shelly being in college in Las Cruces.

"I'm expectin' myself," she said.

"I kinda figured."

She looked down at her belly as if she hadn't noticed it before.

"Ah, hell," Clarence said, patting his gut proudly, "you got nothin' on me."

That almost made her laugh. Or else the single grinning bob of her head was as far as laughter went with her. Clarence drank as much of the cola as he could stomach and was about to thank her and get going, but again she thought of something else to say to keep him there talking to her.

"We went down to some little Mexican town last night," she said.

"That'd be Palomas."

"Wildest thing I ever seen. Not ten feet from America. A whole different world. Everyone was lookin' at me. Every beady little eye. They'd liked to have gobbled me up."

"What'd you all go down there for anyway?"

"To get Trevor's medication. He said it was cheaper down there. Course they didn't have his brand. I could've told him that myself."

Clarence nodded. He glanced up at the mountains. From that vantage they were stunning to behold, a curtain of blue-gray granite blocking out the entire eastern sky, so sharp and clear that it seemed he could reach out and touch them. It gave him a pleasant floating sensation just to look at them, as if all that mass piled up in one spot were exerting a gravitational pull on his insides.

When he glanced back down at her he noticed that the hem of her dress was hitched up to her knees and that her legs were spread enough for him to see that she wasn't wearing any underwear. He caught an eyeful of black pubic hair under the

63

pale dome of her belly before he quickly looked away. He glanced out across the bajada nonchalantly, as if milling something over in his mind.

"Well," he said a moment or two later, "I best be pushin' off."

When he glanced at her again her dress was back over her knees.

"You take care," she said.

———

It took him most of the following morning to think of an excuse to go back up to the camper. His boots made a dry sucking sound in the sand as he followed his own footprints up the bajada, scattering jackrabbits as he went. Already the walk was shorter than before, thanks to the progress he'd been making with the clearing, but it was still nearly half a mile to the camper.

This time he walked right up to it and knocked lightly on the side. He heard some racket like the clanking of utensils in a pot, then she came to the door. She was holding a can opener in her right hand.

"You're gettin' to be a regular neighbor," she said. She stood in the doorway with her hips cocked left, looking down at him as if he were some exasperating kid come to sell her something. She was in the same dress again.

"My wife was curious to know if that stuff I brung you did you any good."

That wasn't true. Last night over dinner Barb had asked him if he'd given it to the woman, but she knew better than anyone that you couldn't expect results overnight. Ideally, it was best taken in conjunction with Good Life Revitalizer and Worry Away.

"It sure did," she said. "I feel like a million bucks. You thank her for me again."

Clarence couldn't help but grin at the obvious sarcasm in her voice.

"You want a drink?" she said.

"I should probably get on back," he said unconvincingly.

She turned from the doorway, ignoring his remark, and was back a moment later holding a clear, unlabeled bottle by the neck. The bottle was half-empty. She gave it a little shake.

Clarence looked back and forth a few times between the bottle, her belly, and her face.

"Well, are you comin' in or you just gonna stand out there in that heat all day?"

Clarence adjusted his hat, gave a little tug to the right arm of his mustache, then stepped up into the camper.

It was tiny inside and suffocatingly hot. The walls were all wood paneling, stained here and there from water leaks. Awkward stacks of apple crates full of rocks stood here and there at every wall. A dirty yellow curtain hung limply to one side of the back window, which was missing altogether its glass and screen. From the bare aluminum undersiding showing through a rectangular section low on the back wall, it looked as though some built-in furniture, probably a sofa, had been ripped out. In its place stood two metal chairs with torn olive-green vinyl seat cushions. A few feet in front of them sat an overturned apple crate with some magazines on it.

Clarence was struck by the feeling, as intense as the first time he had entered a Mexican's home as a kid, that he didn't belong in there. Out of force of habit he took off his hat and looked around for somewhere to hang it before setting it on the seat of one of the chairs. He took off his sunglasses and put them in his shirt pocket.

"You'd never guess from the outside how roomy these things are," he said.

She was standing behind the narrow Formica counter that partially divided the living room, if it could be called that, from the tiny kitchenette. She scooted a Styrofoam cup his way and took a sip from hers.

"I don't guess that's water," Clarence said with a nervous chuckle, stepping over to get the cup.

"Trevor's daddy makes it," she said. "It's strong."

Clarence stepped over to the door and dug the remnants of

his dip out with his forefinger and flung it to the ground. He took a sip and scowled. A glowing coal rolled down his esophagus and into his stomach.

"You ain't lyin'," he said, eyes brimming with tears.

She grinned at him.

"Have a seat," she said.

"Nah, I sit all day. My back ain't so good."

He took another drink.

"This stuff is awful," he said.

"You get used to it."

"Whoa," he said a few seconds later as a warm breeze wafted across his brain. She smiled again. She seemed to be getting a kick out of him. He didn't mind. There was a part of him, not expressed often enough, that liked to play the merry fool.

"You know you ain't supposed to drink when you're pregnant," he said lightheartedly.

"You ain't supposed to fuck strangers neither," she replied, as if it were the most innocent thing in the world.

That made Clarence laugh—a quick sharp bark of a laugh. He stood there for a second, looking out the door, rolling the remark around his mind, in the end deciding it had to be a joke, odd as it was. He laughed again.

"No, I guess you ain't," he said, still looking out the door. A flying beetle buzzed by, a flash of iridescent green in the blinding sunlight.

He took another sip. He could see the strip of naked earth he'd already cleared, and the bulldozer at the edge of it, a speck of bright yellow in a sea of tan. His heart was pumping a little more forcefully than it should have been. He went to take another drink but there was nothing left in his cup.

At last he turned and looked at her. She was on the near side of the counter now, her arms down at her sides. She was staring at him intensely, not blinking at all.

"Your husband carry a gun?" Clarence asked, almost under his breath.

"He's got one in the truck."

Clarence walked over to her and set his cup on the counter.

Her eyes hadn't left him for a second. He tried to look into them but they were too intense. He stared at her belly instead, his heart knocking hard against his sternum now. Then he slowly raised his right hand and set it on her stomach. The fabric of her dress was thin and he could feel the warmth of her body through it, even in that stifling heat. He brought his other hand up. Staring down in dumb amazement he watched his hands roam in tender circles around that lovely sphere. When his fingers grazed her belly button she inhaled sharply then gradually let her breath back out.

"Would he use it if he was to walk through that door right now?" Clarence said without looking up.

"Right now he might not," she said, "but a minute or two from now he probably would."

With that she took a fold of her dress in each hand and slowly began to pull it up, pulling Clarence's eyes up with it as it passed her knees, slid up her pale skinny thighs, up over and around her bulging belly, exposing the fleshy pink clot of her belly button. Beneath it her thick black pubic hair spread out toward the top of her thighs, thinning to a fine line creeping toward her navel. She pulled the dress over her head and off.

The sight of her little freckly tits nearly touching the top of the white globe of her belly just about knocked Clarence over. He stepped back, balanced himself, and teetered there slack jawed, as if on the edge of reason. The dress dropped silently to the floor.

After that it was all panic and fluster, him clutching her ass and sucking at her tits, her fumbling with his belt buckle, both of them grunting and gasping in haste to be done with the preliminaries and find some place to fuck. In the end he turned her around and bent her down against the counter and got up into her from behind, his hands gripping her swaying belly as if for dear life as he banged away against the blunt knobs of her haunch bones. Finally he collapsed against her with a hoarse little bleat, panting, covered in sweat, the whole business having taken less than two minutes.

"Sweet Jesus," he gasped, and stood there for a while breathing hard, still inside her. "I don't even know your name."

———

When he got home that evening some of the ladies were already there for the Wednesday night Vivaway social. They looked up from their brochures and greeted him from the sofa with big, frivolous smiles. Barb came from the kitchen and kissed his cheek and told him his dinner was in the oven.

After his shower Clarence ate his supper alone in the kitchen, staring at the wall. He could hear the ladies arriving, chattering away, laughing, but for all intents and purposes he was still in the camper with Angela's pregnant belly in his hands.

"Now that's a strange sight," Barb squawked, all juiced up on Vivaway vision, when she came in half an hour later to get the snacks out of the refrigerator. Clarence had already washed his plate and the other dishes that were on the counter and was now in the middle of cleaning all the aluminum trays beneath the stove burners.

He mumbled something about burnt gunk.

"You can clean the rest of the kitchen while you're at it," she said on her way out the door.

He did. It was so clean when he finished that Barb had to bring all the ladies in to show them what kind of a man she had. Clarence heard it all from the deck chair on the back porch, where he sat thinking about the silence of the desert at night.

"Is there something you aren't telling us, Barb?"

"Hold on. What's this? He didn't dust the knife holder."

Clarence didn't return to Enchanted View Road for the rest of the week. Instead he joined his crew at the road site near the border. They had been on the site for two months already and were well into the paving. All the men had their jobs and didn't need Clarence loafing around telling them what to do. It was only when he was around, they always said, that they messed things up. As if to prove the point, Hector forgot to load the bitumen into the hopper, and they had to rip up fifty yards of fresh pavement. Still, Clarence felt grateful to be among his men again, good simple men, free of the burdens of shame. Of course they all knew about the Okies in the camper—Ruby had made sure of that—and they wanted to know more. What did the woman look like? What were they doing out there? Did they intend on staying? "How the hell should I know?" Clarence replied to all their questions, bewildered by how much energy it took to say it with just the right amount of feigned indifference.

By Thursday afternoon Clarence was starting to feel bored. Being around the men always got his upper lip twitching with barely restrained frustration. He had a variety of tactics for relieving this tension, one of them being tugging fitfully at the right arm of his mustache. He was also a master of the slow, disgusted shake of the head. Tapping the fingernail of his left pointer against the brass bull on his belt buckle was another. On those occasions when a series of relatively minor incompetencies suddenly flared into a blazing display of ineptitude, he had no choice but to take off his hat and run his fingers through his thinning black hair in stonily silent disappointment.

By Friday morning all his twitchings and tappings and tuggings were back from vacation.

It was a long, dull weekend. He spent all day Saturday working on the front and back yards, mowing the grass, pulling weeds, clipping the shrubs. Sunday after church he settled into a golf tournament on TV. At one point Barb came up behind him and started rubbing his shoulders. Images of the camper, of Angela, of her pregnant belly, flashed across his eyes and flowed up Barb's fingers into her unsullied mind.

"Was that a hole in one?" she asked.

Clarence grunted. He knew what she was after. She always got frisky Sunday afternoons after church, when at last the world was pure again.

"Your shoulders sure are tense," she said. She massaged deeper. He could feel her breasts against the back of his head.

A few putts later they were naked in the bedroom, Clarence trying to maneuver Barb into the doggy position. She resisted. She never liked doing it from behind. Clarence tried to tug her around but she wasn't having it.

"Why do you have to be so damn prissy about it?" he snorted. "Everyone else does it."

She turned around, her neck and face flushed with indignation.

"How do you know what everyone else does?"

"Ah, hell," he said and started getting dressed.

———

Monday morning Clarence checked in at the office and left his truck there and drove back out to Enchanted View Road in the big flatbed hauler. It was time to get the bulldozer out of there.

As he pulled up to the junction of the clearing he glanced out across the bajada. In his own truck he hadn't been able to see it from the dirt road, but the cab of the hauler was higher, affording him a clear view straight across to the mountains. Clarence sat there tugging pensively at his mustache. The fact of the matter was they didn't even need the bulldozer down at the border site. They were well past that stage of things. They didn't need him either. If he didn't carry on with the clearing here, he had no option but to go back to the office and deal with the paper work he'd been putting off for weeks. As much as he loved Ruby, he had no desire to be stuck in the office with her all day.

He pulled out his can of snuff and set a clump in his cheek. He managed to work until ten before the urge to go on up there and say his piece got the best of him. She must have heard him coming, for she was already at the door when he got there.

"Where you been?" she said, an accusatory tone in her voice.

"I had some business to take care of."

She nodded, not impressed. "Must've been pretty important."

On each of his previous visits the sun had been right in her face, but at this time of day she was entirely in the shadow of the camper, and it made her pale skin look almost blue.

"You all right?" Clarence asked her.

"Right as rain."

He glanced over at the crates of rocks, which had multiplied considerably since his last visit.

"Looks like your husband hit the mother lode."

She made no reply. She crossed her arms atop her belly. Her foot was tapping the floor. Clarence looked up at her.

"Is that the only dress you got, woman?" he said and immediately felt sorry he had. It was none of his business. Her foot stopped tapping.

Clarence lifted his hat and ran his fingers through his hair. He'd never felt such confusion. Pity one second, disgust the next. Ten seconds of dense silence hung in the air between them before she spoke again.

"You want a drink?" she said sullenly.

Clarence glanced down for a second then looked up at her again, his heart all knotted up in his throat.

"What the hell's wrong with you?" she said.

Clarence shook his head. He didn't know. He was on the verge of weeping.

"Get over here," she said.

He stepped up to her. She took off his hat and set it on her head. It was too big for her. It nearly covered her eyes. It only made the guilt and pity all the worse for Clarence, seeing his hat on her like that.

All of a sudden he dropped to his knees and wrapped his arms around her legs and sank his face into her belly. He felt a stifled laugh ripple through her body. A moment later she was running her fingers through his hair, pulling his face hard against her. He reached under her dress and ran his hands up and down the backs of her legs, and whatever remorse he was feeling was quickly replaced by a sharp jolt of lust. She went on petting him as he stroked her legs. Then, knowing there was no sense fighting it, he pushed her dress up over her belly and put the knob of her navel into his mouth and proceeded to suck it like some big hairy baby at the nipple of an enormous breast, and the sounds that came from his throat were new to him and not entirely human.

They didn't bother with the drink. As before, they did it up against the counter. Clarence tried to take his time but it wasn't easy, what with the rush of premeditated adultery, the seediness of the camper, even the hard-to-forget fact that the husband carried a gun. Most of all it was her belly. He couldn't keep his hands off of it. He loved the way it hung down when she was bent over, the weight of it, the tightness, how it heaved forward and back in his hands, how it pulled taut the skin around her ribs and backbone, how soft and round and smooth it was, and even the knowledge that another man's fetus was the thing in his clutches did something to Clarence, made him feel more alive than he ever had before. And if there was one point on Angela's body that unleashed this feeling in him more than any other it was her belly button, or rather what it did to her when he touched it. He would push it in and twirl it around between his fingers, and she would let out a stifled, laughing cry, as if she were swallowing a scream, and her knees would start to jitter. He kept pressing it until she was moaning and whining like a sick dog. Clarence had never heard those kinds of sounds from a woman.

Afterward they sat on the olive-green chairs facing the open door. She was back to her terse, inscrutable self. They stared vacantly out at the desert, Clarence upright in the chair with his arms crossed in front of him, Angela reclining with her head against the back of the seat, her legs way out in front of her.

He started to say something, then stopped. He pulled out his can of snuff and pinched a fresh wad into his cheek.

"He don't like doin' it with the baby in me," Angela said. "Says it'll give it brain damage."

Clarence shook his head and nearly chuckled, but she wasn't joking.

That wasn't the only thing that got Clarence thinking that the man had a screw loose. When he asked her about the rocks, what exactly her husband did with all of them, she told him again about the rock shop they'd had back in Muskogee. "Course he burnt it down himself to get the money from the insurance," she said, "only the insurance had done run out. So he stole five hundred dollars from his old man. That helped get us out here."

Clarence frowned in disgust, picturing Ruby's face receiving these new details, but he'd already started lying to Ruby, and to Barb, saying he hadn't paid the Okies any more visits.

It was a while before she spoke again.

"I shouldn't a come," she said. "He wanted me to stay back home but I didn't want to."

"Why not?"

"I can't stand my mama," she said. Again there was a long silence before she spoke again. She said they had been out in some desert in Texas for two months before coming here, that she thought she would go out of her mind out there, just sitting there day after day, nothing to do but stare out the door. "I'm fed up with it. This ain't no way to live."

"Why don't you all just stay in town at one of the RV parks? You could at least take a shower without having to use a bucket."

"We ain't got the money for that."

Clarence put his hand on her shoulder and gave it a sympathetic squeeze. It was strange feeling bone everywhere he touched on a woman. Barb was so much thicker and softer. All the hardness of Angela's life was right on the surface, in her bones and in her eyes. He leaned over and kissed her dry lips. That seemed to strike her as a novelty. She smiled, as one might at the sight of some exotic animal in a zoo.

———

Every day before setting out for the camper he took a minute to scope out the terrain through his binoculars for any sign of the husband, either in his truck or wandering around the mountains, but he never saw a thing. It was as if the man didn't even exist. She was usually sitting there on the step waiting for him. Clarence would go to his knees before her in the dirt, whisk off his hat and sunglasses, pull up her dress, and start sucking on her belly button. More than once he felt a little kick against his lips that spooked the hell out of him but only made Angela giggle. Then, tearing him away from her navel, she would pull him up into the camper.

Afterward they would sit and talk on the olive-green chairs facing the open door. One of the magazines on the apple crate that served as a crude coffee table was an old *Better Homes and Gardens*. Angela said she liked to look at the pictures. One day as she sat there thumbing through it, she asked Clarence if he had a house. "Of course you do," she answered herself. That got Clarence telling her about the hot tub he'd put in a few years back, and how Shelly and her boyfriend had been the only ones who ever used it.

"You let your daughter bring a boy into your hot tub?"

"Yeah, me and Barb had a real argument over that one," Clarence frowned at the memory. "I said that ain't no place for teenagers of the opposite sex to be fraternizin' half-naked. You're just askin' for trouble. But Barb liked to think they were less likely to get up to no good under our nose than out in some parked car somewhere."

"She's right."

"That don't mean I got to like havin' my daughter half-naked with some snot-nosed runt feeling her up behind my back."

Angela grinned at him.

"You got a jealous streak in you."

"Yeah, when it comes to Shelly."

"You got a picture of her?"

Clarence pulled out his wallet, a big fat rattlesnake-skin thing nearly three inches thick, full of credit cards, receipts, notes, bills, business cards. He showed her the picture. It was one of Shelly's prom pictures. She was in a white satin dress with a big pink ribbon around the middle. She had blue mascara on.

"She takes after her mother," he said.

74

Next to it was an older Kmart studio photo of Clarence and Barb. He was in a dark-brown suit with a striped tan-and-brown tie, his hair slicked back. She was thinner and her hair was down to her shoulders. Her glasses were smaller then. She and Clarence were smiling, gazing out into the great blue beyond.

"Now if that ain't the picture of wedded bliss, I don't know what is," Angela quipped.

"Yeah, well, we used to have a lot of fun when we was younger," Clarence replied, ignoring the touch of sarcasm in her voice. "Used to go to the dances all the time. Hell, I ain't complainin'. It's just part of life. You ain't meant to have fun all the time. I done had my fun. I don't need any more."

Angela looked at him.

"Ain't I your fun?"

Clarence set his hand paternally on her knee and smiled.

Meanwhile, the road progressed. Sometimes while he was clearing he'd look up the bajada (he was close enough now for an unobstructed view) and see Angela in the distance, outside the camper doing something—hanging some of the husband's clothes out to dry, taking their garbage out to burn, or just standing there watching him work—and he'd feel that this was the way things were meant to be: the man working the land, his home over yonder, his woman there with a child on the way. It got him thinking about civilization in general. What was it good for? What was everyone working so hard for? What was the point of all these computers and telephones and wall-to-wall carpeting and all the debt you had to get into to pay for it all? He didn't have any answers. He knew Reagan had beat the Russians, which pretty much proved that capitalism was a good way to run things, but sometimes he wondered if it wasn't just a little bit out of hand.

Most days she was happy to see him, but on a few occasions she seemed to be suffering from some pregnancy-related discomfort and wasn't up for any sex; she only wanted to talk. When Clarence asked her if she was taking her Female Vitality, she laughed.

"Is it me you're concerned about or yourself?"

"Come on now," he said.

Those were the days he felt the least comfortable being there in the camper with her, as if friendly conversation were the greater violation. Sometimes he would hear something outside and ask her to be quiet for a second, and he'd sit there, listening, but it was usually a small plane passing overhead, or nothing at all.

"The more I see of this life," she said on one of those moody days, a Friday afternoon, "the more I think it's a cruel thing bringin' a new one into it. Nothin' but lies the moment we take our first breath. Is that what my baby's got to look forward to? A life of lyin' and cheatin'? Is that the way it's gonna be?"

"I've got no complaints," Clarence said.

"Then you're just plain dumb."

"Dumb hell. I'm the smartest guy I know."

Clarence was itching to get back to the bulldozer, to the nice, clean, predictable lines of the road. But she had more to say.

"So after I'm gone you're just gonna carry on with your wife like nothin' ever happened and never mention a word of it?"

"That's right."

Angela shook her head in disgust.

"What kind of life is that? Carryin' that lie around inside you the rest of your life? And her probably carryin' her own lies too."

"My wife ain't carryin' around any lies worth a damn."

"How do you know?"

"Because I know."

"She could be out there fuckin' someone right now, goin' door to door, and you wouldn't even know it."

Clarence smiled at the thought.

"She hasn't got it in her."

"Same thing Trevor thinks."

She got up and walked over to the counter and poured herself a cup of liquor. She stood there drinking it almost spitefully, staring at Clarence. He'd told her more than once that drinking was the worst thing you could do to a baby in the womb. It annoyed him that she didn't seem to care.

"I've seen what it can do to you," she went on. "Carryin' secrets around. It eats a hole in you. Trevor wouldn't need them pills if he just got rid of all the stuff inside his head. He won't even tell me, his own wife. I said to him, 'All right, we'll swap secrets. You tell me what you done in Vietnam and I'll tell you somethin' you don't want to hear.' He said I didn't have anything he didn't want to hear. Well, now I do, don't I? Maybe it's time we had us a little truth swap."

"Vietnam?" Clarence sat bolt upright, aghast at the sound of that word. "You're tellin' me you're married to a Vietnam vet?"

"So what?"

"Jesus, girl. Are you nuts?" He stared at her. "He must be thirty years older than you."

"Well, you ain't exactly no spring chicken yourself."

"I ain't the one married to you."

Clarence stood up and ran his fingers through his hair. He picked up his hat and put it on his head. He walked to the door. He turned and looked at her. "Why didn't you tell me your husband was a goddamn Vietnam vet?"

"What difference does it make?"

"Every difference in the world."

More than once he had come across Vietnam vets living out in a trailer or a shack in the desert, exiled from humanity, as if silence and isolation had become the essential nutrients of their troubled souls. There was something in their eyes that cut right through Clarence, no matter how seemingly friendly they were.

"This ain't me," Angela carried on, oblivious to the state she'd put Clarence in. "I need people. I need people to talk to. This is prison. I've thought about it a lot and this ain't no different from prison at all. It's worse. At least in prison you've got other prisoners to talk to."

Clarence looked her squarely in the eye and said: "Well, why don't you just go on home?"

"I ain't got any money. How am I supposed to go back

without any money? What am I supposed to live on? I can just hear Mama now, 'I told you not to marry that crazy bastard.'"

"Well, how much you need? You could take the bus."

"How should I know? What difference is it to you anyway?"

Clarence opened his wallet and took out a fifty and handed it to her. She looked at it, looked at him.

"Get the hell out of here, you goddamn sonofabitch."

"Hold on, now, Angie. It ain't that way at all."

"Get out!" she shouted.

He did. He turned and walked out the door and didn't look back.

———

Monday morning he drove the flatbed hauler out there again. He thought about her as he walked up the path to the bulldozer. He wished it had ended on a better note, but he wasn't about to make the same mistake twice.

He and Barb had had the nicest weekend. Friday night they'd gone out to dinner and rented a video. Saturday afternoon they drove out to the pond at the El Paso Natural Gas Plant, like they used to when they were dating, and walked around it holding hands, talking about Shelly. Sunday at church Clarence felt his soul being cleansed by the word of God. Afterward he made love to Barb the way she liked it, front to front, and he apologized for being grumpy lately, blaming it on his frustrations with his crew. He vowed to himself that he would never betray her again.

He had just settled into the seat of the bulldozer when he noticed some movement from the camper. He glanced up to see Angela in the doorway trying to signal to him with a hand mirror. But because the sun was behind her the mirror wasn't catching any light.

"What in God's name?" Clarence muttered as he watched her trying without success to get a sunbeam on him. He was sorely tempted to ignore her, just fire up the bulldozer, turn it around, and drive it down the road without looking back.

He sat there for several minutes, waiting for her to give up and go back inside the camper, but she just stayed there in the doorway, pivoting the mirror. There was something conciliatory, something pathetic, in that futile gesture, and Clarence wasn't one to turn a blind eye on someone trying to set things right.

He cursed himself as he got down and set out for the camper. He wasn't too far from it when he noticed that all the crates of rocks were gone. That put a hitch in his stride. He instinctively surveyed the surrounding area for the truck, sensing changes afoot.

She had dispensed with the mirror by the time he reached her. He stopped short of the camper, hooked his thumbs over his front pockets and looked her over without comment, figuring the burden of speech was on her this time.

"We're leavin' tomorrow," she stated flatly.

Clarence looked over to where the crates had been.

"Where is he?" he said.

"Gettin' some stuff in town."

"Why didn't you go with him?"

"What do you think?" she said.

Clarence turned his head and spat.

She settled down in the doorway with her feet out on the step. Clarence looked up at the mountains. The sun was just breaching the crests and there was still a hint of coolness in the air.

"Sorry I yelled at you," she said after a while.

"Forget it."

An image of the camper gone, the road path clear at last, flashed across Clarence's mind, and it pleased him.

"Where you all off to?" he asked her.

"What's the next state over?"

Clarence turned his head and looked out across the desert. The shadows lay long westward of the bushes, insects flitting in the angled sunlight.

"Woman, if you don't know that . . ."

She stepped down from the camper and walked over to him, her flip-flops thwacking her heels with every step.

"I told you I was sorry," she said, taking hold of his hands. "Or ain't my apology good enough for you?"

Clarence looked her in the eyes.

"I told myself I was finished with you."

She pulled his hands forward and set them on her belly. She started moving them around in circles.

"You can be finished tomorrow," she said.

Clarence closed his eyes and, despite his determination not to, began to reconsider things. The sound of her breath as his palm grazed her navel settled it. *One for the road*, he thought.

She led him over to the camper, and he followed her up the steps and in. She went straight to the counter. As his eyes adjusted to the dimness he saw that she was holding a pistol in her hands. It was pointed at him.

Clarence stood there looking at her, offended by the notion that she thought he was someone she could point a gun at.

"What in God's name do you think you're doing?"

"Get them pants off," she said.

Clarence stared at her, not knowing whether to laugh or get mad.

"If it's money you're after, all you have to do is ask."

"You're a fool," she said.

Clarence stared at her for a few seconds, then turned to step back out the door and be on his way. She fired. The blast, or the shock wave it sent down his spine, knocked his hat off and opened a small hole of sunlight in the wall a few feet to the left of his head. The bang echoed through his brain as if through an empty canyon, gradually leveling out to a high-pitched ringing in his left ear.

Clarence slowly turned back around, his hands instinctively rising. "Off," she said. He quickly unlatched his belt buckle and lowered his pants. "All the way," she said. He pulled off his boots and took his pants off and stood before her in his boxers and socks. "Sit on the chair," she said, pointing with the pistol. He went over and sat down. She backed her way to the door, keeping the pistol pointed at him, and stepped down.

She took the keys from the front pocket of Clarence's pants

and the wallet from the back. She opened the wallet and pulled out the photographs of Barb and Shelly. She tucked them into the front of her dress and tossed the wallet aside. Until that moment Clarence had been more pissed off than afraid. Now he felt a cold wave of fear roll through him. If she had taken the money, or the entire wallet, that would have been something he could understand.

"What do you want?" he said, his mouth suddenly dry.

She smiled. "I wish you could see your face."

She draped his pants over her shoulders and turned and set out walking down the road path, the gun in her right hand, Clarence's keys in her left.

When she was about fifty yards away, Clarence got up and went to the door.

"Hey!" he yelled. "Give me my goddamn pants back, you crazy bitch!"

She didn't look back. He watched her walk down to the bulldozer and step up into the seat. She sat there for what seemed like several minutes, looking down at the controls.

Then Clarence heard the rumble of the engine firing up, saw the black exhaust belch from the stack. He watched in stupefaction as the blade jerked up, rose to its full height, then began descending again. The engine revved. The bulldozer jerked backward. It stopped. More time passed. She seemed to be pushing and pulling everything. The blade rose again. Then the dozer jerked forward and stayed in motion.

Clarence stood there in a kind of trance, watching his bulldozer drawing nearer, as one watches in silent awe the needles of lightning flashing in a distant storm. She was bearing down on him with the same dispassion, and there was something both awful and beautiful in her placid face coming at him above the mud-encrusted blade.

It was the sound of a yucca stalk cracking less than fifty feet away that snapped Clarence out of it. He reached for his boots and frantically yanked them on. He grabbed his wallet from the floor, picked up his hat, and jumped out the door, scrambling out of the way just in time to see the blade dig into the side of the camper. The camper leapt up with a piercing squeal. Everything inside flew up and slammed into the back wall. The teeth of the treads caught the undercarriage and gnawed the floor to splinters as the bulldozer rolled up and over the camper, flattening it to rubble as it climbed through it and out the other side.

She managed a wide turn out into the desert and circled her way back around to the road and carried on down it. Clarence stood there barelegged, mouth open, watching her, and as she receded down the road atop his bulldozer it seemed to him as if the sky itself was ripping wide open before her.

Fumble

IT IS STANDING ROOM ONLY tonight at Memorial Stadium, every square inch of the concrete bleachers occupied by eager fans in their thickest winter jackets and warmest hats. Fidgety children line the chain-link fence between the bleachers and the field. Older kids are standing along the high fence at the top of the bleachers, and kids who can't or don't want to pay the fifty cents admission have scampered up the steep concrete barrier outside the stadium and are standing with their fingers curled around the fencing, looking down on the field and calling out to their less brazen friends in the stands. Cars and trucks are parked along both sides of every street surrounding the stadium, snaking around Oak Street clear to the north side of the Girl Scout Park, a slow river of headlights and blaring music flowing in between. Just outside the fence on the east side of the stadium looms the symbol of all that torments the heart of a Wildcats fan, a shiny silver Greyhound bus with a blue-and-white colt streaking across its side, the words SILVER CITY FIGHTING COLTS flowing through its mane.

The voice of Ray Canady crackles over the PA, inviting Pastor Wertz of the Church of Jesus Christ of Latter-day Saints to lead in tonight's prayer. Silence falls over the stadium. No sound in that bright, frigid stillness save the buzz of the floodlights and the empty hum of the loudspeakers. Heads bow. The solemn voice of Pastor Wertz, echoing off the walls of the junior high and the Manor Apartments and the DHS auditorium, humbly beseeches the Almighty to watch over these young men tonight that no harm may come to them in their pursuit of victory. And his words give weight to the hitherto unnoticed ambulance parked in the grass beyond the goal posts at the southern end of the field. Upon "Amen" hundreds of hands touch brows, shoulders, sternums, and the DHS marching band strikes up the Wildcat fight song. Six slender and one plump Wildcat cheerleaders burst into a frenzy of kicks and whoops.

The Wildcats win the toss, and once again these bitter rivals face each other across the cold dead grass of Memorial Field. The drum roll ends on a deep bass boom as the ball arcs, spinning and twirling across the field, dropping at last into the eager hands of David Almanza, Deming's star running back, who proceeds to perform a miracle. David makes an eighty-seven-yard touchdown return without so much as being touched by a Silver City player.

The noise in the Wildcat bleachers is deafening. Even old enemies are standing and embracing. John Rickets, covering the game for KOTS-AM, boldly proclaims when at last the roar relents that tonight may well be a historic night for Deming.

"There's an awful burden on this young man's shoulders tonight, Shanty. But if what we've just seen is any indication . . . "

Freed at last from the ecstatic clutches of his teammates, David scans the bleachers for Cindy as he trots triumphantly, humbly, back to the sideline. He spots her mom and dad in the third row, left of center, but she isn't with them. Carmen Uzueta and Patti Lopez, her *cholitas*, are higher up, but Cindy isn't there. She isn't among the throng of bodies around the concession stands either. She'd been wearing his letter jacket when she came to see him in the parking lot after school and he'd ignored her. He can still see the hurt in her eyes, the reddening before the tears. She should've known better. No contact on game day. That is his rule. And this is no ordinary game. It is David's senior year. The season is over. It is the last chance he will ever get to beat Silver City.

After the kickoff return, things settle back into the usual bruising battle between these historic rivals. Silver scores a touchdown and a field goal before the Wildcats' nerves settle and they begin to move the ball. By the end of the first quarter David has been given the ball only once, for a gain of three yards.

"I really can't understand it," John Rickets tells Shanty Bowman in his earnest nasal drawl. "What is going through Coach Harrison's mind at this point? Why isn't he using his starters? They're all standing there on the sideline like expectant fathers."

Shanty only chuckles. It's early yet to be getting solemn.

Three minutes into the second quarter, after the Wildcats fail to complete a six-yard pass that should have been a handoff to David and an easy first down, David approaches Coach on the sideline.

David watches a few more plays before he speaks.

"I could've had that first," he says.

Coach nods. "I know you could've."

Silver picks up another five yards.

David unsnaps his chin strap with unnecessary force, provoking a sidelong squint from Coach.

There is an unspoken bond between David and Coach, one that predates their actual relationship, for David is an Almanza. Before David, there were his older brothers, Pablo and Ricky, and his cousins Freddy, Angel, and little Ricky. And before them there were his father and his uncles, Pancho and Raul, and all his father's cousins. And way back in the days when Deming used to beat Silver City, there was David's grandfather, Ramon, and his brother Hector. These were the legendary Almanzas of Deming, descended, it was believed, from a warrior of the last tribe of free Chiricahua Apaches, whose chief was Niño Cochise, later known as Ramon Rodriguez, Hollywood actor. As Almanza family lore had it, the warrior whose distant heirs would one day form the backbone of Deming High School athletics fell in love with a Mexican woman from the town of Basaranca, Mexico, where the tribe would journey every summer from their stronghold in the Sierra Madre to stock up on whiskey and hardware. One summer the warrior didn't return to the mountains. He changed his name to Pedro Almanza, got a job in the gunpowder factory, married the woman, and sired a large Mexican family, some of whose offspring would eventually migrate north. Much of the wiry muscularity of the Chiricahua survived in the Deming Almanzas, accounting for their catlike speed and agility, a trait that for half a century had been the saving grace of every Deming coach.

Long before David himself was a varsity Wildcat, he had listened to his brother Pablo's descriptions of Coach's tactics and strategies, his mannerisms and personality, his history. David knew how badly Coach wanted Silver—almost as badly as David did himself. His first season as head coach of the Wildcats, fresh from the glory of his days as assistant coach for the NMSU Aggies, Coach had been bolder with his words, stating in interviews with Billy Armendarez of the *Headlight* that the twenty-six-year losing streak with Silver would end on his watch. Like an overzealous politician, he'd made a promise he couldn't keep, and he'd been eating his words ever since. So when at last it was David's turn to be coached by Coach, it was as if he'd known the man for years. Under the exacting gaze of Coach there was nothing David felt he could not do, no tackle he could not break, no time he could not beat. And if in their three years together they still had not been able to beat Silver City, it was no fault of theirs but the fault of those who played football only for the opportunities it afforded them to get into the pants of chicks.

David walks down to the cooler and tilts his helmet back. Cup to lips he studies his gormless teammates. The sight of them fills him with rage. They look like spectators at some natural disaster. He can see from the slump of their hips and shoulders that in their minds they've been beaten again. He crumples the cup in his fist and tosses it to the ground.

On their next possession David gets the ball only once, for a gain of five yards. On his way back to the sideline he hazards a glance into the stands, a practice he generally avoids, one of his many superstitions. He sees his mother and his stepfather where they always sit. Around them are the parents of the other players: the Ramirezes, the Deals, the Brubeks. His eye quickly passes over them in search of its true object. But he does not see her. Despite knowing that such a quick glance is hardly enough to prove she isn't there, David feels an unmistakable throb of unease roll through him, spawning as it does so a variety of unpleasant scenarios. He is certain now that she isn't there, and this certainty leaves a heavy feeling in his stomach.

At the end of the half the score is 37–21, Silver. Apart from the kickoff return, David has only carried the ball four times for a total of eighteen yards, his worst half ever.

Demoralized after such a promising start, the Wildcats file into the clubhouse beneath the visitors' bleachers and yank off their helmets and bang them against the lockers. Their sweat-soaked heads look tiny between their shoulder pads. They all wear the hangdog expression of inevitable defeat, some of them only to conceal the truth that their hearts were never really in it to begin with.

David stands back from the rest, leaning against the wall, one cleated foot atop his helmet on the floor.

The assistant coaches settle in around Coach, stoically setting their clipboards on the benches beside them. Coach stands, arms crossed against his solid midsection, surveying his players. Through the cinder-block walls come the first muted strains of the half-time show.

"All right, men," Coach begins. "It's time for business."

It's not what the players are expecting. Coach isn't upset at all. If anything he is more confident than ever. He tells them that they're on the verge of victory. Two touchdowns and a field goal. That is all that separates them from a place in the history books of the Deming Wildcats. Everything is going according to plan. Silver has already shot their big guns. They may be ahead but they're on the ropes. They're limping. Muñoz is out, may he mend well for his college career. Coach looks his

B-team boys in the eye and tells them how proud he is of them. They've laid the foundation. Now it's up to the starters to take the ball and run with it.

"I've already seen it," he says. "This game is ours."

Coach's inspiring words have stirred powerful memories in the depths of David's soul, memories of Friday nights long ago when his aunts and uncles and cousins many times removed would converge on the old yellow duplex on Buckeye Street, four blocks east of the high school, to sit and stand out in the dirt yard and drink beer and listen to Mexican music blaring from one of the multitude of cars and trucks parked on the street or in the yard itself. On cold fall nights a brilliant white light could be seen filling the sky behind the houses to the west. This strange, ominous light was a mystery to David. He knew something important to the family was happening in it because their voices would change, their laughter cease when they spoke of it. The men especially. They would point to it and shake their heads and sometimes start yelling at each other. Their bodies would undergo strange contortions when they spoke about the things that were happening or had happened before within it. As the night wore on the men would get sadder and drunker, and sometimes a policeman would come and ask questions, after which all the aunts and uncles and cousins would drive away. Now and then when the music fell silent David would hear a voice in the sky above the light, and sometimes a terrible noise like a lion roaring. For David, this force beyond the houses that he couldn't understand had something to do either with God or the devil. His father would take him by the shoulders and proudly declare that this little man, God willing, would one day put Silver in its place. Even that word, "Silver," had a strange, magical power that both frightened and exhilarated David. These were David's earliest and fondest memories, and rightly or wrongly, over time, they had come to embody in his mind a lost paradise that only he could restore.

Coach's eyes turn to David.

"It's your game now, Almanza."

His teammates turn and look at him. Their eyes are filled

with profound respect. He is different from them. He has always been different. There is a fire in him that never goes out. David revels in the feeling of power reflected in their eyes, his face betraying nothing. This is what he lives for. All he wants now is to get his hands on the ball and run his guts out. He is angry with himself for doubting Coach, for doubting himself, for letting Cindy get to him during the first half. All that matters now is the game. His whole life has come down to this moment.

Coach goes on, detailing the strategy for the second half, but his real message has already been delivered. The gloom has lifted. All that remains in the throbbing hearts of the Wildcats is a burning desire to get back out there and finish Silver off.

The half-time show ends. The Wildcats squeeze into a tight circle, their arms jutting spokelike into the hub of a single giant fist. Three sharp roars and the wheel flies apart. On go their helmets, and a clattering wave of head-bashing rolls through the locker room. David lowers his helmet onto his head and buttons up his chin strap.

"All right, men," Coach says with what only a deeply sad man could call a smile. "Let's see what you're made of."

The crowd roars as the Wildcats sprint out of the locker room, back on to the field. A certain crispness of tone and rhythm, absent for most of the second quarter, has returned to the band. The cheerleaders are hopping up and down, their pom-poms doing delirious loops, their legs kicking out well above their heads.

David tells himself not to but he can't help looking again. If she wasn't there before, she has to be there now. In the Wildcat bleachers pockets of concrete are showing here and there. The kids have left the fences. The cruising around the stadium has ceased. The streets are dark and quiet. In the little time he has before reaching the sideline and turning to face the field, he looks for her in likely spots, but still he doesn't see her. It doesn't matter now. He has work to do.

Silver receives the kickoff and after three quick downs is forced to punt. Omega Atkins receives for the Wildcats and makes it to the thirty before he's cut down.

The starters are back in the huddle, all the familiar faces of the true Deming Wildcats. His men around him at last, David feels within himself the calm lucidity that always precedes his best performances. Brubek calls the play.

They break from the huddle with a clap and fan out to the line. The memories stirred up by Coach's speech are still coursing through David's veins, even more so now that he is out on the field, basking in the very lights that were once so mystifying to him, the very lights that have shone on all the Almanzas before him, none of them except the very earliest able to beat Silver. Until now.

The linemen dig in. Brubek barks the numbers. If only for an instant all motion ceases, on the field and off. Even the icy puffs of breath issuing from every face mask seem to hover, frozen solid, in midair.

Slaughter hikes the ball. Brubek takes the snap and swings out left, faking a handoff to Omega. Silver takes the bait, the defensive line lunging in the wrong direction. David glides around almost leisurely and tucks the ball into the crook of his right arm and continues down the line of scrimmage, his eyes scanning the shifting mass of bodies for an opening. Spotting a widening sliver of field between Deal and Dominguez, he cuts in, ducking through and clearing the line with a sudden burst of speed.

A roar erupts from the Wildcat bleachers. A volley of bass drum booms. Two key blocks from the Wildcat receivers and David is in the clear. He can hear the Silver fans now, a rising murmur of unease emanating from the aluminum bleachers above the clubhouse. Glimpsing the Silver players and coaches standing on the sideline, their heads and eyes pivoting as they track his motion, all those years of yearning to destroy them fills him with an overwhelming sense of power. It seems to him that his feet are no longer on the ground. He is flying. And somewhere out there Cindy is watching, he knows it now, or listening on the radio, her heart overflowing with love and admiration.

At the fifty-yard line, David curves sharply downfield,

opening his stride as he veers gradually back to the center for the final sprint. A swelling roar from the Wildcat bleachers confirms that he's in the clear. For David there is nothing more beautiful than this: the wide, empty expanse of yellow grass, the stark white uprights in the distance, the scoreboard farther on.

The yards fall effortlessly away.

By the time he hears the faint patter of footfalls behind him, it is too late. Just beyond the Silver thirty his legs are yanked out from under him. Both ankles wrapped up tight as a tamale. In an instant all his momentum slides up into his torso, pitching him helplessly forward like a tree severed from its base. Even as he is plummeting to the ground some other part of him, some other self entirely, carries on down the field and glides, wings spread, into the end zone, while the one left behind slams down hard against the cold dead grass. David watches with strange detachment as the ball, dislodged by the force of the impact, hops up and hangs in midair, gyrating almost spitefully before his eyes. He watches, for nothing seems to happen when he reaches out to grab it. He can see his right arm, still cocked at a ninety-degree angle, but, like the ball, it appears to have passed into some other medium infinitely denser than air. Nor will his left arm, somewhere out of sight, respond to his repeated efforts to bring it around to grab the ball. Yet there is movement of a kind. The ball has reached the apex of its bounce, paused there as if resting on some invisible surface, and started back down. David's right arm is drifting forward, the fingers uncurling from his fist as slowly as the petals of a rosebud. By his estimation the ball and his hand should meet near the ground fairly soon, at which point he'll be able to scoop it into his body and safeguard it from the Silver hordes, who must be on their way by now. Meanwhile his body is still sliding forward across the grass, propelled by its own inertia. In fact by the time the ball has fallen halfway back to the ground, David's head and shoulders have overtaken it, putting his right arm in an awkward position underneath the ball. He tries to swing his arm around to the outside of the ball, to bring it down into him, but again nothing happens. All he can do is watch helplessly as the ball gently grazes the back of his hand, rolls over the edge, and disappears from sight.

A streaking white mass crashes down on to David. A pair of black gloves closes around the ball as he is pummeled again, the impact snapping off his chin strap and knocking his left cheekbone into the cold hard grass. Body upon body hurtles on to the growing mass, the force of each impact coursing bone by bone down upon and through him. The grass grows dim, then darkens altogether. He looks for the ball but cannot see it, can see nothing now save a dim confluence of writhing limbs. He tries to move but he is pinned. He is in the very center of the dark heart of the pileup, the weight of the universe upon him. He can do nothing now but lie there in the darkness and listen to the battle for the ball, a frenzied swelter of growling and cursing and jabbing, an untold number of fingers tearing at the seams.

He never should have let himself feel, the voice that counsels his failures tells him. Never allowed himself to be weakened by her. It started with the note she passed to him in algebra. "Good game" was all it said. He liked the brevity. He asked her to homecoming. Afterward, walking her home, sweaty from dancing, he explained to her that football was his life. He had no time for girls during football season. It was his destiny to beat Silver City. She agreed with everything he said. And the kiss at her doorstep was like nothing he'd ever felt. Two weeks later he told her he loved her. They were cruising down Pine when he felt it come over him. He drove with it for a while, wondering what he should do, knowing full well how dangerous it was to be feeling this so close to the big game. Until now he'd only let it happen in the off-season. Last year it had been Michelle Saenz, the year before, Lupe Mendoza. His love for each of them had conveniently withered as those summers drew to a close, making it easy to break it off. Their tears had been no match for the call of duty.

He pulled into the dark and empty parking lot of Napa Auto.

It wasn't something you could just say with your hands on the steering wheel and your eyes on the taillights of the car ahead of you. He turned down the stereo and took her hand and, looking at the front of the building, said it. When he turned to look at her he saw the watery reflection from the streetlight in her eyes. They made out there for a long time, then she asked him to take them somewhere else and he knew what she meant. He drove out on to the old Lordsburg highway, turned down Hermanas Road, and drove another five miles before pulling off on a dirt road between fallow onion fields. They got in the backseat and took each other's clothes off and she told him she was a virgin, the loveliest words he'd ever heard. Afterward, lying against her, feeling her heartbeat tapping his chest, he felt the weakness come over him. He told himself it was only physical. It would pass. But the next morning he awoke with a sickening feeling of dread. It was as if he'd sold his soul to the devil. Not only his own soul, but the souls of all his teammates, the soul of Coach, the souls of everyone in town who'd put their faith in him. He vowed to himself and to God that he would have nothing more to do with her until the season was over. He would simply tell her the truth, that he loved her but couldn't see her, couldn't talk to her, couldn't even think about her until the season was over. Too much was at stake. He called her that afternoon. She was hurt, he could hear it in her voice, but she said she understood. Two nights later they were together again, on the same dirt road.

The bleats of the referees' whistles are getting louder and shriller. A final paroxysm seizes the pile before it goes still. The weight begins to lift. Light returns. Fresh air. Rising to his feet David sees the two referees, the fat one and the skinny one, stooped over and shuffling around to better see which of the two players on the ground, the Wildcat or the Fighting Colt, has more flesh on the ball. David and the other Wildcats are pointing emphatically downfield, the Silver players in the opposite direction.

Alas, the fat referee stands upright, blows his whistle, and knifes his arm upfield for Silver. The familiar pall of defeat steals over the hearts of the Wildcats fans as they futilely boo and hiss.

Standing on the sideline during Silver's possession, David feels the heat of indignation spreading through him, the eyes of the fans on him, their disgust and pity and shame, all equally repellent to him. For David there is nothing worse than letting Coach down. He would rather break a leg than feel that he has disappointed Coach. He keeps his eyes on the game, refusing to turn and look at Coach. He doesn't need to. He knows Coach never shows his emotions. Instead his mouth puckers into a kind of frozen kiss. His normally smooth forehead congeals into a knot between his eyebrows. He stands like a man handcuffed, hands resting palms out against his tailbone, the leather elbow patches of his corduroy blazer echoing in size and shade the bald spot atop his head. A stony silence envelops him, the true object of which would seem to be the moral failings of the whole of mankind.

Due Diligence

ON THE BASIS OF THE facts, it could be seen as nothing other than death by natural causes, though that didn't stop him, in the quiet moments of his day, from feeling like a killer.

There was no motive as such, only an accumulation of what he deemed moral failures, harmless in and of themselves but lethal in their totality. To properly appreciate his guilt, which after all was the only punishment available to him, he had no choice but to go through it all, step by step, again. He always started with the closet, not because it was the true beginning, but because in hindsight the symbols of his blindness seemed richest there.

Claudia had wanted to have the yard sale back in October, but Gary had asked her to hold off on it until after the elections. A yard sale might be misconstrued. As it turned out, with the holidays around the corner and winter setting in, it wasn't until April that she finally asked him to go through the hall closet and take out anything he wanted to get rid of—or, as she put it, anything he hadn't used in the last ten years. She knew that her husband was loath to part with anything once it had entered his life. "You can't just throw these away," he would say of some tattered pair of underwear she was determined to banish from their lives. "I've had these things since college."

But that mild spring evening as he was sifting through all the old junk in the closet—bowling shoes, a Betamax videotape player, a denim jacket with a Mondale-Ferraro badge on it—he was seized by an uncharacteristic urge to get rid of it all. This may have been precipitated by his having just happened upon the box with all the extra buttons and bumper stickers from the campaign in it. As he kneeled there staring at his ridiculous little face smiling back at him from the button—the oversaturated colors made his disembodied head look cartoonish—he couldn't help wondering if all those years of convincing juries of truths that he was rarely certain of himself had made it too easy for him to believe he could be a politician. He realized, in short, that he had made a fool of himself.

By the time he was done with the closet there was virtually nothing of his own left in it. Even his old tennis racket was in the pile of stuff to be purged from his life. It was a Prince mid-size graphite, the very racket he had used when he and Mike Hern had taken second in state in varsity doubles. His mother had given it to him for his sixteenth birthday, and it was that sentiment more than anything that had made him hold on to it all those years. He hadn't so much as set foot on a tennis court since college.

He unzipped the case and pulled out the racket. The original strings were still on it, torqued out of true from the last time he had played. The faded blue sweat grip around the handle was worn down to the leather where his thumb joint had ridden it. He grasped the handle and made a few light forehands through the air, trying to think of some reason to keep it. Golf was his game now, and it was all the sport he had time for. He would have liked to give the racket to his son, but Mark had no interest in sports unless they could be played on a monitor. In the end Gary resigned himself to the fact that it was best to sell it to someone who might actually use it. He zipped it back into its case, sending a little prayer of gratitude and regret to his dead mother, who had always had so much faith in him, and returned it to the pile.

He still had every intention of selling it when, the following Saturday morning, a fat bearded guy wearing a Hawaiian shirt and a red ball cap picked up the racket from the table out in the driveway and said: "How much you want for the racket?"

"Twenty dollars," Gary said.

"Twenty bucks?" the man said incredulously. "This thing's older than Jimmy Connors."

The man fiddled with the strings, frowned at the scrapes across the head guard, swiped it brusquely through the air. Gary had a vague sense, he wasn't sure why, that the man was the owner of the adult video shop that had just opened on West Pine.

"I'll give you fifteen."

"Sorry," Gary said. From someone else, maybe, but not from this buffoon.

"'Packer for the People,' eh?" the man said rudely and pulled a roll of bills out of his front pocket.

The comment hit a nerve. Gary's first instinct was to tell the guy off, but sensing that the man was inadvertently conveying what must have been the general perception of him during the campaign—that he had no real interest in the common man but was in it purely for himself—he held his tongue. The idea of this man walking off with his beloved old racket was now inconceivable.

"I've changed my mind," Gary told him.

"What, so now you're not selling it?"

"That's right."

The man shook his head in disgust, which, given the earlier comment, seemed to suggest an accusation of complete moral bankruptcy.

From that day forward, Gary found himself dwelling on the election all over again, asking himself the same old questions five months after the fact. Why had he run? Why had he lost? Why hadn't anyone stepped up and said, "Gary, you're a great lawyer but politics isn't your game"? Instead, everyone had been so supportive. How could even his own wife have been so wrong about him? Ike Crawford, the seven-time incumbent, had won by a landslide. Gary tried to bear his defeat philosophically, telling his wife and son that politics was no place for an honest man, but in truth he felt humiliated. He had genuinely believed that the qualities he possessed—his personal integrity, his impressive record as a prosecuting attorney, his youth and vitality—were what the people of Deming were hungry for. Instead they had gone and voted yet again for an old alcoholic philanderer perpetually embroiled in scandals.

On the Wednesday following the yard sale, instead of going out to the country club to play nine holes with the DA and the city manager and a couple of retired bankers as he usually did, Gary drove to Family Valu and bought a can of tennis balls. The racket was already in the trunk.

It was two in the afternoon when he pulled up to the courts at the south end of the high school parking lot. It was a perfect day: warm, crystal clear, quiet. The sight of the silent, empty cars in the lot, awaiting the final bell, gave him a pleasant sensation of playing hooky. The four courts, surrounded by a high chain-link fence, were deserted. Above the cinder-block wall of the school administration building behind the courts, the bare branches of the mulberry trees were just beginning to bud.

Gary got out and took the racket from the trunk. Walking across the grass of the embankment, he recalled a black-and-white picture he had taken of Claudia when they were seniors and painfully in love. She was sitting cross-legged there in the grass, leaning forward over her legs with one hand outstretched as if in supplication. He adored that picture. It always reminded him what a lucky man he was that, although they had gone their separate ways for nearly a decade after high school, the strength of that first love had drawn them back together, and they were still the happiest couple he knew.

Gary raised the squeaky U-shaped handle of the gate and walked out on to court one. The surface was in bad shape. All the nets were sagging like overburdened clothes lines. The white stripe across the green plywood backboard was barely visible. Off in one corner a forgotten ball, bleached of all color, cowered like some forlorn little rodent.

The can popped crisply and let out a hiss as Gary peeled back the aluminum lid and dumped one immaculate yellow ball into his hand. He unzipped the case and pulled out his racket. A feeling of long-overdue calmness suffused him as he dropped the ball to the court, swung the racket back, and fired the ball into the backboard.

He didn't last more than twenty minutes that first session, but Gary was surprised by how well his strokes had weathered the years. He couldn't help smiling as his body effortlessly conjured up his old reliable two-handed backhand and his wily top-spin forehand.

The following Wednesday afternoon he was there again. There was something deeply appealing about the desolation of the empty courts baking in the sun in the dead of the afternoon. It was the only time in his week that he was truly alone. The backboard was a kind of mirror that not only let him play himself but gave him occasional glimpses back on to the courts of his memory. He had spent entire summers on these very courts, and every now and then, when he found his rhythm, some long-forgotten image and its associated feeling would come hurtling back at him out of the past, as clear and bright as the tennis ball. He would stop and stand there for a minute with a smile on his face as the memory reverberated through him. He remembered old Mr. and Mrs. Leopold, out there every day, playing each other, and himself telling Mike Hern that he hoped one day he would have a wife he could play tennis with until his dying day. (Claudia didn't play.) He remembered summer nights when at 10:30 sharp the lights would cut out with a startling *clack* and the whole universe would be plunged into impenetrable darkness, over which would burn a ghostly freeze-frame of an unfinished stroke. He remembered Chuck Zemco exploding in frustration at his daughter Missy, and Missy crying, and all their reconciliations. Seldom did he remember his own games and matches from the years he was on the team. Rather the memories that stood out clearest were the ones that had little to do with tennis at all but resonated instead with some mysterious and poignant emotion. While he may not have fully understood at the time that these memories were guiding him back to himself after the dislocating effects of the campaign, the pleasure they gave him, coupled with the visceral joy of watching his body return to form, made his Wednesday afternoons at the courts his favorite time of the week.

His stamina improved quickly. Within a month he was lasting nearly an hour against the wall. He took a bucket from the garage and filled it with new balls and began practicing his serve as well. Sooner or later, he now knew, he would start playing matches again, maybe even enter one of the local tournaments, but for the time being he was content to work alone on restoring his game to at least a semblance of what it once was. He wasn't interested in the kind of sloppy, bungling tennis that the average Joe liked to play on weekends. It was a matter of pride with him that he strove for classic form, in the manner of the pros, however short of the mark he may have fallen in actual execution. For him, tennis was not simply a game. It was, like any endeavor taken seriously, an expression of a moral position. There was a right way and a wrong way to play tennis. Real tennis, like the practice of law, was a sport of the mind. It was about getting inside your opponent's head and having a ready response for all his challenges.

In mid-May, when the schools let out for summer, Gary's solitary Wednesday afternoons were corrupted for a time by noisy kids on the adjacent courts, but the steadily rising heat soon took care of that, further confirmation to Gary's mind that the current generation, of which his son was a prime representative, had no mental fortitude.

One hot Wednesday afternoon in early June an old white VW Rabbit with a blue streak spray-painted across the passenger door pulled up in front of court two, and an old man got out with a wooden racket in one hand and a faded tennis ball in the other. By the looks of it he was at least eighty. He had a scraggly white beard and was wearing a wide-brimmed straw hat and short red shorts. There was something wrong with his hips or his back, judging by the way he shuffled over to the gate with little mincing steps, like an old geisha, the hump of his upper back keeping his head angled toward the ground.

He acknowledged Gary with a stiff nod as he made his way across the court and over to the backboard on court two. Gary couldn't help staring at the guy's ancient wooden racket as he passed. With its long, slender, rectangular wooden shaft, its tiny ovoid head and its striped strings, it looked like something from the epoch of lawn courts and bloomers. Every now and then, as Gary carried on with his hitting, he would glance over to see the old man planted like a tree in one spot, making stiff little hacking strokes at his ball, which always came right back to him.

After about ten minutes the old man shuffled over to the low fence that separated the courts and stood with his forearms resting on the crossbar, watching Gary hit.

Gary carried on with his strokes until, beginning to feel unnerved, he caught his ball and turned to acknowledge him.

"You want to rally a little?" the old man asked him, a child-like eagerness in his eyes. The sharp curving shadow of his hat brim cut just below his big, reddened clump of a nose, leaving the scruffy white beard and hints of a handsome jawline exposed to the sun.

Images of stoically retrieving errant balls flashed through Gary's mind. *Don't be a snob,* he heard Coach Diaz telling him, *there's something to learn from everybody.*

"Sure, why not?" Gary said, taking mercy on the old fellow.

They introduced themselves. The old man's name was Ray. Gary assumed he didn't follow local politics, for nothing registered in his eyes when Gary told him his name, first and last, a professional habit he found hard to break.

Gary grabbed a few balls from his bucket and switched over to Ray's court, and they began to rally. It was almost painful watching Ray play. His strokes were more like flyswatting than tennis, all the action coming from the wrist and forearm, his feet rooted firmly to the court directly below his immobile hips. He couldn't even bend over to get the ball but had to use the racket and the side of his shoe to give it a bounce and dribble it up. But somehow, with that crazy old racket and not an ounce of power in his hips, he sent the ball rocketing back flat and low over the net, catching Gary completely off guard. After two months of playing exclusively to his own rhythms, Gary found himself mistiming nearly every shot. And the way the old man somehow managed to get from one side of the court to the other in time to get the ball back was so uncanny that it produced in Gary a sensation of mild vertigo. One second he would be nowhere near position, and the next, scurrying sideways like a crab, he would be on top of the ball and taking a wicked swat at it.

After about ten minutes of this the old man said he needed a break. He shuffled over to the bench against the fence and eased himself down with a groan and a long sigh. Gary came over and sat down beside him.

"You're pretty good with that old thing," he said with more affability than he was feeling.

"I never put much store in rackets," Ray said in a philosophical tone, gazing out across the courts. "The racket racket. It's the man behind it, like anything else. Not that I'm an exemplary specimen."

Gary smiled. He liked people who didn't take themselves too seriously.

"We'd be better off with clay courts in this climate," Ray noted, appraising the worn concrete. "You wouldn't get all this cracking. They're easier on the joints too. When I lived in Paris I used to play for hours without feeling a thing. Of course I was a lot younger then."

"Paris, eh?" Gary said, surprised and intrigued. "When did you live in Paris?"

"Oh, years ago. Back in the seventies. That's where I took up tennis, in fact. I played at the Loisirs Tennis Club. Beautiful courts. Two or three times a week." He paused in remembrance, an almost beatific smile on his face. "Nothing in this world like a skinny French girl in a miniskirt . . ." He went quiet again, this time for well over a minute. It was the kind of intense, personal silence that one is loath to interrupt. Finally he sighed wistfully. "Ah, Paris. Who was it said that good Americans when they die go to Paris? I'm afraid I don't qualify. Oh well, I got my glimpse of heaven anyway. I had an apartment in the Third Arrondissement, overlooking the Place de la République. Had my dinner every night at Café de Flore."

Gary, staring abstractedly at Ray's pale, knobby knees, found it hard to imagine the decrepit old guy next to him as a young man living the bohemian life in Paris.

"What took you to Paris?" he asked him.

"Well, I'd been in Swaziland for two years and needed to get back to civilization."

Gary turned and looked squarely at Ray. Nothing in the old man's face, at least in the profile of it, indicated that he was pulling Gary's leg. He simply sat there gazing out beyond the courts as if staring across an African savanna, his jaw jutting out nearly as far as his nose. Then, the spell abruptly broken by some mnemonic cul-de-sac, he turned to Gary and said: "You want to play a set?"

Gary looked at his watch. He didn't really feel like foisting the rigmarole of rules on to this choppy, hack tennis, but sooner or later, he knew, he would have to start playing sets again.

"Sure," he said. "Why not?"

Gary suggested that Ray serve first, but Ray insisted on spinning his racket and making Gary choose M or W. Gary guessed wrong, and Ray set about getting the spare balls into the pockets of his shorts. His serve was an ugly, cautious tap, more badminton than tennis. He could barely get his racket over his head, let alone achieve any arc. But the ball always went in. Gary couldn't resist the temptation to hammer it back into the empty corner, but every time he tried he either hit it long or into the tape, and he soon resigned himself to just getting the ball back with meager little pats of his own—proof of the truism that in tennis, as in chess, bad form often befuddles and defeats the better player. As for Gary's own serve, he was so intent on unleashing the beautiful, curving power that had been his trademark in high school that everything kept going long and wide. Soon Ray was up 3–1.

Every time they switched sides, Ray had to take a break and sit on the bench for at least five minutes. Although he didn't need a break himself, Gary obliged him out of consideration for his age. The breaks frustrated Gary's game still further, causing him to cool down and stiffen up, usually right when he was starting to get into some kind of a rhythm. Ray, meanwhile, seemed to enjoy having a captive audience for his reminiscences. By the end of that first match Gary would learn that Ray wasn't from Deming but had lived there for some time in the fifties, that he was originally from Iowa, that in addition to Paris and Swaziland he had also lived in San Francisco and had spent the last twenty years on Pohnpei, a Micronesian island.

These revelations struck Gary as bordering on the fantastic. The only time of any significance that he had spent away from Deming himself was his college years, the four years in Las Cruces and the three in Albuquerque getting his law degree. Even then he was never long away from home. How remarkable, he thought, to encounter such a man of the world on the Deming tennis courts.

"Why did you come back to Deming?" he asked Ray during one of the breaks.

"I came back to die," Ray said.

Gary stopped realigning his strings. He wasn't sure how to respond, it had been stated so calmly, like a passing comment on the weather. He stared down at Ray's new-looking pair of tennis shoes, clownishly incongruent with the stretched-out socks bunched up around his wiry ankles.

"But you're healthy," he eventually replied, an almost defensive tone in his voice.

"No man my age is healthy."

In the same breath Ray began rattling off all his infirmities, which included osteoarthritis, a plastic hip, bad circulation, a leaky bladder, gallstones, rheumatism, gout, hemorrhoids, and heart trouble. He spoke the way old men often do to younger men, with a kind of veiled pride in his ailments masquerading as good-natured advice not to get old, for it isn't for the faint of heart. Gary, playing his part, nodded respectfully.

"But that's all normal stuff," he said. "I mean, it's not like you've got cancer or anything. Right?"

"No," Ray said, giving a little knock to the bench. "I've been spared that one, so far."

"So why did you choose Deming to return to?" Gary asked again. "Of all those places you lived, why Deming?"

"I made good friends here," Ray said as if it were patently obvious. "It always felt like home to me."

Gary liked that answer. He liked knowing that the town he had essentially never left was the one place that a man who had traveled the world would choose to return to to end his days. It made him feel as if his own lack of desire to experience the rest of the world was somehow justified. If you end up pretty much back where you started, why bother leaving? Wasn't it a mark of a higher wisdom to just stay where you had been put and be content with it? The way Gary saw it, what he lacked in scope of experience was compensated for in depth: the depth of his attachment to his hometown, his family, his practice, the people he loved.

"Well," Gary said, beginning to stiffen up, "I guess we'd better finish this thing."

———

It was more than just losing both sets to a nearly crippled old man that so annoyed Gary. However irrational it may have been to conflate these two seemingly unrelated contests, losing so badly to an old man at tennis only stirred up the humiliation still festering in him from the election. It made him realize that he needed much more practice against the wall before he could hope to stand a chance against anyone with a halfway decent game.

When he arrived at the courts the following Wednesday afternoon, it was with a sense of renewed purpose. A quiver of almost greedy anticipation, not unlike that of the painter before a freshly stretched canvas, or the writer facing an empty page, thrilled through him at the sight of the vacant courts.

He had been hitting for twenty minutes when the old white Rabbit pulled up.

Something about that streak of blue spray paint across the passenger door instantly irritated him. It wasn't so much the vandalism that bothered him—he had done stupid things like that himself when he was a kid—as the sense that the old man, if he was aware of it at all, either didn't give a damn or simply couldn't be bothered to get rid of it.

Ray got out with his racket and his ball. Same red shorts, same straw hat. He shuffled across the grass over to the gate. Without so much as glancing at Gary, he went and started hitting against the backboard on court two. Then, after about ten minutes, just as before, he came over to the fence and stood there watching Gary. Gary went on practicing until, sensing he was approaching the threshold of rudeness, he caught the ball and turned.

"You want to rally a little?" Ray said.

The thought of repeating that frustrating experience didn't appeal to Gary at all, but it seemed mean to outright refuse the man when there wasn't anyone else around for him to play.

Gary looked at his watch.

"I can give you about ten minutes," he lied.

"Name's Ray," Ray said, extending his hand across the fence.

"I know," Gary said. "We played last week."

"I don't think so," Ray said. "This is the first time I've been on a court in years."

Gary looked into the old man's eyes and saw with a strange empty feeling that he actually believed what he was saying. Ray's outstretched hand hung there in the air above the fence. Gary went over and shook it uneasily and uneasily said his name, wondering if what he was witnessing was genuine dementia or just the usual faulty memory of advanced age.

"Good to meet you, Gary."

They rallied for a while, and just as before, after about ten minutes, Ray said he needed to take a break and shuffled over to the bench.

"I don't know why we don't use clay courts in this climate," he remarked. "You wouldn't get all this cracking. It's easier on the bones too. I used to play for hours in Paris without feeling a thing. Of course I was a lot younger then."

Again a strange empty feeling came over Gary, a kind of sudden solitude, as if despite the presence of another human being beside him he were sitting there utterly alone.

"Ah, Paris," Ray reminisced, calling up the exact same memories, the same phrases even, as before.

When, right on cue, he made his offer to play a set, Gary, out of both pity and curiosity, couldn't bring himself to refuse. And as he began to lose, it was as if he were playing the exact same match all over again.

During the next break, as a kind of test, he asked Ray his opinion about recent world events, but Ray's lack of knowledge on that score wasn't proof of anything; half the population didn't have a clue what was going on around them. If the old man really did have Alzheimer's, it was remarkable he was out there at all, let alone actually beating a man half his age and in perfect health.

The following Wednesday Ray again showed up and introduced himself as if he had never laid eyes on Gary. Gary realized then that what troubled him most about this ritual to which he had unwittingly become a party was the ghostly sensation that within a matter of days, perhaps even hours, he himself would cease to exist in the old man's mind. He would be completely erased.

Everything was exactly the same. The offer to rally, the introduction, the rest breaks, the wretched sets. It never varied, from week to week. Gary began to dread seeing that white VW with the blue streak across the passenger door pull up and Ray get out with that old wooden racket, that silly straw hat, those red shorts. *Will he remember me this time?* he always thought. The few times that he turned down Ray's offer to rally, saying he just wanted to work on his strokes, he felt so mean and guilty seeing Ray across from him, hitting stoically against the wall, that it spoiled his concentration.

One of the most irritating aspects of playing Ray was having to listen to all his rose-tinted memories during the breaks. Left to his own devices he tended to gravitate to Paris, often repeating verbatim the same stock images and emotions. He was always finding ways to bring up women, always in the same lascivious tone, which got on Gary's nerves. On the few occasions when high school girls in shorts were playing on the other courts, Ray would sit and stare at them like a heron in shallow water. Gary didn't know what was worse, being subjected to an old man eulogizing his dearly departed libido, or pretending he hadn't already heard the story five times.

On one afternoon Gary got so frustrated with the whole introduction business, the whole endless déjà vu, that he looked Ray squarely in the eyes and said: "If we've never met before then how do I know that you lived in Paris in the early seventies, in an apartment in the third whatever, that you were a member of that fancy tennis club, and that you went there mainly to eye up women in miniskirts?"

A look of violation stole over Ray's perpetually congenial expression. He studied Gary's face for some clue as to how this complete stranger could possibly know such intimate details about him. Gary stared back at him, standing his ground, though he already felt sorry he had said it.

"What do you want from me?" Ray said nervously, taking a step back. The sinews of his wrist went rigid as he tightened his grip on his racket.

"I don't want anything from you, Ray," Gary said, startled by the sudden tension in the air. "I'm just trying to help you remember that we've played before. We play here every Wednesday afternoon. My name is Gary."

Ray started shaking his head like a child refusing to eat. Gary pressed on, concealing his own jittery nerves behind the studied calmness of his courtroom persona: "How else could I know all that stuff about you unless you told me?"

"No," Ray said, still shaking his head. "You've been talking to my ex-wife, haven't you? You stay away from her."

Gary smiled in self-defense.

"Come on, Ray. I don't have the faintest idea who or where your ex-wife is."

Ray turned and shuffled quickly off the court, got into his car, and drove away. Half an hour later he was back, looking for a partner, as if the whole episode had never happened. To a disinterested observer, nothing would have seemed out of the ordinary about an old man extending his hand across the fence, a younger man taking it in his own with a cheerless smile.

———

After that Gary was always careful not to reveal to Ray any of his knowledge of the man's past, which made eliciting new information a delicate business. That reference to an ex-wife had struck Gary like a revelation, a chink in the old man's armor, and he wanted to know more. An ex-wife peering over his shoulder was the perfect antidote to the old man's tiresome Don Juan routine.

Gary began slyly yet systematically deposing Ray, as if preparing a case for trial. *Reality v. Ray.* The ex-wife being the key witness, Gary needed to call her back to the stand. It was easy enough to get Ray reminiscing, but it wasn't so easy pinning down the chronology. He sometimes forgot, virtually midsentence, where he was in a memory, and when he carried on he would be in some other country entirely, some other period of his life. To situate him more precisely in his memories, Gary might casually allude to Deming being "as hot as Africa" or make a general comment like, "What I wouldn't give for a vacation on some faraway Pacific island." Once he got Ray relocated and rambling, it was easy to ask him more pointed questions.

In this way, over the course of countless rest breaks, Gary gradually pieced together, like some diabolical jigsaw puzzle, a rough chronology of Ray's remarkable life.

He had joined the navy when he was eighteen and was sent to Guadalcanal for what turned out to be the last push in the

Pacific theater. (Gary later calculated that Ray must have been born in 1926 or '27, making him about eighty years old.) He served two years, most of it as part of the occupying force in Tokyo. Wherever he roamed in his memories there were always women there, frozen in time, his wistful tone sculpting their figures in the air.

After the war he decided he wanted to be a writer, so he went back home and enrolled in the Iowa Writers' Workshop. A year was all he could stand of that, though it didn't stop him from writing, for a while at least. He sold some stories to *Harper's* and other magazines—"dreadful things," he said, shaking his head in self-disgust, thinly veiling his pride. He said he was more suited to journalism. That was what had brought him out to Deming in the early fifties, that and the desire to live in a warm place again. He had contracted malaria on Guadalcanal, and still got the shivers now and then. He stayed in Deming for a decade, writing for the *Headlight*. "Happiest years of my life," he quipped. "Thought I was Hemingway." He told Gary about some of his stranger assignments, like the time he interviewed a circus lion tamer who let the lions hang out with him in his trailer; or the story about the carhop who found a woman's head in the dumpster behind the Triangle Drive-In. Of all of Ray's stories, these were the ones Gary could most relate to, for the obvious reason that they were about Deming. Gary enjoyed the sense of the outsider's perspective on his little town. Ray's stories made Deming seem livelier and stranger than Gary had ever known it. As in every other place he had lived, Ray had his share of women in Deming, all apparently Mexican, one named Carmen featuring more prominently than the rest.

"I bet you married that girl, didn't you?" Gary tried leading him.

"No. Though I probably should have. She was the best cook."

"Better than the woman you married?"

"I'm not married," Ray said.

"But you were once, weren't you?"

"Nope."

Gary wiped the sweat from his upper lip. He drummed his racket against his shoe. It was torture for him not to be able to read back Ray's earlier testimony and remind him that he was under oath.

"Are you *sure* you were never married?"

"That's not the kind of thing a man forgets," Ray stated matter-of-factly. "No, I never could stand being pinned down to one woman."

This response was unacceptable to Gary. He knew from experience that the revelation a man makes in the heat of emotion is always closer to the truth than all his calm denials. For whatever reason, Ray was willfully withholding the truth. Gary didn't believe for one second that Alzheimer's was behind it; Alzheimer's didn't just pluck individuals out of otherwise perfectly intact long-term memories and discard them.

The next stop on Ray's picaresque journey through life was San Francisco, which he had fallen in love with during the three days he had spent there before shipping out for the war. Through a connection he got a job with American Express, and over the course of a few years he rose through the ranks until he found himself handling huge sums of money in international finance. It seemed he had given up writing completely by this point. "It was all a game to me. As soon as I got tired of the role I was playing I just dropped it and moved on to something else." His memories of San Francisco were full of the pleasures of high living, of unforgettable dining experiences, of sunsets he would remember to his dying day, of the joys of wandering around that most enchanting of American cities, all of it utterly cliché to Gary's ears. As always he spoke of the gorgeous girlfriends he had at the time, and he didn't bat an eye when he mentioned that the most gorgeous of them all was a transvestite.

Sometimes, after they got up and headed back onto the court, the sight of Ray's withered body, hobbling away from that nimble, romanticized vision of life, stung Gary like a slap in the face. He didn't want to sit and rest in the first place; in order to beat Ray he needed to wear him out, deny him his breaks. But, hardly realizing it, Gary would get sucked into one of Ray's stories, start to cool down, momentarily forget his frustration. His desire to root out the ex-wife would momentarily eclipse his desire to beat the old man on the court. Then, abruptly, Ray would get up and shuffle back to the baseline, and the illusion of some exotic world would evaporate in the heat of the Deming tennis courts, recreated only by a tedious feat of rhetorical gymnastics ten minutes later, or the following week, and once again Gary would be staring the facts in the face: he was going back on to the court to lose yet again to a senile old man.

Tired of San Francisco and of wearing a suit, Ray joined the Peace Corps and went to Swaziland, where he lived in various villages for a couple of years, teaching English, though of course always finding time to get his fill of African women. "Roughest hands you'll ever feel on a woman. Like pumice." He killed a lion. He ate beetles. He learned to play the calabash. "I'd stashed enough money from my finance days to keep me going for at least a decade in the Third World."

But apparently two years in the bush was more than enough, even for him. "I went a little mad down there," he said with an almost longing look in his eyes. He needed to return to Western civilization. So he went to France and got a position with American Express in Paris. He didn't speak a word of French, but within two years he was fluent. He was now a middle-aged man and felt he was ready to settle down. This was when he bought his beloved apartment in the Third Arrondissement.

"I hear French women make good wives," Gary said, grasping at straws.

"Whoever told you that is full of crap," Ray replied.

"I take it you know from firsthand experience?"

"Nope. I never could stand being pinned down to one woman."

Gary stifled a groan. "So you don't have any kids?"

"Well, probably a few I don't know about." Ray chuckled.

"Do you live alone?"

"You're never really alone in a town like Deming." Ray

turned and looked at Gary. A glimmer of recognition seemed to flit across his eyes. "I'm sorry. What's your name again?"

Gary hesitated briefly before answering. "Chuck," he said, wholly unprepared for the glee that thrilled through him with the lie. "Chuck Zemco."

Ray shook his head quizzically. "Oh. For a second there I thought you were someone else."

"Who?"

Ray scratched his beard.

"Can't recall," he said, glancing skyward. He stared into the sky for at least half a minute before looking back down at the court, perplexed. "What was I saying?"

This was the first time it crossed Gary's mind that he would rather be dead than lose his mind.

Just as suddenly as Ray had left every other place he had been, he decided it was time to leave Paris, do something else. Again he had plenty of money tucked away. He began to feel the urge to write again. He realized that what had stopped him before was that he hadn't lived enough. He had had nothing to say. That was no longer a problem. Partly inspired by a thorough reading of the works of Céline, he decided he would try to write a novel loosely based on his own travels and adventures. To do so he felt he needed to extricate himself from the modern world and all its many diversions. The image that came to mind this time was a tropical island he had seen en route to Guadalcanal. So in the late seventies that was where he went.

Once he was there it didn't take long for him to realize that his vision of being the next Céline was nothing more than a pretext to get him moving again. If he had had too little of life to work with before, he now had too much. The thought of trying to reconstruct it all in words paralyzed him. He couldn't bear sitting alone in silence, staring at a blank page, knowing all the while that real life was there to be lived right outside the door. But he liked Pohnpei, felt something relax inside him, so he bought a little store and started selling office supplies. And there he stayed, amassing a small fortune, for nineteen years. Oddly enough it was Pohnpei, the one place where he had lived longer than any other, that he had the least to say about.

Gary, having seemingly scoured every corner of the globe in search of the ex-wife, now felt certain that Pohnpei was where she was hidden away, somewhere behind those silent decades.

"So you settled down there in Pohnpei?"

"I was there nearly twenty years."

"Sounds like a good place to raise a family."

"As good a place as any, I suppose."

"I bet those Pohnpei women are beautiful."

Ray smiled and looked skyward, his eyes scanning his mind for the choicest images.

"Yeah," he said almost hypnotically. "They're definitely put together right out there."

"You married one of them, didn't you?"

"Nope. I never could stand being pinned down to one woman."

Gary clenched his teeth. It was all he could do to keep from screaming.

"Come off it, Ray. I know you were married once. Why can't you just admit it?"

Ray turned and looked at Gary with an expression like that of someone getting a strong whiff of sour milk.

"What's up your craw?" he said.

"Forget it," Gary said.

"I don't know where you come off, coming out with something like that. I don't even know you. And you sure as hell don't know me."

"Yeah, whatever."

They sat there side by side, staring straight ahead, their knees almost touching. It was mid-July, searingly hot, completely silent. Not a single tweet of a bird. An old, unpleasant memory came back to Gary as he sat there glowering in the silence. He and Mike Hern, in their first tournament as partners, were playing doubles, on that very court in fact, against some awful kids from Lordsburg. He and Mike were destroying them. Then at 5–2 in the first set their game just crumbled for no explicable reason. They were so astounded when they lost the first set that it was almost as if they willed themselves to lose the second, and the match, for confirmation. The strangest thing about that experience, something that Gary and Mike would only be able to articulate to each other years later, was that they both, at seemingly exactly the same moment, were seized by a terrible, crippling fear—not of losing to such incompetent players, but of beating them. It only happened that once. They would go on to become the stars of the team, taking second in state that same year, but the only match that Gary could ever remember from all his time on the team was that humiliation at the hands of the Lordsburgers.

"Come on if we're going to finish this thing," Gary said brusquely. "I don't have all day." He had already lost the first set and was down a break in the second.

Ray grumbled something incomprehensible, and they both stood up and headed back onto the court.

A few games later Ray made a bad call.

"That was on the line!" Gary fumed.

"Well, no, it was a good six inches out."

"Six inches out?! Which side of the line are you looking at? Are you going blind as well?!"

Ray ignored the barb. "Let's play it over."

"I don't want to play it over. It's my point. That's the rule. The ball goes in, the point's mine."

Gary was so vehement about it that Ray, clearly less interested in winning than Gary was, relented and gave him the point. Gary went on to win the set, leaving them tied at one apiece.

Ray wanted to call it a day. Gary could see he was worn out, but that was tough. That was part of the game. If Gary's only advantage was his youth and stamina, if that was the only way to beat the old man, then so be it.

"I'd better not," Ray said.

That really got Gary's blood boiling.

"Look, man, you owe me another set."

"How do you figure that?"

"I've played you every damn time you've asked me, even when I didn't feel like it."

Ray looked at him queerly.

"What on earth are you talking about?"

Gary bellowed in frustration, startling Ray nearly out of his wits. He was instantly embarrassed by his outburst. He hated people who shouted and hollered on the court.

"Well, if we're going to play another set," Ray calmly said after a while, "let's make it worth something."

"All right, you name it," Gary said, trying hard to recover his cool.

"Loser buys dinner."

"All right."

"And not McDonald's either. A real restaurant, like K-Bob's."

"You're on."

At first Ray seemed reinvigorated by the challenge, the prospect of winning a steak dinner. Gary knew that if he could just keep the ball coming back, sooner or later Ray would wear out, and to that end he backed off on his power and just made sure to get the ball over the net. In doing this he discovered a tactic that he should have been using all along: the shallow drop shot, a little dink barely over the net, forcing Ray to run it down forward instead of sideways. This proved virtually impossible for him, though it didn't stop him from trying. In no time at all he had little energy left for the rest of his game, and his shots began sinking into the net.

Gary was up 5–2 when they sat down for what appeared to be the last break of the match. For all intents and purposes it was over. A warm feeling of peace came over Gary as he sat there, sweaty and tired, letting the fact of his long-overdue victory slowly sink in.

"What kind of food do you like?" Ray asked. Other than his name, it was the first question he had ever asked Gary about himself.

"I'm partial to a steak," Gary said. "Medium rare."

Ray nodded.

"You know I was a cook for a while once," he said.

"Were you?" Now that Gary was on the verge of winning he felt more than happy to hear another one of Ray's stories.

"It was in Paris, before I was . . . no, San Francisco. That's right. I wasn't any good at it. I don't like to be rushed. Life should be taken at a comfortable pace. I only lasted there about a month." He drifted off into his memories. "Ah, Paris. A moveable feast . . ."

A few minutes later they were back on the court. At 30–30 Gary sliced one of his drop shots just over the net. Ray made it about six steps forward before he stopped and stood for a moment with an odd expression on his face, the way a man looks when he realizes, as the door clicks locked behind him, that he's forgotten his keys. He bent over a little and brought his free hand up to his heart. Then his knees buckled and he went down. His racket dropped from his hand and hit the court a moment before his upper body slumped down with a dull thud, knocking his hat off his head. The ball went bouncing past him. He lay motionless.

Gary stood there stunned, thinking for some reason that it was a joke.

Ten seconds later Ray still hadn't moved.

Nor had Gary.

In the quiet moments of his day, this hesitation, above all else, seemed to Gary like a dagger with his own hand on it, twisting inside the old man's heart. Not because he believed a quicker response might have saved Ray's life. Rather, what sealed his verdict of guilt, what sent him back to the hall closet to stare again at his own smiling face on the campaign button, was the profound sense of justice, however brief it may have been, he experienced when he grasped that the old man had suffered a mortal blow.

At last Gary ran around the net and knelt down and turned Ray over. A deathly pallor had already stolen over his face.

When his eyes met Gary's a shine of unmistakable love came into them.

"Julien," he said weakly. "Allez, cherche ta mère."

"What?" Gary said, and it seemed to him that these incomprehensible words were the answer to all his questions.

Blanco

THE FAMILY VALU PARKING LOT was strangely empty for a Saturday afternoon. A black pit bull, chained up and panting in the bed of an old Chevy pickup, eyed Kyle as he pulled into a spot near the entrance and turned down the stereo, the better to feel the mixture of peace and dread and intangible yearnings that those first few moments back always gave him. He felt it in his stomach, and near his heart, as if his insides were made of tissue paper, balled up and slowly expanding by some frail inner tension.

Yolanda was at one of the registers with a customer and didn't see him come in. Slow fiddles and slide guitar drifted down from the ceiling as Kyle stood idly turning the keychain rack, listening with half an ear to the nasally twang of Yolanda's customer. He swiveled the rack. The woman ranted on. At last, gathering up her loud plastic bags, she made the obligatory upbeat parting quip and headed for the door.

"Hey, baby," Kyle crooned, sneaking up behind Yolanda and putting his arm around her shoulder. She flinched and turned, staring blankly until at last recognition dawned.

"Kyle?!" She stared at him, as if still not quite sure. "Wow!"

She stepped back and put a fist on her hip. She wasn't much over five feet tall. Black denim pants. Red-and-green floral-patterned blouse. Good ass. Long black hair pulled back with a wooden clip. Ring on the finger. Sparky little Yolanda. It seemed she'd always been at Family Valu and would be there still long after it was gone.

"Wow!" she said again.

He was used to it by now, the bewildered expression, and the effort it took to conceal it. The barber himself had been reluctant, asking him three times if he was sure. The floor around the chair looked like a brown shag rug when the shaver had finally clicked off. It was the strangest sensation, staring at that alien creature in the mirror. The naked white skull looking huge one second, tiny the next. The sudden return of his ears. The weird elongation of his face. All his friends and coworkers were stunned. To them it wasn't just a change of look. He could see it in their eyes, behind their words of approval. The Kyle they had known—the rocker, the partier, the friendly neighborhood dealer—had suddenly and without advance warning ceased to exist. Kyle himself marveled at the feeling of lightness that suffused him, the feeling that along with his hair he had shed something much heavier. A week later he was still catching himself flicking back phantom hair, like an amputee scratching the air beyond a stub.

"You look hot as ever," he said. He'd been flirting with Yolanda Alvarez since he was twelve.

Shooing away the remark, she cocked her hip and looked him over.

"So, what brings you down?"

He glanced toward the office window. "Mother's Day duty."

"Ah. How sweet." He caught her stealing another glance at his head. "God, I just can't get over how different you look. Why'd you . . . I mean, what made you decide to do it?"

Just then the woman who'd been stocking yarn in the crafts aisle walked by, pretending to mind her own business. Yolanda called her over, telling her that the handsome young man before her was Judy's son Kyle, whom she'd known since he was only yay high. The woman's name, which Yolanda pronounced with odd formality as if she were some notable Deming personage, was LaVerne Cass Brown. LaVerne Cass Brown was lumpy everywhere. Lumpy belly, lumpy breasts, lumpy arms, lumpy fingers, lumpy nose. She was holding a pricing gun in her right hand, a clot of white price tags stuck to her wrist.

"Pleasure to meet you." Kyle shook her soft, warm hand.

"You're the musician." A hint of accusation somewhere in there. She too was stealing furtive glances at his head, the skin tone still a shade lighter than his face despite his sitting out in the park every lunch hour last week.

"I play a bit."

"Stop being modest." Yolanda jabbed him. "He's got a CD out."

"Well, isn't that something," LaVerne Cass Brown remarked with genuine, irritating sincerity.

She then started in about some old boyfriend who'd played the fiddle. Kyle indulged her with a nodding smile. He tuned out when she got to the part about how tough the music business was. He glanced around the store, shifting the burden of LaVerne Cass Brown's life story back to Yolanda. They were still selling the exact same stuff they'd been selling for the past decade or so, all in the same places on the same shelves in the same aisles. The arts and crafts supplies. The picture frames. The rainbow coffee mugs. The crocheted pillow covers. The "Footprints in the Sand" Bible placemats.

Kyle took advantage of a pause in LaVerne Cass Brown's reminiscences to excuse himself, making his way to the back of the store, through the double doors into storage and up the crude white stairs two at a time to his mom's office.

"Good Lord!" she exclaimed, taking in the change and setting it aside with a broad smile of unexpected joy. "What are you doing here?"

Judy Martin's voice had the smoky husk of a pack a day for twenty years, less the month here and there of New Year's resolutions. More subtle in her voice was the spunkiness of the big city girl (Phoenix) who'd been kicked around by life but wouldn't have had it any other way.

"Happy Mother's Day." Kyle stepped around her desk and gave his mom a hug.

"Oh yeah. You'd think with all the crap I had to order, I'd've remembered." She pulled a cigarette from the pack on her desk and lit it with a Bic. "So . . . ?" she said, her eyes doing the cranial tour.

He shrugged, saying, "Just felt like it," failing to add that he'd had an anxious eye on his thinning crown for several years. It was obvious she didn't care for the change, but she restrained herself commendably.

He glanced toward the broad two-way mirror in the wall to his left, remembering how he used to sit there on dull summer afternoons trying to scope out shoplifters in the aisles below.

"So, tell me more about this job," she said. "Do you like it?"

He turned from the window. "It's all right."

She took a drag, looking at him. The teeth she'd replaced her naturally crooked ones with when she got the promotion still struck him as too straight and white.

He shrugged. "It's performance." He reached up to flick back his hair, caught himself, lowered his hand. "It's all bullshit."

"Well, I sure as hell couldn't do it."

She tapped her cigarette against the glass ashtray strewn with lipsticky butts. She smiled at him, clicking the fingernails of her thumb and middle finger.

"Listen," she said. "I've got to finish up some stuff. Let's go out to dinner tonight. My treat."

She gave him the key to the house and said she'd be home around six.

———

Driving down shady Platinum Street, Kyle glanced toward his best friend Sam's grandma's house on Buckeye. He considered stopping by and shooting the breeze with the old bird, Mary Margaret Palmer, but he carried on, the heavy dullness of the afternoon somehow at odds with the idea of lively banter. He couldn't help feeling as if some catastrophe had struck town and everyone was gone. He came to a complete stop at the stop sign at Walnut Street, just to savor the stillness. Down the whole length of Florida Street he passed only one car. He thought it was stalled, it was going so slow. All he could see through its windshield were some wispy gray hairs and a pair of arthritic knuckles.

As soon as he was inside the house he pulled the pouch and pipe from his bag and went out to the back porch and smoked a bowl. The yard needed mowing. One of the metal doors of the shed had slipped its groove and was hanging crooked, forming a sharp black triangle out of the darkness within. He unfolded a lawn chair, brushed away the spider webs and sank down into it. A single fluffy cloud hovered motionless in the blue. He sat completely still, listening to the silence. Every little sound, a car driving down some distant street, the buzz of a fly, the twitching of the chair, only made the silence around him seem more vast. He closed his eyes and tried to remember the faces of his high school girlfriends.

By the time his mom got home he'd showered, and the buzz was gone. She was all bustle. "Where do you want to eat?" She suggested La Fonda. "Let me get out of these shoes." They went in her car. She smoked while she drove. The sun was finally on its way down, a little hint of coolness in the air. She told him how happy she was he'd come, as if feeling guilty for not saying so earlier. She said she'd been thinking about him a lot lately. Praying about him.

He held the door for her as they made their way into the restaurant, past the postcard racks and candy machines. There was something pleasingly innocent about the little glass dispensers full of cashews and Spanish burnt peanuts. Those old things were nowhere to be seen in Albuquerque. At least not in the world he inhabited. It was all strip malls and glossy retail up there. He glanced around the booths and tables for familiar faces and was relieved not to see any. He didn't feel like going through the whole catching-up routine, the inescapable sizing up of lives.

They slid into a booth on the left side, out of the sun. A young Mexican waitress approached.

After they'd ordered, his mom told him about her new

boyfriend, Clark. A retail liquidator, whatever that was, who lived in St. Paul, Minnesota. They'd met at a retailers' convention in Chicago. Kyle asked the relevant questions, allowed her her seeming happiness. The waitress brought their chips and salsa and two glasses of water to the table. Kyle tried to make eye contact but she was all business.

"So," his mom said, watching the waitress walk away. "You're a free a man again. How's it feel?"

"Damn good." Kyle chuckled guiltily. They both laughed.

"I had no idea it had gotten that bad."

That wasn't strictly true. She'd known he'd been in therapy, had helped pay for it in fact. Anger-management issues, he'd told her. Of course he hadn't told her all the ugly details. The kicked-in doors. The mad revving of engines. The petty little revenges that chipped away at his spirit. It seemed he'd tapped into some bottomless well of fury he never would have guessed existed within him. But whenever he'd spoken to his mom on the phone he'd toned down the problems until they sounded like nothing more than the usual growing pains of marriage. Right up to the end he was never quite sure if that wasn't all they actually were.

"Yeah, it was pretty much hell," he said.

"You should've told me."

He shrugged and dipped a chip into the salsa.

"Here I thought you two were the greatest couple ever invented. The next thing I know you're getting divorced."

He took a drink of water. The thick red plastic glass felt good in his hand, solid, the lip all scuffed to dullness. She was giving him the maternal look. He glanced aside.

"So how long's he got?" he asked her.

The waitress returned at that moment with their sizzling fajitas, warning them that the platters were very hot. Like you, Kyle heard himself about to say.

"Two years for the armed robbery," his mom said when the waitress was out of earshot. "Another year for the parole violation."

Kyle shook his head, but the truth was, he always appreciated how his own problems seemed to evaporate in the glare of his little brother's. Only in darker moods did he sometimes wonder if he wasn't partly to blame. Maybe he should have set a better example. Given him books instead of joints. But as far as Kyle was concerned, if anyone was to blame it was surely that hard-ass sonofabitch he'd lived under the same roof with for six long years. John White, Kevin's father, a convicted felon himself, presently living somewhere down in Mexico to evade doing time for something or other. Ironically, Kevin was the only one who didn't seem to blame anyone but himself. He'd admitted to Kyle during the month that he was out that he didn't know what to do with himself on the outside. Inside, everything was clear, ordered, predictable. He didn't have to think at all. This quiet resignation, wisdom even, at eighteen years old, floored Kyle. This when Kyle, twenty-six at the time, was still sucking the tit of his rock-star fantasies. He'd carried on pretending to be the magnanimous half brother, the one to be emulated, but at some point he came to realize that their roles had been reversed. Kevin was the one with all the hard-earned knowledge of life, while Kyle, divorce and all, was just another thirty-two-year-old teenager.

They finished their dinner with an order of sopapillas. They tore open the corners of the steaming, bready pockets and squeezed thick honey inside. Kyle snatched up the bill as it hit the table. She argued.

"It's Mother's Day," he countered.

"No it isn't."

"Close enough."

He let her leave the tip.

———

Back at home they sat on the couch and watched TV. He bore it as long as he could, then went back to his room. He stood there for a while, staring at nothing in particular. The pinholes from his posters were still visible in the walls. Hendrix. Satriani. Stevie Ray Vaughn. The laugh track came prancing down the hall.

It was dark outside now. He pulled the bag of weed from his duffel and stared at it for some time before putting it back.

"I'm going out for a drive," he told her, standing beside the couch.

"Okay, sweetie."

He drove around with the stereo blasting, and it seemed to him that he'd never left. He drove up and down Pine Street, from the truck stop to the Mirador Motel and back. The cruisers were out en masse, the lowriders, the pimped-out little pickups, the boring family cars, all shiny from fresh washes, driving up and down the strip at a snail's pace.

The place at Sonic where he used to park being taken, he pulled into a stall under the awning on the "gay side" and cut the engine. The night air was fresh and mild. In the stall directly across from him a group of kids were standing around a shiny black truck. Loitering. That was the word the sheriff used to use during his biannual crackdowns. "No loitering outside your vehicles, ladies and gentlemen." The guys were clean-cut types. Short hair. Athletic bodies. All wearing white high-top basketball shoes. In Kyle's day they'd been called preppies. He didn't know what they were called anymore, if anything.

In a stall a few cars down from them were the usual two guys wearing shades, death metal blasting from their windows, no doubt a six-pack hidden somewhere in their car. That's who Kyle had been. Above it all. Nothing but contempt for "normal" people. What idiots, he thought. Then there were the Mexican couples, who tended to park on the gay side, as he himself now was. He glanced around. Sure enough, it was still the case. They always seemed the most at ease in their cars and trucks. Half the time it was a sixteen-year-old guy with his fifteen-year-old girl who was six months pregnant, and they already looked like they'd been married for twenty years. The preppies seemed like sugared-up two-year-olds in comparison.

Then there was always the guy sitting alone in his car who nobody seemed to know. The preppie girls had a built-in radar for this character. He either gave them the creeps or he was cute and mysterious. Kyle glanced from car to car but didn't see him, not realizing until he caught two of the preppie girls staring at him that of course it was himself. They turned away in titillated embarrassment.

He stayed at Sonic for some time, observing and thinking, then he felt the urge to be moving again. Driving slowly past the preppie camp he waved casually at the girls. They waved back, staring at his face for some clue to who he was. Maybe someone they used to sigh over in their big sisters' annuals.

It was only 8:30. He drove aimlessly around residential streets, buffeted here and there by the flux of memory. He hadn't gotten on the Columbus highway with any goal in mind, only with a desire to be out in the darkness, away from town. Fifteen miles later he was still driving south.

———

He parked in the dirt lot fifty yards from the crossing and walked the rest of the way, a gentle breeze teasing the Mexican and American flags high up the pole near the floodlit fence. He walked through the portal of the Mexican immigration building, exchanging a nod with the two guards in dark-green uniforms leaning against the wall.

On the other side, the pavement abruptly ended, and all at once Kyle felt the assault to the senses that was a Saturday night in Palomas, Mexico. The wide dirt road, split up the middle by broken yellow concrete dividers, was choked with cars. Headlights and taillights shining and wobbling through a haze of dust and exhaust. People cruising in their stripped-down, beat-up heaps. Bald tires. Missing grilles. Unpainted fenders. Windshields caked with dust.

Kyle's joints tingled with nervous energy as he made his way down the sidewalk deeper into the town, the side streets tugging at his insides as he passed them, so dense was the darkness beyond. The smell of fried corn tortillas and beef and chile filled the air, mingling with the bright odor of pine disinfectant. All along the plastered concrete shop fronts, clusters of men were standing in the harsh glare of fluorescent lights. Men in boots and hats and long-sleeve work shirts. Men with thick mustaches and brown teeth, soaking up the night. The men, like the cars, made Kyle nervous. He walked down the sidewalk, trying to look at ease, all the while acutely aware of his own radiant gringoness. His bald, white head, it seemed to him, was a big, throbbing light bulb with "GRINGO" written across it and an arrow pointing down to his wallet.

A few blocks down, on the right side of the street, he came to a bar called Las Cuatro Ventanas, a white concrete cube with no windows at all, let alone four. The painted ads for Corona and Tecate were flaking and peeling from the whitewashed walls. Kyle stood outside it for a minute or so, walked another block to think it over, then turned back.

The small black metal door scraped noisily against the concrete sill and gave way to blaring blackness. What little light there was to see by was emanating from the purple panels of the ear-shattering jukebox, from the string of twinkling colored Christmas lights around the bottles behind the bar, and from a reddish-orange glow of no apparent source. The place was packed. Mostly men. Sitting in the dark booths along the two side walls, along the bar, standing in groups here and there where there was something to lean a forearm on. The few women he could see were at the bar or behind it serving drinks.

Curious eyes followed Kyle to the bar. He took a stool and asked for a Tecate. The bartender, a hefty woman with bronze hair and silver hoop earrings, pulled a can from the icebox and, otherwise paying him little heed, set it before him with a single-holed salt shaker and a wedge of lime.

That first icy sip felt good going down. Like a blade slicing through the bullshit of life. A feeling came over him, one he hadn't experienced in a long time, of being exactly where he belonged. Sitting at the bar, drinking his Tecate, he felt at ease in the darkness and the noise, felt brave even.

Halfway through his second beer a voice caught his attention. Louder than the others, it was obvious by the bad accent that it belonged to an American. Kyle turned his head a little the better to hear it, for there was something crude and compelling in its brazen self-assurance, down there where it didn't belong, speaking Spanish. He listened.

In the moment before he heard the words, something seized Kyle's heart. Some terrible foreboding.

"They can kiss my ass!" the voice boomed in English.

The hairs at the base of Kyle's neck went stiff. He set his beer down. He didn't dare turn around. The voice rang out sharp and clear above all the noise in the bar, above the deafening jukebox, as if it were made of something far denser than air. There was limitless self-confidence in it. Above all there was the certainty that his listener could not help but like this great big force of a man.

It all came back to Kyle now as he sat there staring at the bottles behind the bar. Six long years compressed into a sickening montage of misery. The trailer parks in shithole towns from Yuma to Lordsburg. Never knowing when he'd be woken up in the middle of the night and told to start packing, leaving behind his new friends yet again. The never-ending criticism and humiliation. *Suck in that gut about half a mile, boy. Get that TV off and get out there and rake up that dog shit. Watch that lip, son, or I'll knock you clear to Kingdom Come.* But most of all what came back to Kyle as he sat there riveted by that voice from the past was the absolute menace of the man's body. His bull-like bulk. His thick pink neck with that cinder block of a head stuck on top. His meaty fingers closing into big white fists, half the left pinky left behind in Korea. His long-sleeve button-up shirts, which added strange formality to his menace. His coarse, off-brand blue jeans. And those spotless white tube socks with his feet inside, propped up ever so leisurely on the ottoman. John White. Ex-marine. Purple Heart in the Korean War. This was the man Kyle had once seen beat a man's head in with the butt of a pistol. In his photo album from the war there'd been a picture of him proudly holding a Korean soldier's severed head by the hair. That head had haunted Kyle's dreams for years. Even now Kyle would sometimes awake from a dream in which it was himself hacking off someone's head. Sometimes people he knew. Once it had been his wife's. His therapist had made much of this.

Kyle slowly swiveled his head around to see his former step-father sitting in a booth with two Mexican men. In that quick glance he saw all he wanted to see of the man. He looked exactly the same. Same thick, square head. Same sparse, white hair. Same self-satisfied grin. Same deceptively charming little blue eyes. Kyle had known that John White was living down in Mexico, calling himself Juan Blanco, but he'd thought it was Juarez or Nogales or something. Not Palomas. Fuckin' hell, he thought. Wait till I tell Mom.

He finished his beer and asked for another. As the initial shock began to wear off, Kyle had to admit there was a certain satisfaction in it, an almost perverse sense of irony in hearing John White again, bellowing in Spanish in this dark little hole down in Palomas. At first the idea of sitting there listening to the past from the relative bliss of the present seemed to be enough. But gradually the idea of going over and showing himself began to take hold of Kyle. He didn't know why. Nothing could be accomplished by it. But the longer he sat there, the more cowardly he felt. Just go over there and say hello, he told himself. Be a man, for Christ's sake.

At last he set his empty can back on the bar and got up and walked over to the booth.

John White turned his head as Kyle neared. He leveled his gaze, squinting a little, suspicion in his eyes—the wariness of the perpetually wanted. Kyle could see his mind working, trying to place the face. John White angled his head slightly, glancing up and down Kyle's body. He sat back in the booth. Then it clicked.

"Kyle!" he boomed. "Well, I'll be goddamned."

"Hey, John," Kyle said matter-of-factly, fighting back the nerves.

"Well, I never. What brings you down here, son?"

"I just came down for a drink."

John White shook his head in confounded delight. The Mexicans looked at Kyle.

"I didn't recognize you there for a second. Without the hair and all. How's your mother?"

Kyle nodded. "She's good."

"Well, hell, come over and sit and have a beer with your old man. Hombres," John White said to the Mexicans, "es mi hijo, Kyle."

"Ah," they said, their eyes smiling now, "tu hijo. Vente, hijo Blanco. Vente."

They made room for him in the booth, one of them moving over to John White's side. Kyle tried to think of some excuse for why he couldn't stay. But he had no excuse. He had no reason to leave.

"What're you drinkin'?" John White asked Kyle as he slid into the seat across from him.

"Just beer."

"Ho!" John White shouted at the bar, three fingers and the pinky stub thrust high. "¡Cuatro más! ¡Por favor!"

He turned back to Kyle. "This here's Pablo," he said. "That's Hector. They know English."

Kyle glanced at Pablo. He looked to be in his forties. Puffy cheeks. No mustache. Slightly drunk. The other one, Hector, had on a fancy cowboy shirt, and his knuckles were scabbed. Kyle shook their hands.

"Kevin tells me you've done pretty good for yourself up in Albuquerque. Got a band and all."

"Yeah, I got a band."

"What kind of music you play?"

"Rock, pretty much."

"Can't beat that." John White smiled, and despite himself Kyle felt a small, unexpected warmth begin to quell his nerves. Visions of Saturday afternoons in trailer parks, John White out working on some truck he'd weaseled out of someone, Creedence Clearwater Revival whining from some crappy tape deck as he sang along, tapping his foot, jutting his head like a turkey.

The bartender brought their beers over and they all cracked them open and drank.

"Last time I saw you, you had long hair."

Kyle nodded.

"What'd you get rid of it for?"

He gave it some thought before saying he didn't really know.

"Hey, Juan Blanco," Hector broke in. "Tell him about your cancer."

"Now what'd you have to go sayin' that for, dumbass?" John White took a long guzzle of beer and winced. He leaned forward, looking Kyle in the eyes. "Yeah, I had me a case of gut cancer. They cut a chunk of my intestines out yay long," he said, spreading his meaty hands a couple feet wide and clinching his fists as if holding a rattlesnake between them.

"Sorry to hear that."

"Yeah, laid me out for a good year. Goddamn Mexican doctors. They can kiss my ass!"

Pablo and Hector chuckled and drank some more beer.

"So how's your mother?" John White asked again.

Kyle nodded. "Real good. Real good. They made her manager at the store. She's got a new boyfriend in Minnesota."

John White nodded. Kyle couldn't be sure in that dim light but he thought he saw the man's eyes go a little misty.

Then came a long, uncomfortable silence. They all drank their beers and avoided each other's eyes. The noise of the bar flooded back in from wherever it had retreated to. Kyle began to prepare a parting remark. He was glad he'd come over and said hello. The bastard seemed to have mellowed with age. Kyle couldn't help feeling a little sorry for him, this sick old marine stuck down there in Mexico. On that forgiving note, he reached for the edge of the table and was just about to slide out and wish John White all the best when John White said: "What say we do us a whore?"

Kyle looked at him and chuckled. For some reason the sound of those words in John White's mouth, spoken with such sincerity, such fatherly generosity, struck him as downright funny. At the same time Kyle couldn't help feeling a little touched by the suggestion, intended or not, that they were somehow equals now, two grown men out on the town, seeking the pleasures of the night.

"Them's some good pussy," Pablo quipped, grinning. "Trust me. I know."

At that Hector and Pablo and John White all burst out laughing, Hector and John White ribbing Pablo about being a happily married man. The whores at the bar, keeping tabs on their prospects, turned and flashed their smiles at the table of raucous men.

"What say, kiddo?" John White said when they'd settled back down. "My treat."

Kyle looked at him. He wasn't exactly sure what the man was proposing. He was reluctant to refuse him outright, unable to forget, despite the present joviality, the sudden eruptions of violence he was capable of. But if he was suggesting that they both go into a room and do some whore together like marines on a weekend tear, he was out of his mind.

"Ah, man," Kyle said, half-joking, glancing toward the bar. "I can get better than that for free any day of the week."

"Well, I'm sure you could," John White said, smiling, congenial as a mayor a few votes short, "but this here's the hand we been dealt."

Pablo and Hector, eager to see father and son bond in such high style, reassured Kyle that they personally knew every last whore in Palomas, and they were all as clean as their own sisters. They all laughed again.

Pablo turned to the bar and whistled and the two whores got down from their stools and walked over to the table. One was fat, the other skinny. The fat one was wearing a tight green dress with sparkles on it. The dress was strapless, mounds of flesh bulging over the seams. The thin one wore a red dress. It was either less revealing or else she simply had less to reveal; it was hard to tell in the dimness. Neither of them looked the least bit attractive to Kyle. He didn't go for the gaudy blue mascara and cherry-red lipstick look.

Upon reaching the table, the fat whore proceeded to make

herself comfortable on Kyle's right thigh. The skinny one took a seat on John White's leg. Now that he could see her, Kyle didn't think the skinny one was too bad. Much better looking, to his mind, than the one on him. She was younger, for one thing. In her early twenties. Her makeup didn't look as whorish up close. And she had a lovely, delicate neck, one of his favorite parts on a woman. She smiled at him when she caught him staring.

The next half hour was a flurry of Spanish, everyone but Kyle jabbering away at the same time. Wherever Kyle's eyes happened to roam, to John White, to the accumulating cans of beer, to his own fidgeting hands, they kept returning to the slender neck of the skinny whore. There was something tantalizingly vulnerable about it, all the more so given the man she happened to be sitting on. John White sat there like some kind of lord, his pinkyless hand cupping her bony shoulder, oblivious to the finer qualities of this delicate creature in his lap.

"Come on, son, whaddya say?"

The crack of Kyle's whore's big haunches was burning a stripe up his thigh. She had her blubbery arm around him, her hand stroking his baldness.

"¡Ay, qué calvo!" she exclaimed.

"Sí, y las otras partes también," Hector joked, and everyone laughed. Kyle laughed a little too, at what he wasn't sure.

"She likes you, ese," Pablo slurred.

"My treat," John White offered again.

By now Kyle was starting to entertain the idea. He hadn't been laid in a good three months, and that had been a dismal little post-divorce screw with an out-of-town friend of one of his coworkers. Images of the skinny whore undressing for him in some nasty back room began to flicker through his mind.

He finished off his beer.

"All right," he said at last, nodding toward the skinny whore. "But I want that one."

John White smiled a little.

"But this'n here's mine," he said, cordially enough.

"I'll trade you," Kyle replied, getting into the sordid spirit of it all.

"Thing is,"—John White leaned in—"this here's Juanita. She's my girlfriend."

Kyle looked at him. He couldn't tell if he was joking. You never could tell with him. He used to say the most outlandish things with a perfectly straight face, like, *There's a whole mess of dead birds outside, Kyle. Run on out and have a look.* And there wouldn't be any birds at all. Kyle studied John White's face for any sign of jest but couldn't find any.

"Oh," he said, not knowing what else to say. "I didn't realize."

"Sweet little thing, ain't she?" John White gave her cheek a pinch. She turned her eyes and smiled at him, her big strong Juan Blanco.

Kyle was starting to feel dizzy. His ears were ringing. He was hot. He needed some fresh air. The whore's fat ass felt like an inferno on his leg. Pablo and Hector were telling him how good Lupe was in bed. "She can do some crazy things, amigo." She was still rubbing his head.

"I've got to get going," Kyle said, shifting his weight to try to get the whore off his leg.

"Hey now," John White said. "What's the rush? I ain't seen you in, God, how many years has it been?"

Kyle shook his head. The whore was off him now. He stood up.

"If it's Juanita you're after, I reckon I could let you have her for a spell. If that's what's eatin' ya."

Kyle stared at John White, incredulous.

"I don't want your goddamn whore!" he barked, much louder than he'd bargained for. He certainly wasn't expecting it when the loud rumble of voices all around the bar suddenly faded away to silence. All eyes turned toward Juan Blanco's table. Only the jukebox blared on, the bass throbbing away with ridiculous joy.

There it was, the face that still haunted Kyle's dreams. The little blue eyes slicing into him. The big square skull. The mouth as tight as a boot seam.

John White's left eye narrowed to a squint. Nothing else in

the face moved. Kyle stared back at him, pulsing all over. He was ready for him now. Ready for anything.

"Eh!" the bartender shouted, firing a barrage of irate Spanish their way. John White turned his head and said something to appease her, then turned back to Kyle and went on eyeing him. Kyle's heart was hammering against his ribcage.

A few seconds later John White's face softened.

"Come on now, Kyle," he said with perfect affability. "No hard feelings. We're just havin' a little fun."

Kyle stared at him a little longer, then looked away, his heart throbbing in his throat. All he wanted now was to get the hell out of there. He reached into his pocket and took out some dollars and set them on the table. His hands were shaking.

Someone mumbled something. The song that was playing ended and another began. Slowly the voices returned.

"I should go," Kyle said.

John White nodded, his eyebrows still raised a little. He offered Kyle his hand. Kyle stared at it, telling himself to just turn and walk away.

"Tell your mother hello for me, would ya?" John White said.

The feeling of that pinky stub pressing into Kyle's palm stayed with him as he left the bar and turned down the nearest side street, walking faster as he went, into the warm, enveloping darkness.

The Wildcat Massacre

IT HAD BEEN NEARLY A century since anything of the sort had happened in the area when the defensive line of the Deming Wildcats, celebrating their victory over the Silver City Fighting Colts in the opening game of the District 3-AAA play-offs, were caught unawares in the dry, sandy bed of the Mimbres River and massacred by Apache warriors.

So opens Massey's provocative if ultimately insufficient account of the events of November 6, 1987, otherwise known as the Wildcat Massacre. The factual details of that night are well known and need not detain us here (see Eluard, *The Wildcat Massacre: A Concordance*). The aim of the present study is to bring to the "Massacre discourse" valuable insights from adjacent fields of inquiry, in this case chiefly from the field of speculative linguistics, not with the hope of solving the mystery in the conventional sense, which efforts are better left in the hands of detectives, but rather to give meaning to the mystery itself. To this end we have cataloged, in accordance with the predictions of the Szekeres Principle—which holds that metaphor, far from being a merely linguistic phenomenon, is a universal force of cohesion—ninety-seven identical *living* metaphors contiguous with the Wildcat Massacre. Of that number, the following five are exemplary.

1) The Football Game

The remarkable losing streak of the Deming Wildcats to the Silver City Fighting Colts has been noted in many accounts of the Wildcat Massacre, but always as merely an anecdote, a piece of interesting local color, or, worse yet, justification for the prevailing notion that Deming is a rotten place to live. I have spent seven months there myself and can attest to the spontaneous generosity and warmth of its people.

Though only sixty miles of desert and mountain separate them, the differences between Silver City and Deming, New Mexico, are stark. Silver City, as its name suggests, began as a mining town, the trappings of its heady boom days still on display in the fine brick Victorian homes fronting its tree-lined streets. Deming, on the other hand, was born of the junction of two railroads, a place whose raison d'être was to be passed through. Silver City is nestled high in the cool, forested hills of the Gila Wilderness. Deming lies flat on a parched plain of the Chihuahuan Desert. Silver City has a university. Deming has night classes at the Kingdom of the Sun Retirement Center. I mention these differences not to perpetuate the stereotypes that each town holds of the other but rather to illustrate the class basis on which the historic rivalry between them stands. It is revealing that upon mentioning to one of my informants in Deming that I would be spending a week researching in Silver City, he gave me an almost wounded look and said, "I thought you was one of us." It is not difficult to imagine, then, the symbolic—the *metaphorical*—significance of a Wildcats v. Fighting Colts football game. What is more difficult to imagine is the sheer magnitude of emotion born of a thirty-two-year losing streak.

One senses when watching those old black-and-white films of the Wildcats v. Fighting Colts football games that one is beholding Metaphor in its purest form, shorn of all the trappings of space and time. These aren't merely high school kids playing football—these are nodes of signification, syntagms and morphemes linked like genes along a strand of DNA. The rhythm of their surges and collisions are the very pulse of Metaphor. Almost nothing, it seems, escaped comparison to those games during those three decades. Indeed, the periodic aspect of the encounters dissolved completely into timeless Metaphor, condensing the many disparate games into a single eternal Game whose ultimate value was its resemblance to so many other unbearable but seemingly immutable situations over the years of the rivalry: the Cold War, the Cuban Missile Crisis, the troubles in the Middle East. Closer to home the game was often compared to labor strikes, to the divisions in the House and Senate, to various minority groups' struggles for equality. The changes in Deming during this same period, while perhaps not as far-reaching, were no doubt equally profound for its citizens; a partial list of these changes includes: the coming and going of two mayors, the closing of the old Rexall on the corner of Pine and Gold Streets, and the erection of drive-through teller lanes at both Mimbres Valley Bank and the Bank of Deming. Just before the film clatters off its reel, the teams line up at the fifty-yard line for the ritual handshake. It is here, as the players file past one another, hands outstretched like the tender wings of baby birds, that one feels again the heartrending despair of the Deming Wildcats and the guilty relief of the Silver City Fighting Colts, while on the periphery, in the silent trumpeting of the Wildcat fight song, in the cheerleaders' pompoms hanging limply against their shivering legs, in the fans' return to motion in the bleachers, one feels the stirrings of renewed resolve. This unflagging optimism in the face of a hopeless situation is epitomized by Lester Good's fifth letter to the editor on the eve of the second game of the 1971 season: "Let me put it this way. When you've been down this dadgum long, there ain't nothin' left but up."

Then, on November 6, 1987, after thirty-two years of continuous defeat at the hands of Silver City, everything changed. Here is how Manuel Torres remembers it:

I'll never forget that night. It was so cold. I almost didn't make it. I live out on Hermanas Road [. . .] Well, we won the toss and elected to receive. They kicked off and David Almanza received it and started running up the left side. He made it to the thirty before Silver's guys were on him, then he cut back to the middle, and that's when we all saw it, it was like a tunnel, man, like there was a path of bright green grass right down the middle of that yellow field, and nothing on earth was going to stop Almanza from making it to that end zone. I've told my wife this many times: I believe he could have stopped running right there and walked the rest of the way, and no one would have touched him. I knew at that moment we were going to win this thing. I think the players sensed it too and got nervous. Silver scored on their next drive, and by the end of the first quarter we were down 13–7. From that point on it was trench warfare. I've never seen kids go at each other like that, man.

Mr. Torres's metaphor is not entirely inappropriate. By the end of the game there were two Wildcats and one Fighting Colt in the emergency room of Mimbres Valley Memorial Hospital. But perhaps the severest violence of the night was the rupturing, the killing, of the greatest metaphor Deming had ever known.

In his study on the power dynamics of sports rivalries, Mark Stuckey describes long-term rivalries (defined as ten years or more of complete domination by one team over another) as a kind of dysfunctional marriage, a relationship whose imbalances accumulate gradually over time into "a state of almost unbearable tension seemingly impervious to change." The phrases commonly used by such rivals to describe their relationship are vivid metaphors of powerlessness: "stuck on a sinking ship," "falling into a black hole," "a nightmare I can't wake up from." Though their constituents, their *metaphemes*, may differ, each of these metaphors embodies the same concept: a force of seemingly infinite magnitude oppressing the subject over a duration approaching eternity. The careful reader will have already deduced that herein lies the precise definition of the Apaches' historic struggle against the oppression of the white man. One may be tempted, therefore, to make the assertion that the thirty-two-year losing streak of the Wildcats is itself a metaphor for the two-hundred-year losing streak of the Apaches, but such a reading is a critical distortion of the Szekeres Principle, which holds that identical metaphors, transitive by definition, cannot be subjected to functions of proportion. They are the same metaphor.

2) The Passing of Rex Cameron

Rex Cameron, aged eighty-two, died on the evening of November 6, 1987, at Mimbres Valley Memorial Hospital. His obituary highlights his service to his country in World War II, in particular his courage during the grueling Bataan Death March. After the war he returned to Deming and worked at the Coca-Cola bottling plant until his retirement in 1970. At the time of his death he was survived by his wife, Tricia (deceased 1998), their children (Rudy, Robert, and Caroline), and eleven grandchildren.

Further investigations at the Deming-Luna-Mimbres History Museum, and telephone interviews with daughter Caroline Richards, now living in Baton Rouge, reveal that her father's death brought to an end nearly a century of the Camerons' ties to Deming. Rex Cameron's father, Donald "Red" Cameron (1885–1952), was born in Cochise County, Arizona, on the day of Geronimo's first surrender to General Crook in the Sierra Madre of northern Mexico. Rex's grandfather, Frank Cameron (1857–1921), was said to have taken the scalp of an Apache warrior he killed at Prospector's Farewell while garrisoned there with the Ninth Cavalry in 1875. This scalp remained in the possession of the Cameron family, passing down from son to son, until it was accidentally thrown away by Tricia Cameron in February of 1952. Here is how Caroline Richards recalls the story:

> It was a difficult time in their marriage. Mom was restless and wanted to go back to work. Dad wouldn't

have it. He felt it was more important for her to be at home with me and my brothers. I was ten, the youngest, and Mom felt we were old enough now to look after ourselves. Then Granddaddy [Donald Cameron] took ill, and my dad went with him to the hospital in Cruces. He was gone three or four days. It seemed like a lot longer to me. While he was away, my mom decided to clean out the attic, get rid of stuff we weren't using anymore.

I should backtrack a little. One of our favorite family stories is how on their first date Dad showed Mom his scalp. [Laughs.] The joke of course is that it was the old Apache scalp he showed her, not his own. Don't ask me why he thought a girl would want to see a nasty old thing like that. But I guess it worked; she married him. Anyway, one of the things in the attic of our old house on Nickel Street was Daddy's old army trunk, a big, heavy, green wooden thing. In her cleaning frenzy Mom opened the trunk to put some stuff in it. The only thing in it was the scalp. Mom swore to her dying day that she thought it was the shriveled carcass of a dead rat. She took it out to the alley and threw it in the garbage can. It was a couple days after Daddy got back before Mom mentioned she'd cleaned the attic and found a dead rat in his old army trunk. "A horrible little black thing," she said. I'll never forget the color Daddy's face went when she told him she'd thrown it out. We were all sitting around listening to the radio. I swear he went the color of a stop sign. "The scalp!" he roared and rushed up to the attic, but of course the scalp was gone. "You've thrown away the scalp!" I thought the ceiling was going to cave in. You never saw Daddy mad. It was frightening. He went out to the alley and dumped the garbage cans out and sorted through all the trash, looking for the scalp. By then the garbage had already been taken. He took off from work the next day and spent all day combing through the mounds of garbage out at the dump, but he never found it. Four days later

Granddaddy Red died. That was a bad year for Mom and Dad. A bad year for all of us.

While it is tempting to note the presence of Apaches in the history of the Cameron family, for our purposes it is merely coincidental and ultimately inconsequential. Rex Cameron's death, above all else, must be seen as a metaphor identical to the other metaphors in the skein of the Wildcat Massacre. His departure from life—the end of an eighty-two-year relationship with the living universe—reminds us of the end of the thirty-two-year losing streak of the Deming Wildcats.

3) The Theft of Mateo Sanchez's Tools from 304 S. Gold Street

Mateo Sanchez is, and was at the time of the theft, an auto mechanic at the Deming Truck Terminal, which receives a fair amount of interstate traffic. He was at Memorial Stadium with his family when his tools were stolen. The tools in question, too various to categorize, had been acquired over approximately twenty years. At least a third of them, by his estimation, had been given to him as gifts on various special occasions, Christmas and his birthday being the most common. They were his personal tools, tools he used in his capacity as head of the family, which consists of his wife, Martha, their three children (Paul, Julian, and Sandy), and Martha's mother, Agnes, affectionately known as Memo. Mr. Sanchez, who didn't strike me as particularly introspective, acquired a philosophical air when questioned about what the loss of his tools meant to him.

"It wasn't the money," he said. "I make good money. It was the memories."

He went on to explain how upon returning from the glorious football game—his eldest son, Paul, was the punter for the Wildcats—he had been angry to see that someone had stolen his toolbox from his garage. News of the massacre the next morning and the subsequent turmoil in Deming took his mind off of his private loss for several weeks. After things had settled down he got to thinking about his tools again. He remembered all the projects he had worked on with them, the green picket fence around his house, the back screen door that never closed properly, the shelves for his kids' video games, working on his pickup all those Sunday afternoons. In short, these were the images of his domestic bliss. The true function of his tools, Mateo now saw, was not to repair and build physical things; rather the tools were the bridge between himself and his role as husband and father, the keeper of his place and his people. His wrenches may have been identical in every way to a million other wrenches, but in their role as the tools of—*the tools to*—Mateo Sanchez, they were absolutely unique.

With words to this effect, while we sat out on his front lawn in folding aluminum chairs one mild September night with a can of beer on each of our armrests, Mateo expressed his gratitude to the thieves. The mesmerizing silence of a Deming night, the languor of a heavy meal, the sixth can of beer, must have put Mateo in a reflective state of mind. There was a fine, deep melody in his voice hard to capture on the page:

> After they took my tools I started remembering how I
> was in the early days with Martha. I treated her bad.
> Maybe you don't know because you're not married. All
> the other girls, man, they started to look so good. Las
> nalgas, las chichis. It's like the devil plays a trick on
> you, man. To me it seemed like the end of the world. I
> always wanted to be a truck driver, out on the road, free
> and easy. Now I was hitched, a kid on the way. All I
> could do was watch the trucks come and go. I got in
> fights. I fought Hector Madrid. I fought Nahum Ramirez.
> I fought Ricky Renteria. I fought all those pinches
> cabrones. After Paul was born I got a girlfriend. Ay, Dios
> mío, she was a little firecracker. I used to go over there
> after work. She had a kid too. Martha knew about her.
> We fought like hell, man. We hit each other. Banged
> each other up good. I ain't proud of it. Then after a while

things kind of died down. I used to drink a lot. I could drink a whole case in one night. See that fence there. I built it myself. It used to be white, then we painted it green. Sandy came along, Julian a couple years later. But you know what, it wasn't until they stole my goddamn tools that I saw how good I had it.

Embedded in this telling remark was Mateo's acknowledgment that the theft of his tools marked an abrupt departure from his previous conception of himself. It allowed him to see more clearly what was truly important to him, that his home was his heaven. The tension dating back to the earliest days of his marriage ended forever on that fateful November night.

Feeling a slight buzz myself, I broke my rule of not divulging my theoretical framework to my informants lest they unconsciously shape their experience to fit it. I told Mateo he had experienced the power of Metaphor. He didn't seem to follow.

"Take your tree over there, for example," I said, by way of illustrating the semiotic underpinnings of the Szekeres Principle. "We can make a metaphor out of it. *Marriage is a tree.* Right? It begins small and weak and grows over many years into a big and powerful thing with many branches. That is metaphor, the fusion of two seemingly dissimilar things into something new."

"So my kids are a metaphor of me and Martha, qué no?"

Thrilled by his intuitive grasp of what Aristotle called "the similarities in dissimilars," I went deeper: "Exactly! Now, if within language the fundamental creative force is metaphor, then Metaphor, on a vast scale, is the fundamental generative force of the universe, as you so elegantly put it, the binding agent at the heart of all inertia and creation, the force of attraction, of gravity, the force behind love and desire, the will to live and the will to die; Metaphor, in short, is the purpose of energy."

After Mateo returned with more beer, I went on to explain how after his fruitless studies of the waltz, György Szekeres had returned to his roots in semiotics, to analysis of man-made metaphor, of poetry and stories, seeking not interpretations of their meanings, for he had already discovered their deepest layer, but the impulses behind their creation.

"What he discovered from writers," I said, suddenly feeling as though Mateo and I had known each other all our lives, "was that their profoundest metaphors were born of their profoundest despairs, that Metaphor came streaming into the voids that opened up beneath them, as if to balm their ruptures of faith. From this, Szekeres reasoned that Metaphor must also flow into the interstices of space-time, into the lesions in reality."

The next time I glanced over, Mateo was asleep, the very picture of small-town contentment. I never got to tell him that his abrupt shedding of an outdated self marked the end of a metaphor identical to the one fractured by the death of Rex Cameron, both of which were identical to the one broken by the Wildcats' liberation from their epic losing streak.

4) The Theft of Two Bikes from Nathan Stevens's Shed at 418 S. Platinum Street

Not a native New Mexican, Mr. Stevens, a tall, slender man with thinning brown hair and thoughtful blue eyes, moved to Deming from St. Louis, Missouri, in March of 1987, citing the need for space and aridity as his motive for choosing the Southwest, and the coincidence of a job opening for a dental hygienist, for choosing Deming. He lives alone in a tastefully furnished home on Platinum Street, where the tree branches enclose the pedestrian in a magical tunnel of deciduous foliage incongruous with the surrounding desert. I suspected Mr. Stevens's sexual orientation moments after meeting him, so it didn't surprise me to learn, as we sat sipping *crèmes de menthe* on a black leather sofa in his "lunarium," that both bikes had been men's ten-speeds. Perhaps it was the impulse to candor that one often feels in the presence of a fellow outsider, or simply the generosity of an open soul, that compelled Mr. Stevens to tell me the story of how the theft of his bikes had changed his life.

St. Louis. 1985. Nathan is in love with an X-ray technician named Andre. Andre, ten years his senior, is publicly open about his homosexuality. Nathan is not. Nathan comes from a fundamentalist Christian family. If movies and television are agents of the devil, queerness is Satan himself. Nathan is twenty-five years old and has been living on his own for four years, but shame and fear still hold him in their grasp. He insists that when they are in public, Andre pretend he is just a friend. Andre, who has a supportive family, begins to tire of the charade. After a year of being patient, Andre delivers an ultimatum: "Come out, or we're through." One night Nathan rings the doorbell of his own family home in a cul-de-sac of a quiet suburb in middle America, a man bearing news to unsuspecting parents of the loss of their son. It is the sound of his beloved cocker spaniel's excited barking, more than anything, that sends Nathan running away before the door opens, back into the arms of despair. He and Andre have a painful parting, the worst part of which, for Nathan, is Andre's refusal to take the bicycle Nathan had bought for him when they started going out. The bike had been a gift, a metaphor, Nathan's way of saying, *I love you and want to spend time with you.* Their bike rides together around Forest Park after work had been the happiest moments of Nathan's life. For Andre to refuse to take the bike was to crush like dead and brittle leaves those fragile memories they shared.

What followed were the darkest days of Nathan's young life. One terrible night while standing on the edge of the bathtub with a noose around his neck, he decided he deserved one more chance. A new start. Far away from the world that shaped but could not accept him. His chance arrived from Deming, New Mexico. Among the things he took with him in the U-Haul were two men's ten-speed bikes.

There was a glint of gentle self-reproach mingled with hard-won wisdom in Nathan's eyes as he told me the story of the bikes:

I got out here, and things were great for the first few months, everything was so new and strange. This town is

147

a lot weirder than it looks, let me tell you. The mayor is a gay Hispanic mortician, and no one bats an eye. I get here and decide I'm going to go straight, I even go on a few dates, but the women here are such cows. The truth is, I was in culture shock. I see that now. And I was a horny twenty-five-year-old man! [Laughs] It didn't take me long to find the queers. You should do a study of the Hitchin' Post. It's a little bar on the other side of the tracks. It's right out of David Lynch, dwarves and all, you'd love it. I kind of went wild . . . the Wild Wild West. [Laughs.] I was still mild-mannered Nathan, the dental hygienist, by day, but I was China in a Bull Shop at night! [Laughs.]

So I'd been here about nine months, doing my best to kill the past, when on the night of November 6, 1987, while I was reading a novel—I forget which one—I heard some racket out back. By the time I got out there the bikes were already gone. It was such a horrible feeling, being violated like that. And yet there was something wonderful about it, too, you know what I mean? I can't explain it. It was as if I clearly saw the absurdity of my pointless torment, that all that anguish over Andre was only a measure of my ego. At that moment, standing there staring at that empty space in the shed, I finally understood that my life was irrelevant. That I could vanish in an instant, and the world would go merrily on without me. It was exhilarating and terrifying. You could call it my Buddha moment.

From that moment forward, Mr. Stevens never again tried to conceal his sexual orientation. Indeed he proclaimed it for all to hear.

We talked long into the night, about a good many things not germane to my research. Mr. Stevens has a voracious curiosity, and once again I found myself setting my professional principles aside.

"In other words," I said, scooting to the edge of my seat,

"metaphor is the glue of the universe."

He crossed his legs thoughtfully.

"So you think the Wildcat Massacre was one of these metamorphoses?"

"Meta-*phor*-phoses," I corrected. "Yes, I do. It can't be a simple case of coincidence that all the metaphors in the skein, including yours, are identical."

He pursed his lips thoughtfully.

"But it seems to me," he said, "that you could find this metaphor in anything—two clouds mingling overhead, the end of a movie, the flushing of a toilet."

"You're absolutely, right," I said. "But not all of them would have the same morphemes, the same meaning, unless they were congealing around a rupture in the space-time continuum, some 'supernatural' phenomenon, like pus around a wound. A ghost, a Bigfoot sighting, a UFO. The Wildcat Massacre is just such a cosmic wound."

Mr. Stevens, while not entirely convinced, seemed genuinely surprised when I pointed out that the end of the Wildcats' losing streak was saying the same thing as the passing of Rex Cameron, the same thing as the theft of Mateo Sanchez's tools, the same thing as his own personal loss. All of these occurrences, on the same night, represented the release of entities locked indefinitely in states of unbearable tension. In Mr. Stevens's case, the bondage he had escaped from was not the metaphorical closet but the closet of Metaphor.

5) The Deflowering of Cindy Villegas

The birth records of Luna County indicate sixteen people born between July 6 and September 6, 1988. To determine if any of them were conceived on the night of the Wildcat Massacre I devised a questionnaire and mailed it, with sufficient return postage, to their stated mothers:

1. Where were you on the night of the Wildcat Massacre?

2. Do you recall anything memorable, other than the football game, on the night of the Wildcat Massacre?
3. How would you define your frequency of sexual intercourse in the latter third of 1987: a) seldom; b) frequent; c) very frequent?

I received nine replies, five of which addressed my questions sincerely. Of those five, three emerged as viable candidates. By this time in my research I was a familiar presence on the streets of Deming. I was often approached at the Cactus Cafe or the Hat Creek Lounge by strangers who knew all about me and my project, a testament to the adage that small towns hold no secrets. This was certainly true of these three ladies, who not only anticipated my questions but had much to say, not all of it flattering, about many of the original sixteen recipients of my questionnaire. In the end, considering the competitive spirit with which my survey was received, it is not unjust to call Cindy Villegas "the winner."

Ms. Villegas is thirty-four years old, divorced, and presently employed in a clerical capacity at the Pollard Insurance Agency, owned by a fine gentleman named Dick Noyes. Our first several in-person interviews were not very fruitful. Neither of us was comfortable with so intimate a subject. We spoke mostly about her seventeen-year-old son, Victor. He was a Wildcat football player himself, a tailback on the junior varsity squad. He was a good student but had some troublemaker friends who'd started him smoking pot. Ms. Villegas, a shy but articulate woman with long, straight black hair and delicate little hands, also talked about her nine-year-old daughter, Becky, the child of her six-year marriage to Val Villegas, who now lives in Hurley and pays child support when he has a job. Only after I had earned Ms. Villegas's trust with a sufficiently attentive ear did we begin to approach the night in question.

She told me his name was Chuy Vasquez. He was a senior. She was a junior. They had been "going steady" for about a month by the night of the Wildcat Massacre. That night he picked her up in his truck to take her to the football game, but on the way there he suggested, as if it had just occurred to him, that they "take a cruise" instead. What was the point of watching the Wildcats lose to Silver one more time? This was fine with Cindy, who hated sitting for so long on those freezing concrete bleachers anyway. They cruised for a while, up and down Pine Street, Deming's cruising drag. They got a Coke at Sonic, cruised some more, then Chuy put Cindy's favorite tape in the player and drove her out to a dirt road he knew, out among the onion fields southwest of town.

He parked the truck and they began to make out. The tape had started over twice by the time Cindy found herself facing a common though nonetheless difficult dilemma: 1) stop now and upset her man, or 2) cross the threshold from girlhood to womanhood in a single painful instant, never to return. As is so often the case in this situation, the deed was already done before she had made her decision. They drove back into town, an uncomfortable silence between them that even the throbbing power chords of Chuy's favorite tape could not dispel.

Something was going on in town. There were cars and trucks everywhere, everyone honking their horns. Kids were hanging out of the windows, screaming their heads off. Someone had lit a bonfire in the vacant lot next to Larry's Pawn Shop. For one terrifying moment Cindy believed that all of this was somehow about the loss of her virginity. That is, until their friends began to chastise them for missing the game of the century.

The story here takes a depressingly familiar turn. Cindy's beloved Chuy goes astray. Within a week he is holding hands with Kelly Dominguez. Two missed periods later Cindy discovers she is pregnant. She hides it for as long as she can, then, unable to bear it any longer, she confesses everything to her mother, who, having borne Cindy out of wedlock herself, hurls the wrath at her daughter that her own mother had hurled at her seventeen years earlier. A good Catholic, Cindy's mother tells her she either keeps the baby and pays for her sin for the rest of her days, or she leaves her house now, never to return. This being a purely rhetorical set of options, Cindy gives birth on August 12, 1988, to Victor. She drops out of high school and begins what will be six years of waitressing jobs at several Deming restaurants before she marries Val Villegas, a backhoe operator, in 1994. Freed for a time from the never-ending cycle of work and debt, she earns her GED and steers herself toward office work, where she remains to this day.

At this point in the narrative I feel compelled, for the sake of professional propriety, to make a few personal remarks. For approximately three months I was involved in a fully consensual relationship with Ms. Villegas, during which time many of the conclusions expressed in this paper began to take their present shape. For this gift of insight I will always be grateful to Ms. Villegas, the price I paid a bargain in comparison. There were many things, I see now, that contributed to the spell I fell under in Deming, which challenged—some will say corrupted—my objectivity: the slow and easy pace of life in this enchanted corner of southern New Mexico, the charm and generosity of its people, the long-overdue respite from the burdens of teaching and writing, the intoxication of intellectual adventure. But it was Metaphor alone that drew Cindy and I together.

As already stated, I was an object of some curiosity in town, but little did I suspect, until Cindy made it known to me, that a steady current of gossip had been issuing from my every move. A few of the misconceptions that I was at pains to correct for her were that I was a writer of sports books, a collector of Indian artifacts, a diesel-truck salesman, and one of the dental hygienist's lovers. To explain to her who I really was, I found myself resorting to my uneventful upbringing in a Philadelphia suburb, my embarrassingly long pursuit of higher education culminating in a PhD in a field routinely mocked by popular culture, my first book (an evolution of my dissertation) on the semitribal social structures of East Coast suburbs, my habitation in a number of remarkably similar yet utterly distinct college towns across the country on my slow climb up the academic career ladder, and finally to my unassailable position as associate professor in the College of Letters and Science at my present institution. Cindy's complete disinterest in my vita was a new and liberating experience for me. She was more interested in my love life, of which there was preciously little to tell.

"How can you know that love is really one of these things you're studying if you've never been in love yourself?" she asked me one afternoon while we were sitting at a picnic bench in the courthouse park, our preferred meeting place. It was late October, the leaves of the tall poplar trees golden in the afternoon sunshine. Cindy was wearing a white coat, the thick imitation fur of the hood enveloping her face. The romantic phase of our relationship had yet to begin, but already I was aware of the deep contentment I felt in her company.

"Well . . . how does one know he will die if he jumps from an airplane without a parachute?" I said. "Some things we must trust to the experiences of others."

"Why are you always sucking the end of that pen?"

Every question she asked me was but another piece of kindling on the growing flame in my heart. What did I do for fun? What was the point of such a lonely life? Who read my books anyway? Never in all my years of presenting at conferences had I been challenged so directly.

One evening after one of these pleasant interrogations, Cindy said she wanted to show me something. We got in her car, an orange Chevy Nova in desperate need of a tune-up, and she drove us out onto the old Lordsburg highway southwest of town, then she turned on to a dirt road running between some furrowed fields. After a while she pulled to a stop. There was a nice view from here of the Tres Hermanas silhouetted against the fading sky.

"This is where it happened," she said.

I had forgotten what day this day was, and to be reminded in such dramatic fashion produced a strange, frightening thrill in me. For once, words escaped me.

"You wanted to see it, didn't you?" she said. "For your research?"

I was amazed that she would even conceive of sharing such

a personal experience with me. A surge of warmth spread through my entire being.

"I hadn't planned on it, no," I said, trying hard to conceal my emotion.

"It seems like yesterday," she said quietly.

She smelled so lovely, that musky perfume of hers. I began to sweat. We sat there in the silence for a long time, the last blue of evening fading to black, every passing second paralyzing me with desire for her. I can hardly express the disappointed relief I felt when she finally started the car and drove us back into town.

I was in love. I was seeing Metaphor everywhere—*my* metaphor, me and Cindy Villegas. I saw us in the pair of pillows at the head of my bed, in the merging of shadows from multiple light sources, in the twin stalks of the yucca beside the hotel swimming pool. I felt her in my every basic urge, the desire to drink, to sleep, to walk, to sing, all infused with the power of Metaphor, pulling me ever closer to my opposite half, Cindy Villegas, so unlike me in every way, and yet when we were together I was overwhelmed by a feeling of the inexpressible grandeur of the universe. Cindy Villegas. The sound of her name alone seemed to erase in an instant my entire pallid history, leaving in its stead a future of unlimited possibility.

The details of the physical phase of our relationship are unimportant. Suffice it to say that for three blissful months I floated adrift on a sea of Metaphor. Here is how it ended.

Victor wanted me to buy him some beer. I had never allowed his open hostility to my presence to dampen my spirits, for I was in love with his mother, that sweet creature who had carried in her womb this Child of the Massacre. Nonetheless, like all sonless men, I suppose, I wanted him to like me. More than once I had envisioned a future in which I was his stepfather. So when he came to my hotel room one cold January night and asked me to buy him a six-pack of beer, I obliged him. On our way to the Hitchin' Post I asked him if he kept in touch with his father.

"My father's dead," he said.

This was news to me. As far as I knew he was unemployed and living in Hurley. I asked Victor when he had died. He told me that he'd been killed in the Wildcat Massacre with the rest of the players.

"But Chuy Vasquez wasn't even on the team," I said.

"Chuy Vasquez wasn't my father," he said in a tone that summed up his appraisal of my intelligence. "David Almanza was my father."

I was about to contradict him but restrained myself as the first fissure in my edifice of bliss appeared before my eyes like a crack in the windshield.

"I see," I said.

A trickle of questions soon grew to a raging torrent in my mind. It wasn't until the following evening that I had an opportunity to confront Cindy.

"Is it true?" I barked.

She started to cry. That was too much for me. I felt mean. I apologized. After we had both calmed down, she looked at me and began her story:

It's true that I was with Chuy during the game, but nothing happened. I was mad at David because he didn't want to see me before the game. He was superstitious. He thought it would jinx him. All he ever wanted, his whole life, was to be on the team that beat Silver. So I found Chuy and we went cruising and went over to some guy's house and watched a movie, then we came back and saw everyone going crazy. All I wanted was to find David. I thought my heart would burst if I didn't find him. The team was gone, somewhere. We heard from someone that some of them had gone out to the riverbed to celebrate. I made Chuy take me out there. We finally found them out by Green Sands. They were burning tires to keep warm. There was a keg there, and they were all sitting around it, all quiet. David didn't seem happy to see me. I wanted him to leave. I wanted to be alone with him, but all he wanted to do was stay there and drink beer with the other players. I told him to go to hell, and me and Chuy left.

I waited for her to go on with the story.

"And?" I said after a while. "What happened next?"

"Nothing," she said. "I went home and went to bed. It was the last time I ever saw David. I found out the next day like everybody else."

I was thoroughly confused.

"But what about Victor?" I said.

Now she seemed confused.

"I mean, were you with David before the game, or what?" I said.

"I'm trying to tell you, it didn't happen that night."

I sat thunderstruck, speechless, uncomprehending for a good minute or so, trying to process this information.

"You mean all along . . . " I fumbled for words, the fibers of my heart ripping at the seams. All I could think about was that the most poignant metaphor of the skein (the conception of Victor, the loss of her virginity, on the night of the Massacre) was nothing but a lie. I was very upset. When I had recovered my composure I asked her why she'd lied.

"I wanted you to write it in the book," she said.

When I asked her to explain what she meant she said she didn't know. It was only after I had completely disentangled my heart from hers, been freed from the shackles of metaphor, that I began to understand what all of this meant, began to behold once again, from an appropriate distance, the divine beauty of Metaphor.

Though she had not known it herself, Cindy was already carrying David's child on the night of the Massacre. I found this out from Lupe Mendoza, Cindy's best friend in high school before Cindy stole her boyfriend—David Almanza—from her. Cindy must have sensed this new life growing within her, which explains why she was so desperate to see David before the game, and why his refusal so crushed her that she fled directly to Chuy Vasquez, the boy who had stolen David's previous girlfriend, Michelle Saenz. Upon discovering that the Wildcats had won, Cindy, in her joy, forgot all about her ploy to make David jealous and wanted nothing more than to see him and congratulate him. After all, he was the boy, according to Ms. Mendoza, to whom Cindy had given her virginity only two weeks earlier. So Chuy, undoubtedly against his own desire, drove her out to the riverbed, where the scene already described in Cindy's own words was played out, ending with her lacerating admonition. This moment, not the one two weeks earlier, was the true deflowering of Cindy Villegas, the moment when she ceased to be a child and became a woman, with all the burdens of womanhood now firmly in place.

Of all the metaphors in our skein, this version strikes me as the most unbearable. One senses the razor edge of the Apache blade drawing ever nearer, the metaphors building strength as the hour nears. Cindy turns and walks away with Chuy, her heart tearing in two, leaving David and the other Wildcats to their grizzly fate.

In light of the trauma she lived through, and the guilt she had been carrying for seventeen years that she was somehow responsible for the massacre, that her words had gone straight to the devil's ears, who in turn unleashed his favored spawn, the Apaches, to carry out her request, Cindy Villegas's desire to rewrite history is understandable. I represented an opportunity to create an alternate version of the past, one authenticated by the intellectual rigor of academic publication. I only wish I had enjoyed this enlightened perspective at the time of our breakup. I behaved wretchedly, accusing her of using me for mercenary ends, for it is true that I had purchased several new household appliances for her. I made other unsavory remarks about her character that I am not proud of, which elicited references from her to a certain murderous cousin. Not realizing she was only speaking metaphorically—in the grips of Metaphor everything is real—I packed my bags that night and left my cozy room at the Bel Shore Inn forever.

These five instances of identical, contiguous metaphors are, as stated above, simply the ones this researcher finds most compelling. The remaining ninety-two, none the less remarkable in toto, are treated at length in the forthcoming monograph.

One question that my data inevitably provokes, though tangential to the argument, is this: Why did the metaphorphosis, of which the skein of metaphors is a resounding echo, take such a violent form? Why Apaches? Recent work by psychologists on the notion of a regional unconscious offers a promising avenue for further research. The great unanswered crime in the collective unconscious of southern New Mexico is the decimation of the Apaches, whose ghostly presence still exercises a strong pull on the imagination of the region. Countless tomes of revisionist history and admirable monographs by well-meaning ethnologists have been unable to loosen the bonds that tie the Apache people to the white man's dream of massacre. The essence of this relationship, distilled to an image almost infinitely dense with meaning, is the moment before the blade of the warrior makes contact with the scalp of the white man. Given sufficient force, say, from the energy unleashed from a skein of shattered metaphors, it is entirely conceivable that the collective yearning of the people of Deming to break with the past could have been strong enough to produce the Wildcat Massacre.

Perhaps Szekeres himself put it best: "The truth of Metaphor is not contingent on the linguistic games of man. The linguistic games of man—the conflation of words with reality—are an index to the truth of Metaphor. Man himself is but the *copula* bridging the void on either side of life."

JUSTIN AND MATT HAD BEEN looking forward to the county fair for weeks. It only came around once a year, in late October, when the nights were turning chilly but the days were still warm. Their mom dropped them off outside the main entrance around noon on Saturday, giving the ten dollar bill to Justin and ordering them to stay together. Hordes of people were streaming in from the cars parked along the dirt road far into the distance.

"Be back here at five," she told them, "and not a minute later. You hear me?"

After wasting one of their precious dollars on the price of admission, the brothers joined the throngs inside the Industry Expo building, where they beheld the merits of solar panels, carpet and upholstery cleaners, double-paned windows, water purifiers, weight-loss drinks, and many more aids to better living being championed from flimsy-looking booths by Luna County's entrepreneurs. Also on show in this building, in long plywood-and-glass display cases, were all the winning entries in the domestic crafts: jams and preserves in Mason jars, all sorts of pickled things, baked goods, butters and cheeses, quilts and embroidery, as well as exemplary specimens from the family farm. Matt was delighted by the freakishly large cauliflower that had garnered Leo McKinney a purple "Best of Show" ribbon. Nothing in this building, apart from some protein powder guaranteed to add twenty pounds to your frame in six weeks if you followed the regimen that came free with the tub, was of any interest to Justin, and he hurried his brother through the crowd and out the far doors.

"Let's get a Coke," Matt said.

"No way," said Justin. "We've only got nine bucks. I'm not wasting any on a Coke."

"But Mom said we should get something to drink."

"I don't care what Mom said."

"Ah, man, I'm thirsty."

"Stop whining."

They walked across the wide dirt lot between the Expo building and the building with all the art in it. Beyond the chain-link fence lay the runways of the old World War II air base, now overgrown with weeds and grass. The bright-orange wind sock at the airport a few hundred yards to the north sagged limply against its pole. They could hear the music of the rides now, the rumble of diesel motors, the faint rise and fall of screaming, and it quickened their pace. Just past the Porta-Potties, where all the fat black power cables were coiled, the midway began.

On greased hydraulics the rocket of the Astroliner bucked wildly, the cars of the Tilt-A-Whirl careened around the wavy track, the blades of the Hammer scissored the sky. People everywhere. Lined up along the metal barriers around the rides, pressed against the counters of the game stalls, milling around the streets of this little three-day city redolent of popcorn and cotton candy and diesel fumes. Above all the dizzying motion the Ferris wheel lumbered through its revolutions.

First they just wandered around, reluctant to begin spending the money. Justin gravitated toward the pockets of junior high girls here and there, while Matt was on the lookout for ugly carnies and novelties to amuse his fourth grade friends with.

Near the Haunted House Justin stopped to talk to Mary Troutman and Kepra Nevins. Mary told him that Kepra's lamb had won first place, which carried a prize of a hundred dollars. Matt was astonished by this sum—"For a stupid lamb?!"—and Justin had to flick him on the arm before he said anything else to embarrass him. Just last month Justin had been talking to Diane Smith in front of the house when Matt came up and farted on purpose right in front of her and nearly killed himself laughing. After that, whenever Justin tried to talk to Diane, Matt's fart always seemed to be there in the air between them.

Luckily for Justin, Matt's friend Pete was just walking by and stopped to show Matt the laser keychain he'd bought for two dollars from the hillbilly in the hangar. Pete fired the red dot at the back of a man who was walking by. That was it. Matt had to have one. Pete told him to come on, he'd show him where they were, and as much as Justin would've loved to get rid of his little brother he didn't want to get in trouble. Some mom who knew their mom would mention she'd seen one of them alone at the fair, and Justin would get grounded for two weeks. He promised Matt they would go over there later and get it.

"Have you guys seen Kelly?" Justin asked the girls.

They smiled and teased him and told him no, but if they did see her they would tell her her sweetheart was looking for her. A warm, satisfying blush stole over Justin's face.

The brothers wandered around some more and soon found themselves watching the shooters at the BB-machine-gun stall. Paper targets with red stars on them hung at the back of the stall across from each of the mounted rifles. To win a prize you had to shoot away all of the star before you ran out of BBs. No one was winning until a cowboy came along and fired a square outline all around the star instead of wasting his ammo on the star itself. The whole square tore right out of the paper, taking the star with it. He chose a big stuffed alligator and moseyed off with it. All the kids who'd seen him shoot now knew the trick and tried to repeat it, but their aim wasn't good enough and their stars didn't pop out like his had.

"Do it, Justin," Matt goaded his brother. "Win us those walkie-talkies."

"I'm not wasting a dollar on that. It's impossible."

"That guy just did it."

"Yeah, and he knows how to shoot."

Nor did Justin want to spend any money on the game where

you throw dimes on to glass plates and try to make them stick. Matt said they could win an ashtray for their mom. She had been mad at them that morning because they hadn't done their chores like she'd told them to. They almost hadn't been able to come. But Justin didn't want to waste the money.

The one unavoidable expense was the ride tickets. The cost was two dollars for ten tickets. All the good rides were three tickets each. Justin bought twenty tickets from the lady at the kiosk, enough for three rides each. That left them with only five dollars for the rest of the day.

"We have to save two dollars for my laser keychain," Matt reminded his brother.

"Yeah, whatever."

First they went on the Eclipse. The carnie running it had a cheek full of tobacco that he kept spitting on the ground. That and the fact that he was missing a thumb excited Matt immensely. On the ride Justin spun the car too fast and Matt almost got sick. Then while they were waiting in line for the Scrambler, Ben Vega and Tommy McClendon came over and did elaborate handshakes with Justin and told him he'd missed the fight between Virgil Armstrong and Manny Nava. Tommy was holding a rolled-up poster he'd won. Ben had a new silver stud in his left earlobe. Matt said it looked gay.

"You look gay," Ben fired back.

"Don't listen to him," Justin told Ben. "He eats other people's chewed-up sandwiches."

Matt nodded proudly and grinned like an idiot.

Justin and his friends talked about girls for a while. Some of the good ones had been spotted, but mostly it was all the usual skags. Justin asked them if they'd seen Kelly. They said no. Tommy unrolled his poster for them to see. It was a sexy blonde in a yellow bikini walking out of the ocean.

"She's the best one, but there's a whole mess of them pretty good over there," Tommy said, nodding toward the poster stall.

After parting with Ben and Tommy, Justin and Matt went over to check out the posters. The counter was thronged with kids throwing darts at paper plates mounted on the back wall.

All three walls were covered floor to ceiling with posters—rock bands, hot women, sports cars, animals doing human things—all full of dart holes. The carnie running it was a skinny, middle-aged guy with blue-black tiger-stripe tattoos on his forearms. He had curly black hair that came down to thick, squared-off sideburns that served only to frame the ugliness of his face, the focal point being his short, fat snout of a nose. While the darts flew around him he stood there exuding boredom, smoking, staring out beyond the confines of his stall. Every now and then he'd suck two tusks of smoke from his lower lip up through his nostrils.

Matt decided he had to have the poster of the toilet with the heading "The Throne" on it and arrows pointing to the various features, all of which had equally regal sounding names.

"That's stupid," Justin said.

"It's better than some dumb girl. Give me fifty cents."

"Mom won't let you have that in your room."

"Yes she will. Besides, half the money's mine and I can do whatever I want with it."

"Let the kid have his fun for Christ's sake," the carnie barked at Justin.

The voice was murderous, and yet the man's face showed no sign of emotion. Justin felt a strange twinge of fear roll through him. He reached into his pocket and gave Matt the money and avoided looking the carnie in the eye again.

The carnie set three red darts on the counter in front of Matt and stayed leaning there on one elbow. Matt's first throw flew wide of the mark, sticking into the hood of a silver Lamborghini.

"Use the force," the carnie said drolly, giving Matt a lazy wink.

Matt took the carnie's advice and whooped happily as his second dart hit the plate. He took aim with his last dart, his hand pecking the air for a good fifteen seconds before he finally released it and missed.

"Ah, man," he groaned. He looked again at the poster he'd nearly won.

"Come on," Justin said, eager to get away from the evil carnie. "Let's go."

"Hey," the carnie said as Matt turned to leave.

He put his cigarette in his mouth and reached into one of the cardboard boxes that held the posters and pulled one out. He rolled it up with lightning speed and winked again as he handed it to Matt.

"Cool! Thanks, man!" Matt said as he and Justin walked off.

Matt unrolled the poster to look at it again.

"You didn't even win it," Justin said.

"Who cares?"

"What do you want a picture of a toilet for anyway?"

"It's not a toilet," Matt said in his idea of an aristocratic accent. "It's a *throne*."

At that moment Justin looked up and saw Kelly Pearson over by the Flying Bobs with Annette Valverde and Charlene Frazier, two of her Lady Kitten basketball teammates. He watched her, a feeling of nervous elation making everything around him go soft and quiet. She was wearing her light-blue basketball pants and a hooded gray pullover sweat shirt.

"How much money do we got left?" Matt asked, oblivious to his brother's sudden preoccupation.

Justin looked down at him.

"All right, listen to me, Matt. We're going to go and talk to some girls over there. And you're not going to say anything, or fart, or anything, or you can forget about that stupid laser keychain."

Matt grunted boredly.

"And roll up that stupid poster."

The girls smiled at Justin's approach, for Kelly had already told them about the tacos he had shared with her on Wednesday.

"Hey, Kelly," Justin said, putting his hands in his pockets and shrugging his shoulders like he'd seen someone do in a movie.

"Hey, Justin." She grinned.

Justin said hey to the other girls and they said hey back.

164

"Is this your little brother?" Kelly asked, smiling down at Matt.

"Yeah."

"Hey, Justin's little brother," Kelly said. She had brown hair, little ears, and a crooked incisor.

Matt raised his hand a little and waved and smiled for about a second, then turned his attention elsewhere.

"He's shy," Justin said.

Kelly said she'd heard that Virgil was in a fight, and Justin told the girls what he'd heard from Ben and Tommy.

"I hate Manny," Charlene said. "He's a Satan worshiper."

"They drink goat's blood out at Holy Cross," Annette said matter-of-factly.

"Cool!" Matt exclaimed, then guiltily looked away, afraid he'd blown it.

Justin's and Kelly's eyes met again. They smiled at each other. The cars of the Flying Bobs flew by them, the screams smearing high then low as they passed, but Justin and Kelly didn't hear a thing.

"Hey, do you want to split a Coke?" Justin asked her.

Matt's brows raised in bewilderment.

"Sure," Kelly said.

They all walked over to the concession stand. Justin paid a dollar for a large Coke. Kelly took a sip and offered one to Matt. Matt shook his head no, even though he was thirsty. He felt like kicking his brother. Charlene and Annette, adhering to some previously devised plan, said they were going to go look at the animals and left.

Then at the BB machine guns Justin did it again.

"Oh, look how cute they are," Kelly said, pointing up at the big pink stuffed unicorns. Without hesitation Justin stepped up to one of the rifles.

"I know the trick," he said.

He wasted a dollar proving that knowing the trick had little to do with winning.

"Give me my two dollars," Matt whispered fiercely to Justin as they stepped away from the stall.

Justin shrugged him off and exhorted him with a scowl to shut up or else.

Now Kelly wanted to go on the Hammer, so they went over there and got in line. The two huge handles of the hammers were swooping up and down in perfect symmetry, the cages crossing paths a foot from the ground, hurtling back up into the sky. The old guy running it was friendlier than most of the carnies. He was in overalls. His tanned, sinewy arms were coarse as leather. His ball cap advertised a trucking company.

"Got you a poster," he said to Matt as they neared the stool where he sat working the throttle. "What of?"

Justin flicked Matt's arm. Matt was sorely tempted to ignore his brother and unroll his poster for the old guy. But as long as they had at least two dollars left there was still a chance he could get the laser keychain.

"Has anyone ever died on your ride?" Matt asked the old guy.

"Nope," the carnie said and added with a wink, "but there's a first time for everything."

After a while the hammers began losing their momentum, rocking through diminishing arcs and finally down to stillness at the bottom. The carnie went and opened the doors and released the safety bars, and the kids staggered out pale faced and grinning.

"Wait here," Justin told Matt.

"What?!"

Justin turned away from Kelly so she couldn't hear and said to Matt: "We don't have enough tickets, man. Let me take her on this ride and I promise we'll go over and get the keychain as soon as we get off."

Matt stared dubiously into his brother's eyes.

"You swear?"

"Yes."

"Swear on Dad's grave," Matt said.

Justin's eyes narrowed to a squint. His lips pursed as if he were about to spit.

"Justin, come on," Kelly called out as the carnie began

escorting the riders to their cages.

"Just give me the money," Matt demanded.

"No."

"Then swear."

"All right, I swear," Justin said at last. "Wait here."

Justin and Kelly got into the near cage. The carnie locked the bar over their laps and closed the door. Matt saw their hands meet on top of the safety bar. When the other kids were secure in the other cage, the carnie returned to his stool and fired up the ride. The engine revved loudly and the cages eased out in opposite directions. The engine let up and the cages rocked back. Back and forth they swung through their shallow arcs, a little higher with every pass. Now the screams began as the hammers swooped up beyond the horizontal, the old carnie grinning wryly as he worked the throttle. Matt watched until the cages finally tipped over the top and swooped down as if to pound a giant nail into the earth. It made him woozy just watching.

The urge to pee that he'd been ignoring for some time now grew more pressing. He thought he had enough time to run down to the Porta-Potties and be back before Justin got off, but when he got there, there were ten people waiting to get into two toilets. He thought about going back, but now that he'd allowed himself to feel it the pressure was too great to resist. Knowing that Justin and Kelly might be getting off the ride any second now made the waiting even more unbearable.

By the time he got back the ride was just starting up again. Justin and Kelly were nowhere to be seen.

"Hey, did you see my brother?" he asked the old carnie.

"The one with the girl?" the carnie said.

"Yeah."

"Nope."

Matt stood there for a minute, wondering whether he should stay there or go off looking for them. A nervous flutter in his belly told him he'd better go look for them. He walked down the midway, looking intently at the backs of all the kids at the games. He looked for them in the lines around the rides. When they didn't seem to be there either he began watching the spinning, whirling cars. He went around the whole carnival three times, his poster getting sweaty and dented in his hand.

He went back through the Industry Expo, up and down every crowded aisle. He crossed over to the building with all the art in it. While he was in there he saw his picture in the Smith School booth. It was his best one ever. It was a drawing of a man getting his head chopped off with a big sword. Blood was squirting out of his neck. It pleased Matt to see his bold picture there among the drawings of flowers and airplanes.

He crossed the lot to the hangar. It was one of the old corrugated-tin variety, presently sheltering the small-time hawkers who materialized at all the county fairs across the greater Southwest, selling their assorted wares. Matt went in and worked his way down between the tables until he found the laser keychains near the back. The guy selling them had hair all the way down to the table and a beard nearly as long. He also sold Confederate flags, shot glasses, miniature New Testaments, and other sundry items.

Matt picked up one of the laser keychains and pushed the button but nothing happened.

"There's no batteries in them ones," the man said and handed the display model over to Matt.

Matt shot the laser at the ground. He shot it at the far wall and at the ceiling. He stood for a long time staring at it in his hand.

"They're usually five dollars but I'll give it to you for two," the hillbilly said.

Matt couldn't remember ever wanting anything so badly in his life.

"My stupid brother went and spent all our money on some girl," he said.

The hillbilly nodded, his lower lip protruding knowingly.

Matt stood there for a while, hoping the hillbilly might just give it to him for free. He didn't. On his way out of the hangar, Matt kicked an empty Coke can. It bounced crazily out into the dirt lot.

Next he went over to where the animals were. It smelled good in there, of hay and manure. In the little dirt arena 4-H kids in blue blazers were showing off their goats. The judges were walking by with clipboards, inspecting the luster of hooves, the girth of shanks. Every now and then one of the goats would let out a long offended bleat. Justin wasn't among the people on the small wooden bleachers.

Matt wandered between the rows of wood-and-chicken-wire cages, peering in at all the little animals. Rabbits, guinea pigs, hamsters, chickens, pheasants, pigeons, ducks. Matt fed some hay to a little white rabbit. At one point he noticed a round dropping in the hay at his feet. He reached down and picked it up and put it in his mouth and chewed it.

By the time he went back through the building where all the art was, the Little Miss Deming beauty pageant was underway. On the dais a dozen little girls, some of whom were in Matt's homeroom, were all wearing colorful satin dresses with silver banners slanted across them declaring the names of their schools. They were standing stiffly in a line, smiling. A row of four judges sat near the front of the dais. The folding metal chairs that had been set out in a wide semicircle around the dais were mostly empty, except for the parents, judging by the periodic outbursts of praise and the number of men with camcorders.

Exhausted from his ordeal, Matt took a seat in the back row and watched the girls as they went through the rounds of the contest. They had to turn their profiles to the judges, walk around in a circle together, then each had to step forward individually and say why she felt she would make a good Little Miss Deming. They all spoke of their particular talents, which ranged from tetherball champion to origami enthusiast, and most of all of their love of Deming and their mothers and their fathers and their teachers. Matt started to doze.

He had been there for quite some time, slouched in the chair, his poster across his lap, when a red dot of light fluttered like an insect over his left leg. He sat up abruptly and turned to see Justin approaching with the laser keychain in his hand. He was alone. At the sight of him, all the hurt and anger that Matt had temporarily forgotten returned. He turned glumly back toward the contestants.

Justin came up beside him.

"I oughta kick your ass," Justin said.

"You left me," Matt sulked. "I'm telling Mom."

"I left *you*? I've been looking all over for your fat ass for the last hour. I told you to wait for me at the Hammer."

One of the dads turned around at the sound of Justin's raised voice, and Justin went quiet.

"You went off with that girl," Matt insisted.

"We were looking for *you*. Here's your stupid keychain."

Justin held the keychain out in his hand, but Matt wouldn't take it. A whiff of sour puke assailed Matt's nostrils. He turned to look and saw a damp, yellowish splotch on the front of Justin's shirt. This leavened his heart.

"You hurled," he said, smiling.

"No I didn't. Kelly did."

At that Matt let out a great howl of laughter. That was the best thing he'd heard all day. One of the dads turned and scowled at him. When the dad wasn't looking anymore, Matt grabbed the laser keychain from Justin's hand and shot it at the back of the dad's head.

"Grow up," Justin said.

Justin wanted to go home. All the money was gone, and there was still two hours left before their mom was supposed to pick them up. He decided they were going to walk.

"What?" Matt said. "All the way home?"

"Yes."

"You're crazy. You go. I'm waiting for Mom."

Justin waited another few minutes, then turned and left. Matt sat there for a while, shooting the laser at his shoe. The smell of puke receded. He looked up. The judges were in a huddle. The time had come to choose the winner. The girls were still standing in a line, stiff as mannequins, smiling.

Matt couldn't help himself. He pointed the laser at the girl in the middle and pressed the button. A bright-red dot danced over her purple dress. She looked down, her smile dissolving in confusion. All the parents turned around with fury in their eyes. Matt bolted up from the chair, his whole being infused with wicked joy, and ran as fast as he could to catch up to his brother.

Luminarias

MARY MARGARET PALMER AND HER daughter Judy were the first to arrive. Mary Margaret, who was ninety-two years old, was wearing a black ermine opera coat that may have fit her several decades ago but now cocooned all but her wizened head, from which her big blue eyes still glowed with impish life. She shuffled in, exulting in the warmth and the legions of pretty dishes laid out across the table.

"Good Lord, it's cold out," she gasped.

"Bless you, Mary Margaret." Mrs. Beckett leaned over and hugged her dear old friend. "I'm so glad you could come."

"Everything looks just lovely, Celia," Judy said.

"You better have some of that chile con queso," Mary Margaret threatened cheerfully.

Everyone the Becketts knew had been invited: Mrs. Beckett's coterie of "old biddies" from Golden Gossip; all of Mr. Beckett's Lion's Club pals and their wives; all their mutual friends from the country club; dear family friends of no association other than a lifetime together in Deming; all the Beckett kids and their husbands and wives and friends. The extra leaves had been added to the dining table and the white tablecloth spread over it, and out had come the crystal punch bowls and silver tureens and platters and bonbon dishes and old family china, which for the rest of the year remained sequestered in a secret place that only Mrs. Beckett knew or cared to know of. The dishes were still in the process of being filled, but many of the night's refreshments were already on the table.

"Margot!" Judy exclaimed with surprised delight as Margot stepped down from the kitchen into the dining room, her hands still pink from handling the hot tamales. "How nice to see you."

They embraced and regarded each other fondly.

"Let me get your coats," Margot said.

"I hope we aren't the first to arrive," Mary Margaret remarked.

"Mother," Judy said snappishly, "let Margot take your coat."

"What?"

"Your coat!"

Margot helped Mary Margaret off with her fur, revealing as she did so the shriveled sparrow of a woman beneath, her upper back little more than a knot of twisted bone.

"It's supposed to snow tonight," Mary Margaret remarked.

"A white Christmas." Mrs. Beckett smiled. "I can't remember the last time it snowed on Christmas."

"I'd say it was at least five or six years ago," Judy said. "Were you here that year, Margot?"

"No, I don't think so," Margot answered, adding that it had been eight years since she had been home for Christmas, an admission that, judging by the troubled expression that crossed Mrs. Beckett's face, should have remained unspoken.

"Well, welcome home," Judy said.

Margot set off with the coats. The four grandchildren were kneeling around the tree in the living room, reading the name tags on the presents, tilting and shaking the packages. The tree was a noble fir over eight feet tall that Mr. Beckett and James had chopped down in the Gila Wilderness the previous Sunday, and its bright scent was filling the entire room. In among the blue and white and gold silk-thread balls were the ornaments the Beckett kids had made when they were children themselves: endearingly misshapen flour-and-water figures painted in bright primary colors, a team of reindeer, Santa with his bag, drums and drumsticks. Margot carried the coats across the living room—"Auntie Margot, I know what you got me!"—and down the hall to her bedroom.

She still thought of it as her bedroom, though it had long since ceased to share any resemblance to the room that had been hers in junior high and high school and well into her college years when her mother had finally redecorated it and moved Margot's things into the attic. Now it was a somewhat lifeless guest room, everything in shades of pale sky blue—the walls, the bedspread, the curtains. It was as if her mother had needed to rid the house of those hard years by painting over them with a cheerful color, the color of baby boys.

She set the coats on the bed and stood briefly before the mirror, judging her appearance in light of the arrivals. Her doubts about the green blouse she had chosen in a festive spirit were now confirmed. Nor did the long, brown pleated skirt she was wearing do much to conceal the bulk of her hips. But then she always did look too blocky from the front, low-cut blouse or not, on account of the broad shoulders she had inherited from her father. She studied herself without pleasure, then went to the closet and slid the hangers aside one by one in search of a better blouse.

The sweet adagio of the old Johnny Mathis Christmas record was flowing from the turntable in the living room, the familiar pops and crackles as evocative of years gone by as the music itself. Teddy Beckett, Nathan Stevens, and Rudolph DeLeRee had just come in from lighting the luminarias and were helping themselves to the hot rum punch.

"When's Ray's service?" Nathan asked Teddy in a quiet voice.

"Wednesday," Teddy replied, taking a sip of punch. "He wanted his ashes thrown in his swimming pool."

Nathan laughed heartily. "He did have a mordant wit."

They were standing at the far end of the sunken dining room, down near the bookshelves and the recliners. In the daytime the broad run of windows carried a view of the expansive back yard and the swimming pool. At present they were misted over, more so along the table, muting all the reflections from the dishes and the candles and the fairy lights strung along the sill. A queue was starting to form at the punch bowl, compelling the three young men to speak softly lest they offend somebody with their gallows humor.

"You could clog the filter doing that," Rudolph said dryly.

"I think a man's dying wish is more sacred than a swimming pool pump," Teddy remarked.

He had recently grown a mustache, much like Mr. Beckett's, only brown, but all it did was accentuate the boyishness of the rest of his face and the subtle lilt in his voice.

"I'll have to consult the jus sacrum on that one," Nathan replied.

"We could've done a nice stone for him," Rudolph whispered as Dr. and Mrs. Hossley approached the punch bowl. "Put it right in the wall at the deep end, four or five feet down."

"Poolside service," Nathan joked, his eyes swiveling upward. "Sorry, Ray."

"Where's Manny, by the way?" Rudolph asked.

"He said he'd be coming later," Teddy replied. "He's got two other parties."

"Well," said Rudolph with mock affront.

Just then Teddy glanced over Rudolph's shoulder.

"Well, well," he said, stroking his mustache. "If it isn't the old man himself."

Standing slightly stooped just inside the doorway, clutching a black cane in his big, knuckly hands, was the old state senator (Democrat) Ike Crawford. As old as he was he still stood over six feet tall, with an imposing cranium, a few stubborn wisps of white hair, and large, pendulous ears. As soon as his overcoat was off he began shaking hands vigorously with everyone around him.

Margot could be seen cutting through the kitchen with the coats of the new arrivals, the passage along the dining table being thronged with people as those initially reluctant to tamper with the impeccable display of the night's comestibles began loading up their side plates. Arrayed in a loose circle on the oak cheese board were an assortment of fine aged cheeses, the centerpiece being the squat pillar of Colston Bassett Stilton brought all the way back from England by Charlotte Thurmond, its thick brown rind veined with mold. Flanking the cheeses were two long straw baskets of assorted fine crackers. For those with less refined tastes, two deep cut-glass bowls filled to the brim with potato and corn chips anchored either end of the table, around which were arranged an assortment of dips and salsas in green glass bowls. A host of other treats were spread out in no particular pattern: a silver platter of chilled deviled eggs, the filling swirled and lightly dusted with paprika; a tray of baked ham slices garnished with rings of pineapple; an oak bowl filled with dried figs; a glazed ceramic dish of candied almonds; a large Talavera plate of powdery Turkish delight. Shoulder to shoulder in the center of the table stood six dark bottles of Las Uvas merlot, their corks wedged back in place. Front and center, at the ready to receive Mrs. Beckett's renowned chile con queso, sat a sterling silver chafing dish, a shallow blue flame floating as if by magic in the canister beneath the chafer.

"Oh, I forgot to put out the napkins," Mrs. Beckett chided herself and hurried back into the kitchen.

The swinging door closed behind her, muting the growing rumble of the party. The cool fluorescent light of the kitchen, in concert with the steamed-over window, the bright tiled countertops, the stainless-steel gleam of pots and pans and utensils, stood in almost clinical contrast with the warm, cozy atmosphere on the other side of the door.

"Let me do that, Mom," Suzanne said, reaching up to get the napkins from the cabinet. "Go out and enjoy yourself. You've been at it all day."

"I don't mind," Mrs. Beckett said.

Suzanne rolled her eyes. Like all her siblings save Margot, she was over six feet tall, of a solid, stately build, her blonde hair swooping down to her shoulders in broad bouffant waves just beginning to gray.

"It's a good turnout," Mrs. Beckett remarked, setting some baking trays in the sink and turning on the tap. While the water was running she reached up and adjusted her wig. It was platinum white, coiffed in a loose, wispy style that just covered her ears, from which two gold orbs were swaying to and fro.

"Even Ike made it," Suzanne said.

"Yes, bless him. He looks quite well, considering."

"Yes."

"He's telling his joke again."

"Which one?"

"About them not waiting until he's dead to name the highway after him."

Mrs. Beckett rubbed a swathe of steam from the window with her soapy hand and peered out, glancing upward beyond the leafless branches of the mulberry tree. A soft yellowish glow from the colored lights along the roof was illuminating the top of the hedge.

Suzanne arranged the napkins in the old ceramic Mrs. Claus holder. Seeing her mother staring somewhat solemnly out the window, she put her arm around her shoulders and kissed the back of her head.

"We'll get our white Christmas yet," she said.

Mrs. Beckett nodded as if not quite listening.

"Is Margot all right?" she asked quietly.

"She's fine," Suzanne reassured her. "You know her."

"We've hardly spoken. It's just been nonstop."

"She warned me she's on her period," Suzanne said with a small nasal laugh.

"Bless her."

A wisp of suds inched down the window beneath the clear spot.

"Let me get these out there," Suzanne said, heading for the door.

She went about the rooms offering the napkins to those who had already wandered off in search of somewhere to sit or stand, the noise of talk and laughter all but drowning out the music.

"How is she?" James asked as Suzanne came into the orbit of her brothers.

The three older brothers had managed to part with their wives and were presently standing together by the "good" fireplace. The other fireplace, in the south wall of the living room, hadn't been lit in over twenty years. Its mantel usually served as an all-purpose repository for things in limbo: unanswered letters, overdue library books, objects in need of repair.

"She's fine."

"She ought to have a rest."

"You try telling her."

The brothers stood there saying nothing for a few awkward seconds.

"And the bed?" Pat asked Paul, resuming their conversation.

"Pretty solid," Paul replied. "At least there weren't any ants in it. The place seems a hell of a lot shabbier than I remember it."

"The Ramada was always pretty shabby," James informed his brother.

"We've got a porno channel," Pat said smugly.

"Nice," Paul nodded, adding a moment later: "We've got the real thing."

Suzanne rolled her eyes.

"An Indian family must've bought the place," Paul said. "The guy behind the desk looks Indian."

"Navajo or what?"

"No, Indian as in from India."

"Yes," Suzanne said. "The Patels. Kanta and Manu. Erin has their son Vijay in class with her. They're very sweet."

"Well, they don't clean the place too well," Paul said. "The office reeks of incense."

"They're thinking about opening an Indian restaurant here," Suzanne said.

James shook his head.

"That wouldn't fly."

"I don't know," Suzanne said. "Both times we've gone to that one in Cruces we've seen people from Deming there."

"Cowboys and Indians," Pat quipped, an open invitation to his brothers.

Paul and James groaned but didn't hesitate to take up the challenge.

"Currying favor with the mayor," Paul offered.

"I'll stick to my sacred sirloin," James said sardonically.

Margot stepped over to the tureen and poured herself a cup of eggnog. A lull in the arrivals was giving her a chance to relax a little. She hadn't anticipated so many people, much less the energy required to smile at them all. Her mother had made it sound like just a little gathering of friends. Not since the family reunion of '74, when relatives she had never even heard of and would never see again had shown up from as far away as Ireland, could she remember there being so many people in the house. Her eyes wandered, taking in all the faces and bodies, settling eventually on her brothers and Suzanne talking by the fireplace. It gave her a strange, almost dreamlike feeling seeing all her siblings in the house again. It was rare enough that she saw one or two of them together anymore, let alone all of them at once. She had never been particularly close to her three older brothers. They were already teenagers when she was still in grade school. She remembered them mainly as a whirling mass of gangly limbs and croaking voices that, fearing injury, she had always given a wide berth to. As kids they had been inseparable, and there was still an effortless unity in the way they were standing now, practically shoulder to shoulder facing each other, as if once again they were fomenting some devious prank to pull on their sisters. All three of them were married and had kids whom Margot occasionally suffered guilt over for not remembering their birthdays. The three brothers—"My Three Sons," Mrs. Beckett used to joke, Teddy being essentially another one of the girls—had always been their mother's pride and joy. As a child Margot had eagerly looked forward to the day when the house would finally be free of them so she could get a little attention herself. But when they did eventually go off to pursue their dreams, they only left a vacuum in their mother's heart that Margot, try as she might, never quite managed to fill.

Margot watched her brothers and sister with strange detachment, as if she were spying in through the windows on someone else's family, someone else's Christmas party. Stranger still were all those old family friends, familiar faces and voices from the long-forgotten past. That too was like a dream, and all those old Christmas decorations that she had helped haul up from the basement and set up were part of it: the red plastic bells softly blinking along the mantel of the unused fireplace, the little illuminated ceramic country pub on the windowsill, the papier-mâché snowman and snowwife that she and Teddy had made when they were kids. Even the stockings were out, hanging side by side before the crackling fire, all their names emblazoned in gaudy gold letters down their lengths.

The voice of a red-faced old woman a few feet away derailed Margot's train of thought.

"I took it out to thaw this morning," the woman was saying.

"How big is it?" another old woman asked.

"I can't remember. Fourteen or fifteen pounds, I think. It's a Butterball."

"Oh, they're good."

"How do you do your stuffing?"

Margot stepped up into the living room, returning the smiles she met, and soon found herself standing beside the unused fireplace, talking with Gabe Ochoa, the artist.

"I'm sorry about your father," she said after the obligatory niceties.

Gabe nodded and dissembled as if he were mildly embarrassed to be implicated in matters as grave as death. He gave the subject its due pause, then changed it by asking if she'd had a good flight.

"What's a good flight these days?" Margot joked.

"I guess surviving it," Gabe said, chuckling.

Margot had always liked Gabe. It was impossible not to. He had a mildly nervous, self-deprecating manner, was quick to

181

laugh, and perpetually nodded in assent. He nodded not only with his head but with much of his upper body, almost Japanese in manner. He also had an adorable fluffy black mustache, now graying at the roots. As far as Margot knew he had had the same job as a teaching aid for remedial readers at Martin Elementary School for twenty years. He still lived with his mother and father, or it should be said with his mother, for his father, who had driven the hearse at Garcia's Funeral Home until his cataracts got the best of him, had died three months earlier.

"I still have your painting on my bedroom wall," Margot said.

Gabe winced, as if that admission caused him some pain.

The painting in question, a New York panorama, captured a New York that every now and then could still stop Margot dead in her tracks in a moment of perfect bliss. Rendered in bright, solid poster paints verging on fluorescent, it was the happy, razzmatazz city she had fallen in love with in her twenties, full of Gabe's splendid little cartoony characters: bankers striding with their briefcases among the skyscrapers, joggers panting across Central Park, people of all ethnicities on the streets wearing bright, happy smiles. The cops had keystone helmets and carried truncheons. There was a bulby little plane flying past the Statue of Liberty. It was New York through small-town eyes, and it had helped Margot through many a winter.

Gabe asked about her work and she told him about the Christmas campaigns her firm had been working on since June. It all sounded very exciting to Gabe, and Margot didn't feel inclined to disabuse him of the notion that advertising was a glamorous profession. He chuckled and nodded and made little jibes at Deming and laughed at them himself while Margot sipped her eggnog and envied him the world he possessed. She congratulated him on his recent successes in various El Paso and Las Cruces galleries, but he was even less comfortable with success than he was with empathy. It was hard not to feel perverse and cynical and capable of infinite cruelty in Gabe's presence. It seemed to Margot she could tell him she had just murdered someone and he would just chuckle and nudge her arm conspiratorially and ask for the details.

"Are those your forebears?" Gabe asked during a lull in the conversation, nodding toward the large framed black-and-white photograph hanging on the wall above the mantel.

Margot laughed at that odd choice of words.

"That's my great-grandfather and grandmother," she replied.

J. A. McMahon, the pioneer and proprietor of McMahon's Furniture & Hardware and McMahon's Funeral Home, was wearing beneath his bowler the standard stoical expression of nineteenth-century portraiture. Beside him stood his equally staid wife, the brick facade of their store close behind them. Other people could be seen in the background of dusty Gold Street, around a bandstand busy with flags.

"Who's the kid in the wagon?" Gabe asked.

Margot smiled at the word "kid," so incongruous with the stern dignity of those ancient personages. "Forebears" was actually closer to the mark.

"That's my grandmother Elleanore. She was an old battle-ax."

Gabe smiled and nodded as if this were a wonderfully scandalous admission, which only encouraged Margot to scandalize him further.

"I remember going over to her house after school and eating jelly beans. She loved the black ones. 'Save me them niggerheads,' she'd say. She had the foulest mouth on a woman I've ever encountered. I was the only one in the family she really got along with."

Thinking back on those afternoons on her grandmother's porch on Pine Street, the sunflowers poking up above the sun-cracked railing, gave Margot a keen ache of nostalgia. Her grandmother was the one who had encouraged her to get the hell out of Deming and do something with her life. Margot had followed her prescription, the first half of it at least. Whether or not she had actually done something with her life was another matter. If being well paid, single, and childless at forty-six constituted doing something with one's life, then she had succeeded.

"I like all the hats," Gabe said, pointing at the people around the bandstand.

Margot's eyes settled on the fine dark hairs running along the side of Gabe's hand, and to her nostalgia was added a warm surge of longing to touch him.

"It was the celebration of Luna County's division from Grant County," she said.

"'Brewery,'" Gabe said. "That's great. Nice and simple. I wish we still had signs like that."

"That's where Hallmark is now."

"Wasn't it Ruby Jewelry before that?"

"Yes, and before that it was Wheeler's Shoes."

"Wheeler's Shoes," Gabe reminisced. "Damn, I remember that place. Do you remember that old woman who used to work there, with the white hair and the blue mascara?"

"Delma Schiamanna. Henry Schiamanna's mother. Henry was the principal at Smith School when I was there. I was well acquainted with his paddle."

Gabe chuckled.

"I was terrified of that woman," he said. "I thought she was the Wicked Witch of the West."

"You did? Why? I thought she was sweet."

"The first time my mom took me in there for new shoes it was Halloween, and she was dressed up like a witch. After that she was always a witch in my mind. I thought my feet would fall off if she touched them."

Margot and Gabe stared at the picture, their minds aroused by memory.

"What about the little bakery that used to be there next to Wheeler's?" Gabe said.

"No, that was on the other side of the alley, where Copper Travel is now."

Gabe nodded. "My dad used to send me down there to get doughnuts on Saturday mornings."

Mindful of her unofficial role as coat checker, Margot glanced over to the dining room where some new arrivals had just come in. In that first glance she didn't recognize him. Her attention was focused on the woman. She clearly wasn't from Deming. The coat alone was enough to give her away. Margot knew it to be current season, for she had seen similar coats in the windows on Fifth Avenue. Judging from the heavy wooden toggle buttons, the large flap pockets, and the unmistakable velvety nap of wool and cashmere—camel in this instance—she guessed it to be Burberry, which placed it in the roughly thousand dollar range. Around her neck the woman wore a cream cashmere scarf, the slack artfully draped over her left shoulder. She looked to be in her mid- to late thirties, a brunette of delicate features, her hair elegantly swirled atop her head.

Curious to see who it was accompanying this ethereal being, Margot turned her attention to the man and felt a sudden jolt, as if a large wave had just rolled beneath the house, as his momentary vagueness came into focus. Her pulse quickened as she watched him embrace her mother, who looked as surprised as Margot, though genuinely delighted, to see him there. He gestured toward the woman, who gracefully removed her gloves and shook Mrs. Beckett's hand.

Margot stifled an urge to quietly turn and disappear into her bedroom as her mother turned her head to look for her. At that moment Johnny caught sight of her. He waved nonchalantly, as if he had just popped over from across the street. Margot smiled and waved back, the easy lie of pleasant surprise quelling some of the heat in her face as she excused herself from Gabe and made her way across the living room, weaving around the legitimate guests, and down the steps into the dining room.

"Johnny," she said with feigned composure. "My goodness." They embraced.

"Margot, I'd like you to meet my wife, Elaine." He smiled. "Elaine, this is Margot Beckett, my high school sweetheart."

Elaine offered Margot her hand. It was a beautiful hand, as fine to the touch as it was to the eye, the knuckles like polished stones beneath the cool, silky skin.

"It's a pleasure to meet you," she said in a strong Texan accent, squeezing Margot's hand and tilting her head earnestly to one side as she smiled.

"Likewise." Margot returned the smile. "Let me get your coats."

Johnny held the shoulders of his wife's coat while she undid the toggles and slipped out of it with an effortless roll of her shoulders.

Margot was trying hard not to stare at him. Perhaps more bewildering than the sudden, unexpected presence of Johnny Edwards in her house was the fact that he had aged. His face had thickened almost beyond recognition. In fact his whole head seemed to have thickened on account of how much hair he had lost. He was bald clear back to the middle of his crown, and his sideburns and the hair around his baldness were gray.

"I never realized New Mexico got this cold," the wife said brightly.

"Oh yes," Mrs. Beckett replied. "We usually get a little snow every year. We're expecting some tonight."

"We heard on the radio."

Johnny folded the coat in half lengthwise and passed it and the scarf to Margot. He took off his own coat—a long, dark-brown rain slicker that struck Margot as wholly inadequate for the weather—revealing a thickness of body in keeping with the transformations of his face. A flicker of awkwardness passed over his otherwise congenial expression as he handed his coat to Margot. She draped the coats over her arm and carried them off across the party to her bedroom.

The bed by this time was piled thick with coats and scarves, and here and there a gentleman's hat or two. Margot set the coats on the pile and stood peering down at them, still feeling in the pit of her stomach the turbulence of the wave that had rolled through her at the sight of him.

She couldn't remember the last time she had seen him. A phone call, shortly after his first marriage, came to mind. Though she couldn't recall the pretext, she remembered well that he hadn't been thrilled to hear from her. Without exactly saying it, he had given her the impression that there was no conceivable reason for them to communicate anymore. And there wasn't. At that point it had been at least nine years since they had dated, in high school no less. Before then it must have been several years since she had actually seen him, probably on one of her trips home from college, a Christmas break most likely, as she had rarely come home during the summers. At least twenty years had passed since that call. Every now and then for the first ten years or so after she had started working she would hear something about him from her mother or Teddy. She knew, for instance, that his first marriage had lasted only two years, a fact that had always given her some satisfaction, for somewhere in her heart she believed that neither of them could ever truly love another the way she and Johnny had loved each other. Even now, after all these years, he still made regular appearances in her dreams—intense, heartrending dreams of longing and loss—in which he was eternally young. And it had always been Margot's belief that some younger version of herself likewise inhabited his dreams, tending the small flame of their enduring love. The fact that he was suddenly there in her house, in the flesh, with his wife, seemed to Margot a gross and insensitive faux pas.

She picked up the wife's coat again and ran her fingers over the luxurious sleeves, still chilled from the cold night air. The ease with which Johnny had made that little addendum about her being his high school sweetheart astonished her, not so much on account of the wife, which implied a relationship seemingly free of the standard jealousies, as for the implication that the intense love they had shared, however brief it may have been, had in the end become something generic and classifiable for him, something essentially insignificant.

Margot set the coat back on the pile and carefully folded the sleeves one across the other in front. A high screech of laughter pierced the low rumble of the party.

Totsie Seybert, the junior high American history teacher, was getting tipsy on rum punch. She got loud and flirtatious with a little booze in her. She was laughing boisterously at a story Miriam Flynn was telling her about a woman named Ruby Hyatt Grimes, whose husband always used to call her "Pet." *Can you get me a drink, Pet? That was a fine dinner, Pet.*

Have you seen my watch, Pet? Until one day she got fed up with him and killed him with a hatchet blow to the back of his head. She threw him down a mine shaft and apparently lived happily ever after. Totsie was getting a kick out of that. Fred Seybert was somewhat less amused but nonetheless indulged the old widow and his wife with a polite smile of appreciation for such colorful Deming lore. The conversation soon turned to the bitter weather and in turn to a yearning for spring.

"We thought we'd take the kids to Yosemite this year," Totsie was saying. "See Old Faithful and all."

"Is that where Old Faithful is?" Ms. Flynn asked. "I thought it was that other park."

"I'm pretty sure it's Yosemite. Well, hold on. Gosh, now you've got me thinking. Fred, what's the name of that—"

"Yellowstone," Fred said.

"Well, I knew it was one of those parks that started with a 'Y,'" Totsie declared, promptly cackling at her blunder.

"It's nice getting the summers off, isn't it?" Ms. Flynn remarked, a retired teacher herself.

"Oh, it is. But I'll tell you, Miriam, you need it after nine months with these kids. They're a whole different breed these days. We're getting some real scary ones. There's just no respect for authority anymore. I've had kids call me things to my face that I can't even repeat. It's not just me. Everyone's getting it. I don't know what it is. Can you imagine talking like that to a teacher when we were kids?"

A momentary dip in the volume of the party attracted Fred's attention. He turned his head slightly.

"Listen," he said, raising a curious finger.

Totsie and Ms. Flynn broke off their conversation. A moment later Totsie exclaimed: "Carolers!"

Other conversations likewise began tapering off until soon the sound of singing children could distinctly be heard coming from somewhere outside the house.

Against Suzanne's protests for her to stay put and let someone else get the door, Mrs. Beckett set off in a fluster across the living room. Suzanne caught her father's eye—he was chatting with the senator by the good fireplace—and they shrugged and shook their heads hopelessly.

The brightness of the carol instantly flooded the house as the dining room door swung open.

"We *wish* you a Merry Christmas! We *wish* you a Merry Christmas! We *wish* you a Merry Christmas . . ."

"It's snowing!" Mrs. Beckett turned and proclaimed to the party, adding impetus to the general exodus from the living room that was already underway.

"Damn," Teddy cursed.

"They'll be fine," Nathan reassured him. "After all, how can a snowflake survive in a burning flame?"

"Dante?" Rudolph asked.

"No. Master Kusan," Nathan replied. "Zen Buddhist monk."

"It's not the luminarias I'm worried about," Teddy said as he watched Mary Margaret trying to work her old bones up from the couch with her daughter's impatient help. "It's the ancient ones."

On the other side of the living room the senator grabbed his cane from its clever resting place among the fireplace tools and set out at a stately pace, he and Mr. Beckett steadily losing ground to Miriam Flynn and Dr. and Mrs. Hossley. Totsie Seybert banged her shin against the corner of the coffee table and cursed under her breath as Fred rearranged the unsettled miniature nativity scene. Teddy, Nathan, and Rudolph reluctantly parted ways with their cozy corner, whose proximity to the tureens was allowing them to keep tabs on who was getting sloshed. Everyone crowded along the table and around the door of the dining room, the better to hear the children's gift to them.

Margot stepped over to the banister and leaned forward to have a look. A breath of cold outside air curled around her ankles as her eyes settled once again on Johnny's bald head. He was standing near the back of the gathering with his arm around his wife's waist. Again she felt something akin to offense, to betrayal even, at the sight of his thick, middle-aged body there in her house.

The carolers stared straight ahead as they sang, their cheeks and fingers pink from the cold. There were eight of them, four boys and four girls, the taller ones in back. Behind them stood Ms. Guthrie, dedicated member of First United Methodist Church, her firm silence giving the children courage to stay the course. Through the darkness beyond the cover of the porch the snow was lightly falling. It looked more impressive through the dining room windows, drifting down at a steady angle, swirling around the thick trunk of the oak tree that dominated the back yard, floating softly down into the dark, empty basin of the swimming pool.

At the sound of the four grandchildren hopping up and down behind him trying to get a better view, Johnny glanced back and noticed Margot alone. A moment later he excused himself from his wife and made his way over to her. Stepping around to her left side, he set his hands beside hers on the banister. It was a while before either of them spoke.

"I certainly wasn't expecting to see you here," Margot said.

"I didn't know you were in town," he replied.

Margot kept her eyes on his hands. Those slender, delicate fingers that she had held and kissed so many times now looked pudgy and coarse. The skin of his ring finger was bulging slightly around the thick gold band.

"My mom told me about your mother," Johnny said. "I thought I'd just stop by to say hello to her."

"That was thoughtful," Margot said after some hesitation. A burst of applause erupted from the dining room. She glanced over at the crowd around the door, realizing now that they all probably knew. It was more than Christmas Eve that had brought them out on such a frigid night. She applauded lightly along with everyone else, and the children launched into "O Little Town of Bethlehem."

"If I'd known you were here," Johnny said, "I probably wouldn't have come."

"Why?"

Johnny looked down and smiled a little at the effrontery in Margot's voice. Then he changed the subject.

"Are you still in New York?"

She answered that and the other well-meaning but superficial questions about her career, and he did the same for her.

"What happened to the saxophone?" she asked to his guilty revelation that he had become a lawyer.

"No money in it."

Then Johnny took out his wallet and showed Margot the picture of his daughter from his first marriage. It was a high school graduation photo of a pretty, brown-haired girl looking somewhat dubious about her accomplishment. Margot smiled and told him, trying hard to keep the tightness in her chest out of her voice, that she was lovely. More than the picture of this girl who was the same age that Margot had been when she was so in love with him, it was the sight of Johnny's fingers proudly cupping the wallet that got to her. The tender sincerity of the caroling children only exacerbated the ache around her heart.

Johnny closed his wallet and returned it to his back pocket. He and Margot stood listening to the carolers.

"I shouldn't have come," he said quietly after a while.

Margot finally turned to face him. She didn't know what to say. She had imagined meeting him again so many times, but always in some random encounter on the streets of New York, where she would have had the advantage of her busy life around her. Never once had she dreamed that they would be standing together in the house in Deming, listening to Christmas carols. It was all too much like the first time he had declared his love for her. That had been Christmas Eve as well, she remembered now with mild shock—nearly thirty years ago! He had come over to play music with the family. They used to bring all the oddball instruments up from the basement and make merry noise with them in the living room. Johnny had won the family over with his jazzy sax renditions of the Christmas standards. He had even played along masterfully with the Johnny Mathis record, to Mr. Beckett's great delight— the final stamp of approval. She had driven him home that night, for it was well past midnight when they had finished. Before getting out of the car he turned to her and said he had to tell her something. He then proceeded to sit there for nearly half an hour, unable to speak, shivering as much from nerves as from the cold. Finally he had blurted it out and opened the door and run off before she could even respond. Never before or since had there been a moment quite like that in Margot's life, when she had felt in a single instant the full terror and joy of love. When she got back home she went and opened his present and wept at the sight of it.

Margot set her hand on his and looked directly into his lively blue-gray eyes, the only part of him that hadn't changed, though time had etched around them a network of fine lines. He glanced down uneasily at her hand but let it stay.

"Do you remember that Christmas when you got me the sword?" she said.

"A sword?" He searched her face for signs of jest, and finding none he lowered his head in thought.

"You don't remember the sword?" Margot said, surprised that he could have possibly forgotten.

"A real sword?" he asked doubtfully.

"Yes. You got me this big samurai sword, or whatever it was, and you put it in this long cardboard box filled with pampas grass."

Johnny smiled, vaguely remembering. A flush stole over his face.

"Jesus. What the hell was I thinking?"

"I loved it," she said. "All the time it was under the tree everyone kept wondering what in God's name could be in that box. Coming from you they figured it had to be something strange."

He looked down again and shook his head.

"Did they guess?"

"Of course not."

"Your poor mom and dad. What must they have thought of me, giving their daughter a sword for Christmas?"

"It didn't surprise them. Dad just said something like, 'To fight off the suitors.'"

Johnny grinned.

"Do you still have it?"

She shook her head. "No. I did keep it for a few years. Took it to New York."

"To fight off the suitors?"

"Hardly. I figured it would come in handy if anyone ever broke into the apartment. I used to have it on the wall. It was a great icebreaker."

"Literally," Johnny joked. He paused briefly then said: "So what happened to it?"

"I threw it off the Brooklyn Bridge," Margot said.

Johnny looked at her, smiling a little to hide his abashment, then he looked away. An uneasy silence crept back into the air between them. Margot removed her hand from his. They stood side by side facing the dining room windows, watching the snow falling silently through the darkness.

Two songs would have been more than enough. Anyone could see that despite their earnest performance the children were eager for the moment when at last the door would close behind them and they would be back in the darkness, free to relax. At present they were battling nobly through the slumberous deeps of "Silent Night."

"Your wife is lovely," Margot said, trying to dispel some of the chill.

Johnny turned to look, as if in verification.

"Thank you," he said. He told Margot they had been married for five years, that they had met at a charity ball. Her father was one of the founding partners of his firm. "And you? Is there anyone in your life?"

Margot smiled at the coyness of the phrase.

"I have a boyfriend, if that's what you mean."

Despite her good intentions, Margot couldn't keep the brittle edge out of her voice. She would have liked to tell him that all that adolescent hormonal melodrama was so much water under the bridge, that she had long since become a strong, independent woman of the world; and maybe that was true back in New York, but here, tonight, back in the house in Deming with everyone there, just like it used to be, it was as if nothing had changed at all. She couldn't help feeling that with every passing minute she was becoming that same confused teenager all over again, desperately yearning for something solid to hold on to.

Again a chill silence enveloped them.

"How bad is it?" Johnny asked after a time.

Margot glanced at her mother, who just then had her mouth open wide in laughter. She looked a bit tipsy as she set her hand on the shoulder of her old friend Bessie Puckett and went on laughing.

"James says maybe a year," Margot said matter-of-factly, grateful for the change of subject. "He's not exactly objective, is he?"

Johnny put his hand on Margot's and squeezed it. He had always had a peculiar fondness for Mrs. Beckett, often coming by to visit her when Margot wasn't even there. That too had been a source of jealousy, one he never could get his head around. He never did understand why Margot couldn't get along with her mother.

"I think losing her hair is more painful to her than losing her life," Margot said.

"Don't say that," Johnny said with such sincerity that Margot instantly felt a lump of regret lodge in her throat.

At last the children finished "Silent Night." Everyone clapped and beamed, and the children, each in their own timid way, acknowledged the joy they had brought to the strangers. Ms. Guthrie stepped forward, deferring to her charges with evident pride. She waved and said hello to her friends among the party. Mrs. Beckett invited them all in for something warm to drink. Ms. Guthrie at first declined, but Mrs. Beckett wouldn't hear of it. It was snowing, after all. She didn't want the children getting sick. Ms. Guthrie happily relented and the party made way for the children, who shyly entered the wondrous coziness of the Beckett home where they were promptly fawned over by all the ancient ones. The less reserved among the carolers hurried to the table and began snatching up cookies and fudge. The gay noise of the party soon returned to its previous level as the guests slowly fanned back out to the living room.

"Something you said to me once has always stuck in my mind," Margot said, sensing she might never get another chance to say it. "You said that someday we'd get back together, you didn't know when, maybe after we were both old and divorced. Do you remember that?"

Johnny smiled to himself.

"I do," he said.

This caught Margot off guard. Not only that he remembered, but that he answered without hesitation. She looked at him. She had the impression that he wanted to say something more, but just then his wife, perhaps feeling that she had left her husband adrift in his youth for long enough, was making her graceful way back to him and Margot.

"I've never been in such a delightful town," she said upon reaching them. "Everyone is just so nice."

She glanced at both of them in turn, tacitly acknowledging their shared history.

"Is this your first time here?" Margot asked her.

"Yes," she said, giving her husband an admonitory sidelong glance. "I've heard so much about it too. I've been trying to get Johnny to bring me out to Deming for ages, but he's hardly had time to come up for air these past few years."

Johnny smiled solicitously.

"Well, I'm glad you finally got a chance to come," Margot said.

"Your mother is such a jewel," Elaine said. "She was telling me all about your family's history here."

Margot nodded, smiling.

"And do you still live here?" Elaine then asked.

"No," Margot replied. "Queens, New York."

"Oh, I just love New York. I'd move there in a heartbeat if I had the chance."

Johnny glanced at his watch.

"I'm sure you could find a firm in New York," Margot said to Johnny, to which he could do nothing but smile amiably.

After a sufficient interval of similarly fatuous exchanges, Johnny took his wife's hand and said that they should probably be on their way. Elaine protested that it was terribly rude to show up at a party unannounced only to turn around and leave so soon. Margot sounded convincing as she urged them to stay at least for the luminarias. But Johnny, pleading exhaustion after the long drive from Houston, insisted regretfully that they really should be going. Margot acquiesced and set off to her bedroom to get their coats.

Johnny's and his wife's coats were still on top of the pile, lying side by side, and it struck Margot now as she stood looking down at them that the way she had arranged the wife's coat, with the sleeves crossed in front, gave the coat, and by extension the woman, a satisfying air of prim vulnerability, as if it and she were protecting some secret weakness.

She picked up the coat and raised it to her face and sniffed the collar. It was a musky, department-store scent that instantly called to mind a range of impressions about the woman and the life Johnny shared with her in Houston. The starkest image, the one Margot would have used if asked to design an ad campaign around their marriage, was of a spotless, cream-colored carpet, the same color as the wife's scarf, sprawled across a vast, modern, sterile suburban living room, in the middle of which, in a vase atop a glass coffee table, stood a single fake red rose.

Margot sniffed again, a stronger whiff of the same impression. She stood there for some time, holding the coat, her heart thumping hard against her breastbone, the drone of Deming's aged luminaries rolling in over her like a tranquil surf. But the image would not leave her. She backed slowly toward the door and closed it behind her. Blissfully alone in the murmuring pale sky blue, she pulled up her skirt, pushed her panties down and pressed the silk lining at the back of the coat up between her legs and held it there, pressing it in a little with her fingers. A warm feeling of perverse pleasure spread down her legs and up around the base of her skull. Far away, in some other world, a doorbell was chiming.

Mr. Beckett, perhaps sensing a certain emptiness behind all

the laughter and talking, excused himself momentarily from Ray Canady and went to turn over the record. Though no longer as tall as his sons, Mr. Beckett was still a man of imposing stature, with a fine squarish head of Irish origin and a full mustache that for thirty years had been the same steel gray as his hair. His wide shoulders were presently filling a coarsely knit maroon sweater, over the neck of which the collar of his shirt was protruding, lending a certain boyishness to his otherwise sedate demeanor.

Soon the happy melody of "Winter Wonderland" was prancing through the party once again.

"He wants to add another bedroom on to the house," Mr. Beckett said upon his return to the fireplace.

"Oh? Which way, toward the back or the south side?" Ray Canady asked.

"I figured I'd go on to the southwest corner. There isn't but thirty feet to the Yokellys' wall."

Just then the four grandchildren filed into the living room from the hallway and rushed over to their grandfather.

"Grandpa," Tyler said excitedly, "can we open a present at midnight?"

Mr. Beckett peered thoughtfully down at the children. All four of them had blond hair and blue eyes, and their plump little faces were full to bursting with Christmas joy.

"Well, now, that's up to your mother."

"She told us to ask you."

"Did she? Well, it's fine with me if it's all right with her, only you oughta wait until after the luminarias."

"Yay!" yelled the kids and ran back down the hallway. Mr. Beckett stood there, staring down at the floor with a glazed expression. The double chime of the doorbell rang sweetly from the depths of the house.

"That must be Manny," Teddy said as Tyler, thrilled to still be awake at that time of night, raced back out across the living room, jumped down the steps and ran past his grandmother, beating her to the door.

Indeed it was the mayor, wearing an ankle-length black

wool overcoat, the mouths of his leather and rabbit fur gloves protruding from the pockets. A light dusting of snow lay atop his shoulders and in his hair.

"It's about time," Mrs. Beckett chided him familiarly, spreading her arms to embrace him as she advanced along the table.

"I was detained at the Halls'," he said in the quiet, understated way he had, which belied his ambitious nature. He gave Mrs. Beckett a firm hug.

Teddy caught his eye and waved. Manny nodded and allowed Mrs. Beckett to remove his overcoat, underneath which he was wearing a dark-gray suit, a white shirt, and a pale-yellow tie. A yellow silk handkerchief bloomed artfully from his suit-coat pocket.

"Tyler, honey, close the door," Mrs. Beckett said to her grandson, who was gazing out with rapt fascination at the falling snow.

"It's really coming down," Manny said, lightly brushing snowflakes from his hair.

He was a slight, gentle Hispanic man in his late forties. Regardless of the season, there was always a ruddy tinge to the skin of his face, which was pocked from some childhood illness. He wore his hair in a youthful style, light and buoyant in front, feathered at the sides. If there could be said to be any breach in the good taste of his grooming, it was that he tended to wear too much cologne, perhaps a consequence of his calling: he had made his fortune in the mortuary business. In addition to the chapel in Deming, he now had branches of Garcia's Funeral Homes in Lordsburg and Silver City.

Excusing himself from Mrs. Beckett, who was looking all around for Margot, Manny made his way over to Teddy and Rudolph, his favorite employees, Nathan having just then been lured away by Dr. Hossley's chance comment that faith was dead in the modern world.

"And how are the Halls?" Teddy asked his boss.

"Not too happy at the moment," Manny said. "There are all of six people at their party. By the way, the luminarias look fantastic."

"Are they holding up?" Teddy asked.

"There's a few out. I saw you have some going down Hemlock."

"Yeah, Wendell Faught had his cousins from Minnesota out there this afternoon shoveling sand."

"Let me get you something to drink," Rudolph offered, and after some haranguing the mayor acquiesced to a glass of the Las Uvas.

"Your mother looks great," Manny said to Teddy as Rudolph set off to get the wine.

"Margot got her the wig in some fancy shop in Manhattan. It was supposed to be a Christmas present but Mom couldn't wait."

"Where is Margot anyway?" Manny said, glancing around. "I should say hello."

"She's somewhere around."

It was time for the carolers to be moving on. Ms. Guthrie gathered them up and shepherded them to the door, some of the children grabbing one last cookie on the way out. Everyone said farewell and merry Christmas. The children were told to thank Mrs. Beckett, and they did so in a resounding chorus and slipped back out into the snowy night to continue their rounds of the neighborhood.

Tyler nearly collided with Margot as he was running down the hall with the mayor's coat.

"Just set it on the bed," Margot told him, tussling his hair.

She made her way across the living room and down to the dining room where Johnny and his wife were talking cheerfully with Dr. and Mrs. Hossley near the door.

"Do you really have to be going so soon?" Margot said to Johnny's wife. "You'll miss our little tradition."

"It does sound lovely," Elaine said. "What do you think, John?"

"I'd love to but I'm just exhausted from the trip. We really should be going." He took her coat from Margot and spread it open and held it for her while she put her arms through the sleeves. "We'll have a little stroll down the block on the way out."

When they were all bundled up Johnny said he had better go say good-bye to the rest of the family, and he set off for the living room, leaving Margot and his wife alone beside the table. In his absence, Johnny's wife adopted a tone of easy candor as she confessed to Margot how hard it was being away from her own family this Christmas. Margot knitted her brow sympathetically. They spoke also of the weather in Houston, of mosquitoes, of Broadway musicals, and of the merits of winter fashion. All while they were chatting so amiably, Margot kept seeing in the back of her mind the dark splotch of blood still clinging to the inner lining of the woman's coat.

At last Johnny returned and gave Margot a heartfelt hug and told her how nice it was seeing her again. Margot saw them to the door and opened it for them. The snow was coming down hard, the flakes big and fluffy. Johnny and his wife stepped out and, ducking their heads together, made their way gingerly across the stretch of open patio before the gate.

"Merry Christmas," Margot said as they opened the gate and turned to say farewell. "Drive safely."

"Merry Christmas," they said.

Johnny raised his arm and waved as one does from the deck of a cruise ship leaving port. It had been one of his rituals, an exaggerated farewell whenever he left Margot at her door, his way of trying to end the night on a lighter note after one of their soul-searching make-out sessions at the foot of the fireplace. That self-conscious wave of his had always made Margot uneasy, for in it she had sensed the truth of his relief to be leaving her. She felt that now as the gate clicked shut behind him.

———

Old Mary Margaret was asleep on the couch. Beside her Gabe Ochoa was telling Miriam Flynn all about the features of his new digital watch. The senator, looking cadaverous, was sitting erect in Mrs. Beckett's yellow wingback armchair. The leather recliner was presently occupied by a dozing Mrs. Hossley.

Those still standing were shifting their weight from hip to hip with increasing frequency. Johnny Mathis was dreaming for the fourth time that night of a white Christmas.

Mrs. Beckett stepped down from the kitchen with the last of the rum punch in a pitcher and made her way with it to the tureen. She glanced at the clock.

"Oh dear," she said to Beatrice Basch, who was trying to decide between another piece of Turkish delight or the last piece of fudge. "I completely lost track of time."

After pouring the punch into the tureen she stepped up into the living room and glanced around.

"Celia, for heaven's sake sit down and have a rest," Miriam Flynn scolded her. "You've been flitting about all night like a three-legged roadrunner."

Mrs. Beckett smiled. Her eyes were somewhat glazed with wine and she swayed ever so slightly as she stood looking around the living room for her daughter. She walked over to the banister.

"Teddy," she said, "have you seen Margot?"

Teddy glanced around.

"She was here a minute ago. She must be in the bathroom."

"Could you help me with the coats?" she said. "I think we should get started."

In the hallway they met Margot coming from the bathroom. Her face was flushed and a little puffy.

"Dear, are you all right?" Mrs. Beckett asked her, a look of concern wrinkling across her brow.

"I'm fine," Margot said, looking away.

Teddy gave his sister a knowing glance.

They went into her bedroom and gathered up into their arms all the coats and scarves and hats. They carried them out to the living room and draped them over the back of the couch and the armchairs, and Mrs. Beckett raised her voice to say that it was nearly midnight and whoever cared to join them for the luminarias should find their coats and make their way to the door. A slow-motion slapstick routine ensued as the tired and tipsy, the aged and infirm, began sifting through the various piles in search of their coats, only confusing each other further with their efforts to help.

"Bill, here, this one's yours."

"That's not mine. That's black."

"It looks blue to me."

"You need to get your eyes examined."

"I think I've got yours, Bea."

"This old thing could use a cleaning. It was my mother's, you know."

"Your arm's in the wrong hole, Totsie."

"So it is. Ha!"

A great peal of laughter erupted when it was discovered that the mayor and the senator were wearing each other's overcoats, both of them being of the same brand, color and style. It was only cleared up when the senator reached into the inner pocket of the coat the mayor had on and removed with a triumphant flourish his brass-and-leather whiskey flask, a gift from his first wife. When all the Becketts had returned with their own coats on and everyone was bundled up, a glacial movement in the direction of the dining room door began.

"Mother," Margot said with unconcealed annoyance upon glancing down at her mother's feet, "you can't possibly be planning on traipsing out in the snow in those shoes." Which remark invited everyone within earshot to weigh in on the matter.

"Oh, I can't be bothered to change them," Mrs. Beckett said dismissively. "We'll only be a few minutes."

"You'll break your neck," Mr. Beckett said flatly.

"I should be so lucky." Mrs. Beckett laughed. "Come on, everybody. Out, out, out!"

It was past midnight by the time everybody was ready at the door, and they all had to stop again and wish each other a merry Christmas.

"Shall we?" Mrs. Beckett called out.

In pairs and singly they filed through the door, past the old plastic Santa lit up on the porch, out into the falling snow. Outside the gate they all stopped and marveled at the snow swirling dizzily through the coronas around the streetlights. Already nearly an inch of it had blanketed the cars and trucks parked here and there along the street. It was coating the hedges and fence posts, the mailboxes and fire hydrants. A thin powdery layer covered the sidewalk, but as Mrs. Beckett remarked, it wasn't slippery at all. Only the streets remained defiantly black.

The party of more than twenty shuffled tentatively down the sidewalk over to the corner of Tin and Maple. Teddy came up behind his sister and took her arm.

"What happened?"

"Nothing," she said.

"Fibber."

At the corner there was a general gush of joy at the sight of the luminarias flickering softly all up and down the street, from Ash clear to Hemlock, parallel rows of golden-brown candlelight emanating from thousands of little sand-filled paper bags placed a few feet apart along the sidewalks on both sides of the street, lining the edges of driveways and walkways, along roofs, atop walls, the snow around them softly aglow. The flames were flickering erratically, pulsing and surging as snowflakes struck the wicks. Here and there some of the candles had gone out, leaving gaps like missing teeth in the rows of amber light.

There were almost no cars out on the street, and the few that came down Tin crawled along with only their parking lights on. The uncommon sight of candlelight in the snow seemed to silence the party. They shuffled north up Tin without a word, past the Pearsons' and the Millers' and the Harrisons', where the Christmas trees were still alight and twinkling gaily in living room windows. Fairy lights and big colored bulbs with textured tin petals traced the dead branches of the elms and mulberry trees that lined the sidewalk. In this direction the snow was coming down full in the face, making it difficult going for those who had trouble enough seeing on a clear summer's day.

Margot caught up with her mother, slipped her arm through

hers, and walked along slowly by her side. Mr. Beckett, seeming to think they wanted to be alone, walked up ahead and joined Suzanne. Paul and Pat and James were farther along with their wives and the children. Teddy, Nathan, Rudolph, and the mayor were at the head of the gradually elongating group to the rear.

"I'm glad you could come," Mrs. Beckett said.

Margot nodded. The episode with Johnny's wife's coat was beginning to recede, leaving a mild twinge of shame hovering around her heart, but she was glad of it. It made the luminarias seem all the more pure and beautiful.

They walked along in silence, Margot looking down at her mother's toes naked to the snow. Past Hemlock the luminarias tapered off, and everyone crossed over to the other side of the street, to the sidewalk in front of the library. Here Margot paused briefly with her mother. She could never pass the library without feeling again something of the magic she had discovered there as a child. All those beautiful worlds she had escaped into were still there behind the walls of that little stucco building. Everything about it—the bike racks near the doors, the roots of the huge poplar buckling the sidewalk, the steel plate of the book drop in the front wall, the flyers for read-a-thons taped to the windows—everything about that little building seemed imbued with the magic of the worlds it housed within it.

Gazing at the luminarias leading up to the glass double doors, Margot felt as if some part of herself were melting, flowing down the walkway, into the library. It was a wonderful sensation. Something told her she would never forget this moment. The falling snow. The luminarias. Her mother clutching her arm in the silence. She would have gladly indulged the feeling forever, but as they were standing there one of the luminarias flickered and went out. It was startling, that sudden cold pinch of darkness. Somehow it seemed terribly poignant, the symbolism inescapable. Margot bristled at her own sentimentality, knowing it was in lieu of the genuine grief that would only come when her mother was actually dead.

"Your feet must be freezing, Mom," she said with annoyance.

"I don't even feel it," her mother replied.

Margot shook her head. They carried on. They were now in the rear of the group, behind Teddy and the mayor. They walked along, the snow pelting their backs and heads. More of the luminarias along the sidewalk were going out now, their bags caving in wet and sodden with snow. Mrs. Beckett asked Teddy why all the luminarias in front of the Brubeks' were still going strong, and he answered that it was because the Brubeks were such fine people, which Mrs. Beckett, knowing as Teddy did plenty of dark Brubek secrets, cackled at. A few minutes later, perhaps inspired by her son's irreverence, Mrs. Beckett leaned over and said into her daughter's ear: "I never did like Johnny."

Margot turned and looked at her mother, surprised to hear this.

"Is that right?" she said.

"He was always full of shit."

Margot smiled and squeezed her mother's arm, marveling at the sudden feeling of joy in her heart. At the corner of Birch they crossed the street once more and headed back up the sidewalk toward the house. People were getting cold now, and the fear of illness hastened many of them to speedy departures. By the time the group made it back to the front of the Beckett house there were only a dozen or so people left, including the Becketts themselves.

"Blitzen's gone out again," Teddy alerted his father.

"On strike," Mr. Beckett said.

They were staring up at the roof of the house, where a life-size Santa and his reindeer team appeared to be coming in for a landing, Santa's arm flung back in merry cheer for all.

"He's not doing much blitzen tonight," Paul remarked.

"Donner probably ate him," James said.

"That would be a sin," Pat said. "A *venisin*."

Everyone went about wishing each other a merry Christmas for the fifth time of the night, and a prosperous new year, shaking hands, kissing cheeks, hugging. Then came the flurry of thank-yous to Mrs. Beckett for such a memorable Christmas Eve, the most wonderful and memorable yet. One by one they came up to hug her: the mayor, Totsie and Fred Seybert, the Hossleys, the senator and his daughter, Mary Margaret and Judy. When everyone had had their turn they said one last farewell to the family and set out for their cars and trucks parked all around the house, leaving the Becketts standing together on the sidewalk in the snow, waving at every car that slowly drove past them, the dark figures inside waving in return.

Those of the family who were staying in motels or had their own homes to return to kissed their mother and father good night, begging their mother to leave the cleanup for them to do in the morning. The grandchildren were dying to get back in and open a present. All along the street the luminarias were going out en masse, the bags sagging from the wetness and weight of accumulating snow. Those that continued to burn seemed to burn all the brighter for the darkness deepening around them.

Acknowledgments

I am grateful to the following publications, in which some of these stories originally appeared:

Connecticut Review: "Darling Courts"
Dublin Review: "Due Diligence"
Fiction: "Midnight Pools" and "Blanco"
Georgia Review: "The Wildcat Massacre"
Iowa Review and *Road to Nowhere and Other New Stories from the Southwest* (UNM Press): "Road to Nowhere"
South Dakota Review: "Double Feature"